Praise for Robert Gregory Browne and
Kiss Her Goodbye

"A smashing good read. It moves at such a breakneck pace that you'll scarcely have time to take a breath."
—Tess Gerritsen, *New York Times* bestselling author of *The Bone Garden*

"[A] provocative . . . breathtaking debut."
—*Publishers Weekly*

"Get ready for one hell of a ride."
—*New York Times* bestselling author Kay Hooper

"An adrenaline-pumping thriller."
—*Midwest Book Review*

"All the elements of a terrific novel are here—a compelling, three-dimensional hero, a brilliant and evil villain, high stakes, a ticking clock, real emotion, and Browne's visceral writing style . . . a strong, striking debut thriller."
—Mark Terry

"Nonstop pacing, breathless prose, and page-turning urgency . . . heart-stopping fiction."
—Kathy Mackel

"From rich characters to heart-pounding suspense, *Kiss Her Goodbye* explores not only the deadly terrain of murder but the nuances of the soul. It's a first-rate novel that will glue you to your chair until you finish the last satisfying word."
—Gayle Lynds

"This debut novel by a successful screenwriter is a fast-paced thriller that you will want to devour in one sitting. Edgy suspense mixed with a touch of the

supernatural keeps pushing the reader forward . . . This is a writer whose name will soon be a household word."

—Bookfinds.com

"A taut, absorbing page-turner. Robert Gregory Browne makes his mark with a compelling thriller filled with twists and surprises. A writer to watch!"

—Carla Neggers

"[A] cat-and-mouse game between two desperate men . . . a nerve-wracking race against time."

—*Kirkus Reviews*

"The writing is wonderful. . . . Donovan is a strong man, tested to his limits. Gunderson is just as strong, a worthy opponent. Browne has the pacing down, the tensions down, all the twists and turns one expects from a good thriller."

—ReviewingtheEvidence.com

"Screenwriter Robert Gregory Browne creat[es] a compelling plot: The characters have to want something—and want it badly."

—*Mystery Scene*

"Provocative and gritty."

—*Tucson Citizen*

"A classic 'race against time' thriller told with the originality of a very different perspective."

—Crimesquad.com

"Part-mystery, part–soul journey, and completely surprising . . . Browne's tale rockets to warp speed after the first third of the book, ending with a surprising jolt."

—*Authorlink*

"[P]art-Thomas Harris, part-Dante's *Inferno*."

—*Tampa Tribune*

St. Martin's Paperbacks Titles by
ROBERT GREGORY BROWNE

Whisper in the Dark

Kiss Her Goodbye

WHISPER IN THE DARK

Robert Gregory Browne

St. Martin's Paperbacks

This is a work of fiction. All of the characters, organizations, and events portrayed in this novel are either products of the author's imagination or are used fictitiously.

WHISPER IN THE DARK

Copyright © 2009 by Robert Gregory Browne.

Cover photograph © Jack Hollingsworth / Getty Images

For information address St. Martin's Press, 175 Fifth Avenue, New York, NY 10010.

ISBN: 0-312-35866-0
EAN: 978-0-312-35866-2

Printed in the United States of America

St. Martin's Paperbacks edition / February 2009

St. Martin's Paperbacks are published by St. Martin's Press, 175 Fifth Avenue, New York, NY 10010.

10 9 8 7 6 5 4 3 2 1

For Leila

ONE

The Woman Who Wasn't Quite Myra

Chapter 1

It was a pretty uneventful night until the naked lady tried to kill him.

Dubosky was just coming off a twenty-hour shift, had just dropped off a couple of Latino kids who had gotten frisky on his backseat, when he decided to forgo the usual last lap around the neighborhood and head straight for the cab shack.

His dispatcher, Freddy, a waste of space if there ever was one, was on the radio trying to get him to respond.

"Hey, numbnuts, I got another pickup for you."

Dubosky ignored him.

He couldn't count the number of times he'd heard that phlegm-throttled voice telling him to get his ass in gear, telling him he was one step away from the unemployment line, telling him if he put even a single dent in his rig, it was coming out of his own pocket.

Numbnuts, huh?

Fuck him. And fuck this job, too.

Dubosky didn't know whether it was age or sheer exhaustion that made him feel this way, but after eighteen years on what seemed like an endless circling of the city, he was ready to crash this friggin' rig, grab a shotgun, and start blasting away.

Freddy was first on his list.

Dubosky had been working twelve-, sixteen-, twenty-hour shifts for the better part of his life. He couldn't pick his kids out of a high school yearbook, and if his poor wife hadn't taken on a lover by now, it was a miracle, because he didn't have the energy to eat, let alone screw. Even half a dozen hits of extra-strength Levitra wouldn't get Old Rusty to stir.

There comes a point in your life, he told himself, you gotta ignore all good sense, forget about doing the right thing, and think about one person: you.

Which was exactly what he planned to do the moment he got back to the cab shack. Tell Freddy to shove this job up his stinky little bunghole, then get out into the world and breathe some free friggin' air. Fill his lungs and keep filling 'em and never look back.

By the time he turned onto The Avenue, he was already lost in a daydream about a weeklong cruise in the Greek Islands, Judy hooked on one arm, sipping a piña colada, as they headed back to their cabin to put Old Rusty to the test.

He was pretty deep into it when a shadow flashed under a nearby street lamp. Before he knew Christ from Hosea, a figure darted in front of his windshield.

Dubosky slammed the brakes, his rear end fishtailing, his tires making a sick squeal beneath him. Squeezing his eyes shut, he waited for the inevitable thud of bumper against bone.

But it didn't come.

Instead, he skidded to an unimpeded stop in the middle of the street and looked out to see nothing, nothing but the streetlights and the parked cars and the stark empty blacktop with its newly painted lines.

What the hell?

Instinct drew his attention to a space on his left. Huddled between two parked cars, trembling in the cold night air, was a street hag—this one more street than hag—about thirty or so from the looks of her, and as naked as a two-year-old at bath time.

Except for the blood all over her hands and face.

Jesus. Had he hit her?

Dubosky cranked the parking brake, then threw open his door and took a tentative step toward her. "You okay, lady?"

It was a ridiculous question. She was, after all, crouched there in her birthday suit, covered with about a year's worth of grime and fresh blood, a skinny little thing looking what could generously be described as disoriented. As he approached her, he realized it didn't much matter *what* he said. She was tuned to another frequency.

He was about three feet away from her, trying not to stare at her tits—which were, admittedly, pretty remarkable despite the circumstances—when she suddenly looked up at him with fierce, untamed eyes.

Then she pounced.

It was only then that Dubosky realized she was holding a pair of scissors. They arced high in the air—the windup before the pitch. Halfway through the pounce, Dubosky did the instinctive thing again and put a fist in her face.

The woman went down with a whimper, scissors clattering on the blacktop, and stopped moving.

Friggin' nutcase.

Dubosky crouched beside her and winced. She smelled like roadkill. But she was still breathing. And despite the blood, he couldn't see any major damage.

Was it even hers?

Glancing at the scissors, which also had a fair amount of blood on them, he wondered if this was the first time she'd tried to use them.

The radio squawked behind him. "Where the hell are you, you goddamn potato chugger?"

Dubosky grabbed a blanket from the trunk, then got on the radio and told Fuckhead Freddy to shut his cake eater and call the cops.

Solomon St. Fort was coming up on the Dumpster behind The Burger Basket, looking to score a late-night snack, when he heard someone crying. It came from inside the alleyway, the deep, wracking sobs of a soul in pain.

Solomon hesitated, listening to the sound, torn between hunger and curiosity.

His gaze drifted to the Dumpster. The Burger Basket routinely dumped their leftovers, filling the bin with stuff they couldn't unload before closing time. Solomon could smell the chili dogs from ten yards away.

But the Dumpster wasn't going anywhere, and the sobbing intrigued him. Moving into the alley, he headed toward the source of the sound, stopping short when he saw a man in a ratty overcoat sitting in the narrow space between two overflowing trash cans, knees to his chest, head in his hands, crying like a lost child.

Solomon immediately recognized him. "Clarence?"

The man looked up sharply, tears streaming, ragged tracks on a dirty face. The sobs grew louder when he saw Solomon. "She's dead, man. She's dead."

Solomon frowned. "Who's dead? Who you talkin' about?"

"Who you think? Myra, that's who."

Myra was a stone-cold junkie who had hooked up with Clarence about six months ago. Fine-looking white woman who used to be a swimsuit model, although she didn't have much meat on her bones these days. Solomon had just seen her this afternoon, over at the Brotherhood of Christ soup kitchen, thinking she didn't look quite right.

"What happened?" he asked.

"I told you she was sick, man. Coughin' up all that shit. Then she goes and puts the needle in her arm and bugs out right there in front of me, eyes rolling up inside her head. Next thing I know she's on the ground and she ain't movin'."

Solomon felt gut-punched. He hadn't known Myra very long, but he liked her. Had a kind of fatherly affection for her. "How long ago was this?"

"I don't know. Couple hours."

"And you just left her?"

"She's dead, man. What am I supposed to do?"

"Don't you know nothin' about junkies?" Solomon said. "Just 'cause they stop movin' don't mean they're dead. You shoulda got some help."

"From who?" Clarence cried. "The cops? They ain't interested in some hopped-up street whore."

"Bullshit. You got scared, so you run away."

Solomon remembered how Myra had once shown him a picture from a magazine. Kept it folded up in the back pocket of those ratty jeans she wore. It was an old ad for men's cologne, a younger Myra staring out at the camera with pouty lips and fuck-me eyes.

He heaved a weary sigh. "If she wasn't dead then," he said, "she probably is now. Where'd you leave her?"

Clarence wiped his face with the sleeve of his overcoat. "Over at our place, under the lean-to."

"Come on." Solomon said, then reached out and pulled Clarence to his feet.

"Where we goin'?"

"Where you think we're goin'?"

"No way, man. I don't wanna see her lookin' like that."

"I don't give a damn what you want. We're gonna do right by Myra. She was a good woman."

Clarence started crying again. Solomon threw an arm

around his shoulder and the two men walked the three blocks back to the freeway underpass, where Clarence and Myra shared a small cardboard lean-to among the litter of street people who called the river bottom home.

When they got there, they were surprised to find the rutted earth beneath the lean-to was empty except for Myra's dope kit, a jumble of plastic bags she used for blankets, and her clothes, which were scattered in the dirt.

No sign of Myra anywhere. Dead or otherwise.

"You sure this is where you left her?"

"I may be a drunk," Clarence said, "but I ain't crazy. She was right here."

"Well, she ain't here now." Solomon picked up Myra's jeans, dug in the back pocket, and found that same folded magazine page she'd shown him. He opened it up and stared at it, thinking how pretty she looked, thinking what a shame it was that she'd let the needle get ahold of her.

Clarence was crying again.

Then a voice from the darkness said, "You looking for the white girl?"

Solomon turned and saw Billy Eagleheart, a burly Mitskanaka Indian, curled up under his own lean-to.

"Yeah," Solomon said. "Somebody come and collect her?"

"Collect her? Last I saw, she was up on her own two, more or less."

Solomon and Clarence exchanged looks, and Clarence immediately stopped crying. "She's alive?"

"Stood right where you're standing," Billy said, then nodded to the jeans in Solomon's hand. "I don't know what she was on, but she was ripping off them rags like they were burning her skin. Had me wishin' I had a handful of dollar bills." He grinned at the memory.

"Don't you be playin' with us, Billy."

"I ain't playin' with nobody. Watched her stumble on up that hill, naked as a goddamn prairie bird. Looked like she was on a mission." He chuckled. "Maybe she needed some new shoes to match her ensemble."

Solomon turned, looking at Clarence. "You hear that? All that crying for nothin'."

"No way," Clarence said. "She was dead. I know dead when I see it."

"Yeah, and I know dumb when I'm lookin' at it."

Solomon nodded thanks to Billy, returned the magazine page to Myra's pocket, then gathered up the rest of her clothes and hooked a thumb at Clarence. "Let's go round her up before the cops do."

As they headed up the embankment toward Main Street, Billy said, "You find her, let me know what she does for an encore."

Betty Burkus found the body.

She was an old woman who had trouble sleeping, the extra weight and the constant heartburn and the sleep apnea making life twice as miserable as it should have been. She had rolled out of bed a little after one A.M., hoping a glass of ice water would kill the fire in her stomach.

Standing at the refrigerator in her small courtyard apartment, she glanced out her kitchen window and noticed that, across the way, the Janovic door was hanging wide open.

She sighed. Carl Janovic had been a pain in her backside since the day he moved in. The way he and his friends paraded in and out of that apartment, she might as well have had a revolving door installed. It was times like this Betty wished to God she'd never agreed to take on management duties. A two-hundred-dollar rent reduction was hardly worth all the fuss and bother.

Moving to her phone, she picked up the handset and

pressed number three—she had Janovic on speed dial, that's how much trouble he was—then listened to it ring and ring. Not too surprised when she didn't get an answer, she sighed again, cradled the phone, then threw on a robe and headed into the courtyard.

She was halfway to the Janovic apartment when she started to reconsider this little excursion. It was, after all, well past bedtime for most normal human beings, and an open front door at almost one-thirty in the morning was not a sign of welcome. Especially when you factored in the complete lack of lights. No porch light, nothing in the foyer, the place as black and silent as an abandoned mine.

But despite her complaints, Betty had always believed that if you take on a job you should *do* that job, so she soldiered on, trudging up to the open door and peering inside. "Mr. Janovic?"

She waited for an answer and got none. Also not a surprise. Chances were pretty good that Janovic had gone out with one of his light-in-the-loafers boyfriends and was so busy playing grabass he'd forgotten to close his door. Not that Betty had anything against his type. They could do whatever they wanted in the privacy of their own homes, but did they always have to flaunt it?

She leaned past the doorway. "Mr. Janovic?"

Still no answer. She was about to say to hell with it and pull the door shut when an odd smell wafted into her nasal radar. Betty frowned, sniffed. It smelled like . . . well, to be frank, like someone had fouled his pants.

Was it a plumbing problem? Had Janovic gone and clogged up his . . . Oh, God, the visual popping into her head right now was too awful to even contemplate.

Yet that smell was unmistakable. And if the plumbing *was* clogged, that meant it was up to her to get it taken care of.

Betty sighed again. Why, oh why had she ever taken this stupid job? Stepping into the foyer, she fumbled for the light switch. There wasn't much point in saying anything out loud, but she nevertheless tried a third time: "Mr. Janovic? Are you home?"

She flicked the switch, half expecting to find a pile of excrement in the middle of the polished wood floor.

What she found instead was Carl Janovic, lying faceup in a pool of blood, wearing only a bra, panties, and a shiny blond wig, his eyes wide and lifeless, his bare chest and abdomen covered with dark, gaping puncture wounds.

That was when Betty Burkus backed out of the apartment and vomited a night's worth of antacids, thin mints, and leftover Hamburger Helper into the ficus tree on Janovic's front porch.

Chapter 2

"Hiya, Frankie boy. Where's your partner?"

"I'm dining solo these days."

"Yeah? There's a nice little after-dinner snack waiting for you inside."

Frank Blackburn had just pulled up to the crime scene, an upscale courtyard apartment complex called the Fontana Arms. The crime tech wagons had beat him there and Kat Pendergast, a cute, coltish patrol officer, was waiting for him at the gated entranceway.

"You the first responder?" Blackburn asked.

"Me and Hogan, yeah."

Kat opened the gate and motioned him past. They moved together into the courtyard, where a platoon of crime scene techs flowed in and out of an open apartment doorway. Across the way, a fat woman in a faded bathrobe watched the proceedings from her kitchen window, hand clutched to her throat in horror.

Blackburn turned to Pendergast. "How many units this place have?"

"About ten."

"You scare up any witnesses?"

"Not so far," Kat said. "Hogan and a couple of the backup boys are shaking 'em out of bed as we speak."

They moved up to the doorway, Blackburn taking in

the glassy-eyed twenty-something who lay in the middle of the floor. Jesus, what a mess. The bra, panties, and wig were a nice touch—and the reason they'd dragged him out of bed. Even a hint of sexual assault and it was his squad's catch.

Special Victims.

"Lovely," he said. "Who is he?"

"Carl Joseph Janovic. Twenty-four years old. Moved in about three months ago. Landlady thought it was important to let us know he's a high-octane butt pilot."

"Looks like somebody was afraid to fly." Blackburn stared at the dark wounds and the blood, which had splattered just about every surface within a three-foot radius. He sighed. "Why do I always get stuck with the nasty ones?"

"Because nobody likes you."

Blackburn shot her a look and Kat threw her hands up. "Don't kill the messenger. Just ask Carmody."

"Carmody can kiss my ass," Blackburn said, then offered just enough of a smile to let her know he was kidding. Which he wasn't.

Truth be told, Blackburn had never been a particularly popular addition to the unit, a fact he attributed to his unbridled insensitivity and severe lack of social skills.

His ex-partner, Susan Carmody, an uptight Republican Goldilocks who was more suited to a career with FOX News than a detective squad, seemed to take offense to his occasional remarks about her rear end—which, Republican or not, was quite formidable.

Blackburn had grown up with four older brothers, in a household where such lapses of decorum were not only encouraged, but served as a measure of your masculinity.

So could she really blame him?

Apparently so. Six months after they partnered up, Carmody stopped just short of filing a grievance against him and transfered to Homicide. Rumor had it she was already screwing a White Shirt and was up for promotion. Seemed she had no trouble *using* the rear end she didn't want Blackburn making remarks about, but that was neither here nor there.

Bottom line, the unit was short a body and he was an army of one right now. And when it came down to it, that was just fine by him. That way, he didn't have to spend every ten seconds wondering whether he was properly navigating the battlefield of political correctness.

Besides, Blackburn wasn't here to win a popularity contest. All he wanted to do was work the case and make a collar.

He looked at the body again. "I can already see this one's gonna be loads of fun. You got a cigarette on you?"

"I thought you quit."

"A temporary solution to a long-term problem."

"Uh-huh," Kat said. "You know what they say, don't you?"

"What's that?"

"It's just an oral fixation."

Blackburn grinned. "You speaking from experience?"

She rolled her eyes. "Why don't you chew on a carrot or something."

"You got a carrot on you?"

Pendergast shook her head, stifled a smile. "You're too much, Detective." Starting back across the courtyard, she said, "I'm gonna go give Hogan a hand."

Blackburn watched her go, his eyes fixed on what was, without a doubt, another formidable rear end.

Careful, big guy.

Sometimes they bite.

Determining time of death was a science that Blackburn had no real interest in understanding.

Oh, he had learned the basics: body temperature, corneal cloudiness, potassium leak rate, parasite infestation, but anything beyond that was a foreign language to him and he'd never been good at geek. All he was interested in was the final determination, and preferred to be spared a detailed road map of how the medical examiner got there.

Some might say that made him a lousy investigator. And who knows? Maybe they'd be right. But Blackburn had proven more than once that he wasn't all that concerned with what some might say. He'd cleared enough cases to shut most of them up.

The assistant M.E. assigned to the case, a chisel-jawed Swede named Mats Hansen, was something of a wiz at pinpointing time of death. He usually proffered a guess right there at the scene that, more often than not, proved to be accurate.

"So what do you say, Mats? What's the magic number?"

Hansen was crouched over the body, staring intently at Janovic's bloody chest. "This one's pretty fresh. I'd say two hours, give or take."

Blackburn checked his watch. "So . . . what? Around midnight?"

"Glad to know you can subtract."

The world was full of wiseasses.

"I wouldn't want to second-guess anybody here, but is it safe to assume he was stabbed to death?"

"Cardio-respiratory arrest is more likely," Hansen said, then smiled. "Caused, of course, by the stabbing."

Comedians, too.

"Thanks for the clarification. What kind of weapon are we looking for?"

Hansen leaned in for a closer look at one of the puncture wounds. "A single-edged blade," he said. "I'm guessing a steak knife, about half an inch wide. We've got six fairly forceful hits to the chest and abdomen. At least two of them pierced the breastbone, probably ruptured the heart."

"Wonderful," Blackburn said. "He didn't happen to spell the killer's name in his own blood, did he?"

Hansen, being infinitely more adept at social niceties than Blackburn, chuckled politely and said, "Sorry, Agatha, no such luck. My guess is he was dead after the first hit. The rest were just for good measure. A lot of rage there. And check out the hands and forearms."

Blackburn looked. "No defense wounds."

Hansen nodded. "Happened so fast he didn't have time to react. No sign of forced entry or a struggle of any kind. Front security gate wasn't touched. This guy knew his attacker." He gestured to a crimson smear on the floor. "And it looks like we have a partial footprint."

"Oh?" Blackburn crouched down, studying the smear, but couldn't make heads or tails of it. Or heels or toes, for that matter.

"And when I say foot," Hansen continued, "I mean barefoot. Whoever left it wasn't wearing shoes, and it's most likely a woman."

Blackburn stared at the smear a moment longer, wondering if Hansen had quit smoking too, because you'd have to consume a whole shitload of carrots to see all that.

But if Hansen was right, then the rather obvious theory that had been percolating in Blackburn's brain—that this had been the work of a jilted gay lover—had just fallen victim to a busted pilot light.

Hansen launched into his usual disclaimer about providing a more definitive analysis once he got back to the lab, but Blackburn tuned him out. If the murder happened around midnight, then one of the other tenants might've been awake and seen something useful, like Cinderella fleeing the scene without her slippers.

Who knows, maybe he'd get lucky with this one. Not that he and Luck were on speaking terms, but you never knew.

No sooner had he thought this than his cell phone rang.

It was Kat Pendergast. "I've got two words for you and I think you're gonna like them."

"Don't keep me in suspense too long."

"Naked lady," Kat said.

Blackburn paused. "There's a couple ways I could respond to that. What exactly does it mean?"

"I just got a call from dispatch. Seems a cab driver almost ran down a naked woman about two blocks from here on The Avenue. She's covered with blood."

Blackburn felt the hairs on the back of his neck stand up. "You gotta be kidding me."

"I kid you not," Kat said. "And when the cabbie stopped to help her? She tried to stab him."

Chapter 3

Solomon and Clarence weren't having much luck finding Myra. They tried the usual haunts: the strip mall that held a Rite-Aid drugstore, a Von's supermarket, a fast-food Chinese joint, and a Taco Bell. Then they checked the 24-hour laundromat behind it, where a lot of folks gathered to get warm on chilly nights like this one.

No sign of her.

They wandered up The Avenue, checking the dark doorways of the discount dental offices and pawn shops. Still nothing.

Where the hell had she gotten to?

They were about to give up when Solomon spotted the flashing lights of a police cruiser and an ambulance up near DeAnza Drive, where The Avenue abruptly turned from brown-skinned working class to white yuppie paradise.

A couple of paramedics were loading a woman onto a gurney in the back of the ambulance, her bony bare legs hanging out of the blanket wrapped around her. She looked unconscious.

"Shit," Solomon said. "We're too late."

"What?" Clarence squinted into the darkness. He'd

broken his glasses a couple weeks ago and Solomon knew he couldn't see worth a damn. "Is that Myra?"

"How many white women you know walkin' around butt-naked at two o'clock in the A.M.?" He gestured for Clarence to follow. "But let's go make sure."

Clarence didn't move. "I ain't goin' near no cops."

"They got their hands full. They ain't gonna be fussin' with the likes of you."

"That's right," Clarence said, "'cause I ain't stupid enough to get that close." He turned and started in the opposite direction.

"Come on, man. Why you always gotta run?"

"That's what keeps me alive. I ain't goin' down for no junkie-ass whore. 'Specially a dead one."

"If she was dead, they'd be loadin' her in the back of a coroner's van. Least we can do is find out where they're takin' her."

"Be my guest," Clarence said. "But count me out."

A moment later, he was across the street and gone.

Solomon shook his head, wondering what Clarence's tears had been about. Did he care about Myra or what? Then a sudden realization hit him. Maybe Myra hadn't shot herself up, after all. Maybe it was Clarence who gave her the needle. She goes flatline, and it was panic, not grief, making him cry.

Solomon had always thought Myra was too good for the sonofabitch anyway.

He worked his way up the block toward the police cruiser and ambulance. There was a Seaside Cab parked several yards away, its driver leaning against the left front fender, quietly sucking on a cigarette.

By the time Solomon got close, a late-model sedan had pulled up to the scene, and a big guy in a suit and tie climbed out. A plainclothes detective.

What the hell did *he* want?

One of the uniformed cops called him Blackburn and they exchanged pleasantries that, to Solomon's mind, weren't all that pleasant.

A small crowd had gathered, a lot of folks standing around in their pj's, and Solomon did his best to blend in. He still had Myra's filthy clothes tucked under one arm. A coupla house hens took one look at him, crinkled their noses, and stepped aside, giving him wide berth.

So much for that plan.

The cop named Blackburn took a look into the back of the ambulance, then turned to one of the uniforms as he gestured toward the cab driver. "I hear she tried to stab him."

Solomon's ears pricked up. Myra?

"So he says," the uniform told Blackburn. "Came at him with a pair of scissors."

"Scissors?" Blackburn seemed surprised.

"That's right." The uniform went to the front seat of the cruiser and brought out a plastic bag carrying a bloodied pair of sewing shears.

Blackburn took the bag, studied it for a moment, then handed it back. "He say what direction she came from?"

The uniform pointed across the street, which was lined with apartment houses. "Over that way. Looks like she could've cut right through from Hopi Lane."

Blackburn turned to one of the paramedics. "How bad is she hurt?"

"She's got a pretty good knot on her cheek where the cab driver thumped her, but the blood isn't hers, if that's what you're asking. Got some cuts and bruises, but nothing that would cause that much bleeding."

Hearing this, Solomon felt relieved. If that was Myra in there, at least she was okay. But what was all this bullshit about her trying to stab somebody?

Not the Myra *he* knew.

He wished he could get a closer look.

"We've gotta sit on her until the assistant M.E. gets here," Blackburn said. "I need a sample of that blood."

"We should've been on our way to the ER by now."

"And I should be in bed with a beautiful blonde, but that ain't likely to happen anytime soon."

Before the paramedic could protest, Blackburn turned and walked over to the cab driver, flashing his badge. They exchanged a few words and, from Solomon's vantage point, it looked like Blackburn was trying to bum a cigarette.

Solomon turned his attention away from them and looked in toward the woman on the gurney, figuring now was as good a time as any to get a better look. He stepped forward, moving closer to the ambulance. He wasn't halfway to it when one of the uniforms spotted him and came over.

"Hey, hey, what're you up to?"

"I think she's a friend of mine."

The uniform looked him over, barely disguising his contempt. "You been drinking, pops? Figure maybe you can sneak a peek at a naked lady?"

Solomon ignored him. "Her name is Myra."

"Well, what do you know." The uniform turned to his partner. "You hear that, Jerry? She's got a name and everything—and it ain't Tina Tits."

His partner chuckled and Solomon took an instant dislike to both of them, the way they were disrespecting Myra. He had the terrible urge to lash out, but kept himself under control.

The cop named Blackburn was coming over now, no cigarette in evidence, and he didn't look happy. "Toomey, do us all a favor and shut your fuckin' yap."

The partner, Jerry, quickly averted his eyes, but the one

called Toomey shot Blackburn a look. There wasn't any love lost between these two. For a moment, Solomon thought they might come to blows, then Toomey backed off, joining Jerry over by their patrol car.

Blackburn turned to Solomon. "You say you know this woman?"

Solomon nodded. "I think so. I just need a better look."

Blackburn gestured and they walked over to the ambulance. "Go ahead."

Solomon glanced around, felt all the eyes on him, then stepped up into the back of the ambulance.

The woman had blood on her and some of it had soaked into the blanket. Her left shoulder was exposed and Solomon immediately recognized the faded Hello Kitty tattoo adorning it.

Myra had once told him that they'd called her that when she was modeling. Kitty. She'd walk into a studio and they'd all go, "Hello, Kitty." Kinda laughing when they said it.

He let his gaze drift up to her face, but was surprised by what he saw—and it wasn't the blood that startled him.

Taking a couple involuntary steps backward, he almost fell out of the ambulance.

The cop named Blackburn steadied him. "What's wrong?"

"Nothin'," Solomon said. "She . . . she looks different, is all."

"Different? Is she your friend or not?"

Solomon was momentarily at a loss for words. How could this be? When he found his voice, he said, "I *thought* she was, but now I ain't so sure."

"What do you mean?"

Solomon swallowed. "That looks like her body, all right. But there's something wrong with her face."

Blackburn frowned at him. He looked as if he was about to respond when the woman's eyes flew open, as wide and frightened as a trapped animal's. Her mouth started moving, words tumbling out so rapidly they were barely intelligible:

". . . a lie stands on one leg, the truth on two . . ."

What the hell?

". . . a lie stands on one leg, the truth on two . . ."

Her gaze focused on Solomon.

"Two times four is a lie, two times four is a lie, two times four is a lie, two times four is a . . ."

Then, with a cry of rage like Solomon had never before heard, she sprang up from the gurney and lunged at him.

Blackburn had never seen anyone move so fast.

One minute she was babbling incoherently, the next she was launching herself at the old homeless guy like a charge from a shotgun.

Blackburn immediately grabbed for her, but she spun on him, catching him off-guard, swinging a bloody fist at his head.

He stumbled back, and before he knew it she was out of the ambulance and running. Toomey and his partner and the EMTs all stood around with their heads up their asses as Blackburn regained his footing and took off after her.

She plowed through the crowd, screams and shouts erupting around her, then cut diagonally across the road, heading for a narrow side street crowded with parked cars and boxy, rundown houses.

Blackburn heard an engine start up behind him—the patrol officers finally getting their shit together—but the psycho bitch cut sideways, heading into the darkness between two houses.

Jerking his Glock out of its holster, Blackburn followed, picking up speed, then slowing as he reached the mouth of the passageway. He listened for sounds of movement, but all he could hear was the commotion behind him, the distant barking of a dog, and—

—what?

Psycho Bitch, babbling again. Barely a whisper.

"A lie stands on one leg, the truth on two, a lie stands on one leg, the truth on two, a lie stands on one leg, the truth on . . ."

Blackburn took out his Mini-Mag, flicked it on, and pointed it into the passageway.

Psycho Bitch sat huddled near the wall of one of the houses, next to an old, rusted bicycle, the blood on her face shining garishly in the light, her eyes alive and frightened.

"Two times four is a lie, two times four is a lie, two times four is a lie, two times four is a lie . . ."

Blackburn slowly moved toward her. "Easy now."

One of her hands dropped to her side, fingers groping in the dirt, searching for something, then latching onto a small, dusty chunk of brick. Her inner arm was mottled with bruises. Needle tracks.

"Drop it," Blackburn said. "Put it down."

"Two times four is a lie, two times four is a lie, two times four is a lie, two times four is a . . ."

"Come on, now, nobody's gonna hurt you. Put the brick down and step away from the wall."

He knew it was probably pointless talking to her. She was deep inside her own head. But he kept trying anyway, wondering where the hell his backup was.

"Put it down," he told her again. "Put it down and we'll find someone to—"

There was a shout behind him as a car screeched up and—

—suddenly the fingers hurled the brick, forcing Blackburn to duck. Psycho Bitch sprang from her crouch with an animal-like agility and threw her arms around him, knocking him against the adjacent wall. The Mini-Mag flew out of his hands as—

—the shouts grew louder and then Toomey and his partner were there, pulling her off him and wrestling her to the ground as Blackburn got to his feet, struggling to catch his breath.

He stared down at them, annoyed.

"I can't believe you morons didn't cuff the bitch."

Still rattled, Solomon edged away from the ambulance, watching as the crowd of onlookers moved across the street, then down toward where the cop car had screeched to a stop.

The EMTs had already followed on foot and now they were bringing her out—the woman who wasn't quite Myra—carrying her between them, her hands cuffed behind her, her bruised and bloodied body exposed to the world.

Solomon thought about her face, about how different it had looked. And about those wild, terrified eyes.

A sudden thought occurred to him then—a memory of his childhood in St. Thomas and a grandfather who liked to tell tall tales.

Tales of darkness and death and resurrection.

And as he thought about those tales and what they'd meant to him, a single phrase crowded his brain. One that had given him nightmares for years:

Enfants du tambour.

Children of the drum.

TWO

The Man Who Couldn't Let Go

Chapter 4

Nothing good comes from a phone call at three in the morning.

Tolan had learned that the hard way, when he first got the call about Abby—exactly one year ago today. It had been a morning a lot like this one, chilly but not cold, and he'd been standing in an overheated hotel room instead of lying in his own bed.

He thought about that morning a lot. Especially when he couldn't sleep. His frequent bouts of insomnia were the aftereffects of the tragedy, and the grief that accompanied them was as palpable and unrelenting as an electrical storm.

These days, however, that grief was shadowed by a twinge of fresh guilt. Not the usual feelings of culpability—those were a constant. But something new. Different. Because the woman who had been there for him, who had nursed him through those impossible first days, was now sleeping quietly beside him, the calm amid the chaos.

Tolan lay there, staring into the darkness, listening to the nearly imperceptible sounds of her breathing, feeling the warmth of her back against his, and tried not to think about Abby and how she had once occupied that very same spot.

Then his cell phone vibrated on the night stand.

He glanced at the clock: 3:05.

Scooping up the phone, he flipped it open and checked caller ID. Blocked. He thought about letting it buzz, but was afraid the sound might wake Lisa.

Climbing out of bed, he slipped into the bathroom to answer, catching it just before it kicked over to voice mail.

"Hello?"

"Dr. Tolan?" A man's voice. Little more than a whisper.

"Yes?"

"Dr. Michael Tolan?"

"Yes," he said, not bothering to hide his impatience. "What is it?"

"Today's the day, Doctor. The day I've been waiting for."

"I'm sorry, who is this?"

"You'll find out soon enough," the caller said. "I just wanted to wish you a happy anniversary before I slit your throat."

Then the line clicked.

By the time his phone started vibrating again, Tolan had convinced himself that there was no reason to be alarmed. The caller was undoubtedly an old patient of his, playing mind games.

He'd dealt with a number of difficult cases back in his days of private practice, and this wouldn't be the first to entertain himself at his expense. Such threats were a hazard of the profession.

There had, however, been something uniquely unsettling about the caller's voice. That almost-whisper laced with a touch of menace.

And despite reassuring himself, he couldn't help feeling his discomfort deepen as he watched the vibrating phone shimmy on the surface of the bathroom counter.

For a moment he wondered if it might be one of his current patients, someone from the hospital. But it was unlikely that any of them had access to a phone. Especially at this time of morning.

He reached out, picked it up. Answered it.

"Dr. Tolan?" Not a whisper this time, but forceful, self-confident.

"Look," he said. "I know you're having fun, but I'm really not in the mood. If you want me to recommend a new therapist—"

"Sorry, Doc, I think you've got me confused with somebody else. This is Frank Blackburn."

Surprised, Tolan hesitated. "Who?"

"Frank Blackburn, OCPD?"

It took him a moment to find the memory. "Ahh, right," he said. "Sue Carmody's partner."

Carmody was a Special Victims investigator he had consulted with on a couple of cases. Their collaboration had been successful both times out, but he had never been able to warm up to her. She was a typical anal-retentive with control issues that he'd found just barely tolerable.

"Carmody transferred to another unit," Blackburn said. "But that's a conversation we'll reserve for a later date. Right now I need your help."

"Is this about one of my patients?"

"I don't think so." Blackburn sounded surprised. "Why do you ask?"

He considered telling Blackburn about the phone call but decided against it. "No reason. What can I do for you?"

"You still run the EDU over at Baycliff, right?"

"I'm the director, yes." A sixty-bed facility, the Emergency Detention Unit at Baycliff Psychiatric Hospital handled a large portion of the city's mental health emergencies, usually picking up the overflow from County General.

"I've got a Girl Gone Wild here I need you to take a look at. Real whack job."

Tolan bristled. He had never appreciated the dehumanizing slang cops used to describe the mentally ill. Not that he was a saint, but his patients were troubled human beings who deserved respect, not scorn.

"The Unit's staffed twenty-four-seven, Detective."

"I'm sure you've got a wonderful crew, Doc, but I need the big guns on this one. The way you handled that kid we brought in a few months ago was nothing short of magic."

"Is this another rape case?"

"At this point I'm not sure what it is. That's why I need you."

Tolan sighed. He'd already given up on sleep, and lying in bed dwelling on his grief wasn't doing him any good. Still, he needed time to decompress.

"Go ahead and have the night staff process her. I'll let them know you're coming and meet you there in a couple hours."

"Thanks, Doc, you're a peach. Sorry if I woke you."

Somehow Tolan got the feeling that Blackburn was never really sorry about anything.

It was a state of mind he envied.

When he got out of the shower, Lisa was awake and waiting for him, towel in hand, a look of concern on her face.

"How are you feeling?"

"I've been better," he said, taking the towel from her.

"You were asleep when I came home."

Tolan shook his head. "Playing possum. Didn't want you to worry. You came in pretty late. I figured you were staying at the beach house."

"We went to Isabel's after the movie, and you know what happens when you get four women in a room talking about men. We all start sharpening our knives."

He tried to laugh, but all he could manage was a weary smile. As he finished drying off, Lisa moved in close, slipping her arms around him. "You look miserable. Maybe you should talk to Ned again."

Ned Soren was Tolan's ex-partner. He was also his therapist.

"He'd probably just try to get me back on the fluoxetine," Tolan said. Unlike Soren, he was a strong believer that psychopharmacology was a last resort. "Drugs or no drugs, you'd think that after a year I'd be making more progress."

"There's no time limit on grief, Michael. You know that."

"Clinically, yeah. But emotionally . . . I just want to get past this. It isn't fair to you."

"You don't owe me anything."

"Bullshit."

"I just want you to heal," she said. "No matter *how* long it takes." She gave him a squeeze, kissed him. "You'll be marking this day for the rest of your life, Michael. But it'll get easier. I promise. You'll come around."

"Is that what you told the girls last night?"

"It's what I always tell them. I wouldn't say it if I didn't believe it."

"You're too goddamn good to me."

Lisa smiled. "Don't you ever forget it."

He considered telling Lisa about the phone call, but what good would that accomplish? He was certain now that it had been nothing more than a cruel joke perpetrated by a sick mind, and telling her would be equally cruel. As grounded as she was, Lisa was also a worrier. And what she worried about most was Tolan.

Why throw gas on the flames?

He thought about all the years they'd known each other

and how their friendship had only recently blossomed into romance. They had met as undergrads at UCLA, had shared a house with four other students in Westwood. There had been a fair amount of flirting at first, a night of drunken kisses that never led anywhere, and they'd quickly settled into friendship mode. Thanks to similar paths in grad school, they'd kept in touch ever since.

Lisa had served on staff at County General for several years, then signed on as head psychiatric nurse at the Baycliff EDU about six months before Tolan came on board. Shortly after Abby's death, she had encouraged him to take the director's job, and they had been working together ever since.

Truth was, she had awakened something inside him he'd thought would lay dormant forever, and the feeling was both unexpected and welcome.

He needed her. Not at the same primal level at which he'd needed Abby, but Abby had been his soul mate and there was no competing with that.

Lisa was, for lack of a better word, his savior. And if he could keep his remorse from dragging them down, they might have a future together.

By the time he was dressed, Lisa had brewed a pot of coffee and handed him a cup as he entered the kitchen. Her shift at the hospital didn't start until later that morning, and she was wearing only a T-shirt, which barely covered her ass. Her hair still had that tousled, just-got-out-of-bed look.

Tolan suddenly remembered the first night they'd made love and felt his body reacting to the memory. Maybe *that* was the date he should be marking on his calendar. Celebrate the bliss, not the pain. Anything to get him through this godforsaken day.

"Feeling any better?" she asked.

"Getting there. You look great, by the way." He set down his coffee cup. Smiled. A smile she was getting to know quite well.

"Don't even think about it. You don't have time."

"We could *make* time."

"I thought you said the police are waiting for you."

Tolan's smile broadened. He was starting to feel better now. Much better. Decompression nearly complete.

"Let 'em wait," he said.

Chapter 5

Blackburn was in the staff parking lot when Tolan pulled in.

Tolan had met the man only once, several months ago, when he and Detective Carmody brought in a young rape victim who was suffering from trauma-induced mutism. Tolan had managed to get her to talk, giving them just enough of a description to eventually help nail her attacker.

This had more to do with the girl than Tolan, but no matter how much he tried to dissuade them of the notion, the partners were convinced he'd pulled a rabbit out of his hat.

As Tolan killed the engine of his Lexus and climbed out, Blackburn came over. He was big and lean and distinctly urban. Someone you wouldn't want to piss off.

His smile, however, immediately softened him.

"Hiya, Doc. Thanks for showing up on such short notice."

It was approaching five-thirty now and Tolan was late, but if Blackburn was bothered by this he didn't show it. Tolan noted that his shirt and jacket were stained with blood.

They shook hands. "I assume she's been admitted?"

Blackburn nodded. "The doc on duty said they were gonna clean her up and put her in a cell. She's pretty docile right now, but if you're smart, you'll strap her to the goddamn bed."

Tolan nodded, gestured. "Let's walk and talk."

Baycliff Psychiatric Hospital was located on Pepper Mountain Mesa, overlooking the Pacific Ocean, and what the cluster of colorless buildings lacked in character was made up for by their surroundings.

The walkway leading to the Emergency Detention Unit was edged by neatly landscaped grounds full of oak and bigleaf maple. There was a good breeze blowing, and the leaves, a rusty yellow-gold, floated like confetti and cart-wheeled across the lawn.

Off to their right, and some distance away, was a forest of California pepper trees. A narrow pathway snaked through them, its mouth blocked by a thick chain holding a NO TRESSPASSING sign, warning off the curious.

A good quarter mile up that pathway, nestled in the Pepper Mountains, stood the remains of the old Baycliff Hospital, a once majestic structure that had been abandoned after a severe earthquake and fire over half a century ago. It remained untouched and forgotten, except by the occasional adventurous gang of teenagers looking for a midnight thrill.

The current hospital, located on what the geophysicists considered more solid ground, had been built in the late 1960s and looked it. Except for the view, it held little of the grandeur of the older model. And none of the allure.

As they walked, a sudden memory assaulted Tolan: he and Abby exploring the ruins of the old hospital one afternoon. His calendar had been free and she had closed her studio for the rest of the day, both of them hoping the adventure might help them recapture some of the energy that had been draining from their marriage of late.

As they explored the grounds—Abby furiously snapping photographs of the massive, burned-out building—they had joked of ghosts and demons, and had marveled at the courage of those who chose to visit late at night, tempting fate.

Three days later, Abby was dead.

"Here's the thing," Blackburn said as he and Tolan continued toward the EDU. "I've got a guy on his apartment floor with a ventilated chest. Less than two blocks away, your new patient shows up bare-assed in the middle of the street and tries to use the business end of a pair of scissors on a cab driver."

"I assume this isn't a coincidence?"

"She had what looks to be the victim's blood on her, including traces on her left heel, and we found a matching footprint at the scene."

Tolan sensed some hesitation. "So what's the problem?"

"A couple of things. First, the crime scene techs say the splatter pattern doesn't mesh with the blood we found on her. Thinks it's more likely she put her hands in it, then rubbed her face."

"Uh-huh," Tolan said. "What else?"

"The scissors."

"What about them?"

"They don't match the wounds. So if Miss Nature Lover is my suspect, why the sudden switch of utensils? It doesn't make sense."

These things rarely do, Tolan thought. "Have you considered she might also have been a target? Maybe she picked them up at the crime scene in an attempt to protect herself."

"I was thinking the same thing," Blackburn said. "The blood on them probably came from her hands. But to be honest, I don't know *how* she's involved—and I'd sure as hell like to find out. Unfortunately, she's a complete schizo."

Tolan bristled again. Most people who used such terms knew nothing at all about schizophrenia or mental health in general. He laid the blame for that squarely at the feet of a syndrome he called BTS—

—Bad Television Shows. And the treatment was simple: selective use of the remote control.

"You say she was naked, so no ID at all?"

"Nope. We ran her prints and got a big fat zero. Some old homeless coot thought she might be a friend of his, but he turned out to be a nut job too."

Tolan stopped just short of the EDU lobby doors and looked at him. "Listen, Detective, if we're going to work together, let's get something straight. They aren't nut jobs or whackos or schizos or loonies or maniacs. As far as I'm concerned, the only difference between my patients and a guy battling a heart arrhythmia is the organ under distress."

"Easy, Doc, I'm not trying to offend anybody here. Hell, my old man was manic-depressive."

"Then you of all people should know how damaging labels can be."

Blackburn shrugged. "The only label we had for him was asshole. But if it'll make you feel any better, consider me duly chastised."

Tolan said nothing. Truth was, he'd heard a lot worse coming out of the mouths of his own colleagues. Looking back on the year he'd spent as a medical resident, he could remember when burn victims were crispy critters and terminal patients were GPO—Good for Parts Only. Such language was a release valve, a little dark humor to help get them through those long, hard hours of sobering reality. He doubted it was any different for cops.

But for some reason he'd been particularly touchy lately. Was it the insomnia? Had his yearlong battle with sleep deprivation somehow robbed him of his capacity for tolerance and turned him into a high-minded, judgmental prick?

Taking a long, deep breath, he sighed and said, "Don't mind me, Detective. I'm a little oversensitive these days."

"That just about makes us polar opposites," Blackburn said. "But I can live with it if you can." Then he smiled. "Call me Frank, by the way. Some people tell me it's a name that suits me."

Tolan managed a smile in return. "I'm beginning to see why."

He pulled open the lobby doors and gestured Blackburn inside. He had been coming to the EDU almost daily for over nine months now and still couldn't get over how drab it looked. Faded green walls, a row of metal chairs, battered end tables carrying the requisite out-of-date news magazines. Function over aesthetics.

Adjacent to this was a wire-mesh security cage that led to the maze of hallways that made up the detention unit. A lone guard sat at a desk just inside the gate, and a sign above it read ESCAPE RISK.

Thanks to funding cutbacks, both public and private, institutions like Baycliff tended to use such facilities until their last living breath. This one was definitely in the gasping phase.

All in all, it was a far cry from the upscale office suite Tolan had once shared with Ned Soren. And the world of book signings and television appearances and standing-room-only speaking engagements seemed like another life, belonging to someone completely foreign to him.

Normally Tolan wouldn't bother coming through the lobby. Like all the other doctors on staff, he carried a special key card that got him in through any of the three private entrances located at the sides and back of the building. But hospital policy forbade allowing outsiders such access, and with Blackburn tagging along, they had to take the traditional route.

As they approached the security gate, Blackburn said, "I don't think I have to tell you that time is of the essence."

Tolan nodded. "I understand. But if she's suffering from any real psychosis, it could be weeks or even months before she opens up."

"That's not what I want to hear, Doc."

"I'm not a miracle worker," Tolan said. "Far from it."

"Maybe not. But you're the closest thing I've got."

Chapter 6

Solomon never did get his chili dogs.

After the incident on The Avenue, he'd lost his appetite and spent the next couple hours wandering the streets, feeling like somebody had ripped the guts right out of him.

He couldn't stop thinking about those wild eyes. The ones that should've belonged to Myra, but didn't.

Around about 5:45, he found himself standing in line at the Main Street Mission. They served a decent enough breakfast, and he figured, hungry or not, he'd better get some food in him before his body staged a revolt.

One of the folks in line, a young tweaker named Trinity, took one look at him and said, "You okay, Sol? You look like you seen a ghost."

Solomon had seen something, all right, but it wasn't any ghost. Ghosts were bullshit. The kind of thing you'd see in some cheesy chick movie, like that one with Demi Moore making clay pots and staring dewy-eyed at Patrick what's-his-name as he professed his everlasting love.

Ghosts were all Hollywood, and Solomon was convinced that what he'd seen this morning was pure Louisiana. Not the Louisiana of po'boys and Zydeco and drunken college girls flashing their headlights at Mardi Gras. Not even the Louisiana of shrunken heads and mojo beads. But the one he'd known as a child, the one his grandfather had taught him about, where bad things lurked and faith was as much a weapon as it was a source of comfort. Where the divine vision was sometimes accompanied by the beat of a dark drum and the smell of rotting flesh.

When he was nine years old, Solomon and his little brother, Henry, used to take the caps off soda bottles, jam them into the soles of their tennis shoes, and head on down to the Quarter, where they'd tap dance for nickels and dimes.

One day, they were headed back to St. Thomas, their pockets full of change, when Solomon got distracted by a discarded hubcap, thinking it would make a pretty good tip jar.

Henry, who wasn't quite six and had about as much sense as a brain-damaged cocker spaniel, wandered into the street without looking, and got himself hit by a police car.

Solomon looked up just in time to see his little brother go under the front bumper, tumbling beneath the car like socks in a dryer, only to be spit out the back looking as if every bone in his body had been busted.

Along with his head.

A spray of nickels and dimes littered the street around him.

The cop brought the car to a sudden stop, threw open his door, and staggered out. He had a bottle in his hand. He took one look at Henry, threw up on the side of the road, then climbed back into his car and hightailed it out of there.

A little while later, more cops showed up and Solomon

told his story. Then his mama came and his grandfather, too, and pretty soon there was a lot of crying and screaming going on, most of which he didn't want to remember.

They never found the cop who killed Henry. Never even tried, according to his grandfather. But one night, shortly after the funeral, when Papi was tucking him into bed, he kissed Solomon on the forehead and said, "Don't you worry, boy, Henry got The Rhythm on his side now. And when those drums start beating, he'll rise up, and he won't stop until the world's been synchronized and he gets the one who wronged him."

At the time, Solomon wasn't quite sure what his grandfather meant by all that, but he was smart enough to know that it couldn't be good. Because in Solomon's mind, *he* was the one who had wronged Henry. If he hadn't been playing around with that hubcap, if he'd been watching his brother like Mama always told him to, then Henry would be alive and cuddled up next to him right now.

Solomon started to cry then, thinking how much he missed his brother, and he almost wished the stupid little runt would rise up from the grave at that very moment and come after him, because *he* was the one who deserved to die.

He cried well into the night and every night after that for almost a month. But the drums never beat and Henry never showed up. And Solomon would be lying if he didn't admit that he'd felt just a touch of relief.

A year later, almost to the day of Henry's death, he was staring at the *Times Picayune* over Papi's shoulder when he saw the picture of a cop who had blown his own brains out in the middle of the county morgue. The cop had gone there late at night to investigate a break-in. Why he'd decided to shoot himself was a mystery to everyone concerned, but Solomon immediately recognized him and pointed him out to Papi.

Papi nodded. "That's right," he said softly. "Your brother did good."

After sixty-six years living in poverty, Solomon was finally driven out of Louisiana by the bitch herself, Hurricane Katrina. The night the levees broke, he was stuck in a jail cell on a drunk and disorderly, watching from a wire-mesh window as Katrina unleashed her fury.

He didn't know if the cops had forgotten about him or left him there intentionally, but they were long gone by the time the storm was in full bloom. Before the night was over, Solomon found himself waist deep in water, calling out for help.

But no help came.

Three days later he was still there, huddled on the top bunk of his cell, stinking of his own bodily waste, alive thanks only to sheer willpower. All the strength had been sapped out of him, but he still managed to call out every once in a while, hoping someone might be within earshot.

Then, finally, thankfully, a face appeared at the window. A kid of about fourteen. "You okay, mister?"

"Besides the fact that I'm hungrier than a motherfucker? I'm doin' just fine."

The kid grinned, then said, "Hang on," and a moment later he was banging at the mesh with something solid, looked like a crowbar. It took awhile, but he managed to pry enough space for Solomon to slip through, then pulled him into the battered row boat he was piloting.

"Got me a bus," the boy said, handing Solomon a hunk of beef jerky. "Just across the way. I'm headed up to Houston. I hear they been takin' folks in."

"Must be pretty bad, they takin' us to Houston."

"Bad ain't the word, mister. We been fucked, and no-body gives a good goddamn."

Solomon pulled himself upright then, taking in a full view of what he'd only been able to see a slice of from his jailhouse window. There was destruction in every direction. The city he'd spent his entire life in had been bull-dozed, drowned, and left for dead.

Bodies floated in the water. Old folks. Young. Even lit-tle babies. It was only then that Solomon realized just how lucky he was.

The kid rowed his boat up a river that had once been a street, picking up a few more survivors, people looking as weak and shell-shocked as Solomon felt, all of them happy to be alive. Then the kid steered them to a patch of dry land, a debris-covered road where a beat-up old school bus was waiting.

He drove them all the way to Houston.

Every once in a while Solomon would catch the boy staring at him in the rear-view mirror. About halfway through the ride, a thought occurred to him—one that had been stirring at the periphery of his tired old brain ever since he'd seen that fourteen-year-old face in the jailhouse window:

The boy looked a lot like Henry. Or at least what Henry might've looked like if he'd lived that long.

Solomon could almost hear Papi's voice.

Your brother did good.

Those words kept rolling around in his head as he let the low rumble of the bus lull him to sleep.

He never did return to Louisiana.

Reconstruction had been stalled by empty promises and government bureaucracy, and Solomon had no fam-ily left to go home to anyway. After he left Houston, he'd decided a new start was in order, so he used the few dollars a relief worker had given him and caught a Greyhound bus to Ocean City, California—part beach community, part urban melting pot.

He washed dishes for a while at a little bar and grill near the ocean called Riley's House, but that ended when Riley burned the place down for the insurance money.

Despite all the smiling millionaires on TV talking about spikes in the stock market, times were hard for folks like Solomon. The days of tap dancing on bottle tops were long gone, and the nickels and dimes didn't come easily. Without any marketable skills, jobs were scarce, and he couldn't make rent at the shitty little hotel-apartment he'd been staying in.

So he wound up on the street. Spent some time wandering from shelter to shelter before migrating to the river bottom, where much of the city's homeless lived.

Now here he stood, waiting in line for a plate of eggs he didn't much feel like eating, thinking about the woman who wasn't quite Myra and wondering where they'd take her.

She was dangerous, he knew that much. Hell, everybody did—but they didn't really know what kind of danger. Not like Solomon.

Somewhere in his head he heard the beating of dark drums, and despite his fear, he wondered if he should do something about it. Warn somebody.

Because whoever had wronged that poor woman, whoever had caused the pain that was keeping her hostage to that unrelenting beat—

—was about to wish he'd never been born.

Chapter 7

"Jane Doe Number 314. Brought in on a 5150."

Clayton Simm was at the tail end of his shift and looked it. His eyes were bloodshot and the circles under them were as dark as camouflage paint.

A native of Seattle, Simm had only recently moved to the Ocean City area. He'd been recommended for a staff position by an old Harvard classmate of Tolan's and, in his short time here, had proven to have good diagnostic skills and even better instincts.

Tolan had quickly warmed to him. Especially after he'd agreed to work graveyard.

The three of them—Simm, Tolan, and Blackburn—stood near the EDU nurses' station, where Simm stifled a small yawn and continued his recital of the facts.

"She was cleaned up and clothed by the nursing staff. I did a basic physical and found her to be malnourished but in fairly good health and free of injury, except for a few minor contusions on her arms and feet, and a pretty significant one near the right cheekbone. No sign of sexual assault. She appears to be about thirty-two years old, with a clear case of heterochromia."

"Hetero what?" Blackburn asked.

"Heterochromia," Simm said. "Her eyes are two different colors. Green and brown. It's pretty rare in humans, but it does happen."

"Any sign of glaucoma?" Tolan asked.

"Retinal exam came up negative, with no indication of hemorrhage or injury. If I had to guess, I'd say the etiology is genetic."

"I don't remember anything hinky about her eyes," Blackburn said.

"It's not always obvious," Tolan told him. "Especially under less than optimal lighting conditions."

"The patient has no other identifying marks or scars," Simm continued, "except for a small tattoo of what looks to be a cartoon cat on her left shoulder. On arrival, she presented signs of mild catatonia. Offered no resistance to taking blood and urine samples, which were sent off for testing. The EMTs reported that just prior to transport she had an acute violent outburst accompanied by hysterical, disorganized speech."

"A lie stands on one leg, the truth on two," Blackburn said.

They both looked at him. "What?"

"That's what she kept saying. A lie stands on one leg, the truth on two. Over and over again."

It was a quote from one of Tolan's favorite books. Abby had given him a copy for his thirty-seventh birthday.

"*Poor Richard's Almanac*," he said.

Blackburn shrugged. "You think her behavior could be caused by the drug abuse? Maybe she got hold of some bad powder or some PCP."

"That's always a possibility."

"True," Simm said. "But I didn't notice any overt signs of drug use."

Blackburn stared at him. "You're kidding me, right? She's a goddamn junkie. Got like a thousand needle marks on her arms."

Simm's gaze went to Tolan, then shifted back to Blackburn. "Are you sure we're talking about the same woman?"

"I know who *I'm* talking about. Do you?"

"Sorry, Detective, but I examined her thoroughly. There was minor bruising, yes, but I didn't see any needle marks."

"Now, wait just a minute," Blackburn said. "The eyes are one thing, I'll give you that, but I know smack tracks when I see 'em." He turned to Tolan. "What's the story here, Doc? You letting the inmates run the asylum now?"

Tolan grimaced. If blunt were an art, they'd be calling this guy Picasso.

He exchanged looks with Simm, whose body language spoke of a sudden distaste for all things Blackburn. Tolan had a hard time believing Simm would make such a blatant error, but sent him an unspoken message to keep his cool.

It took obvious effort, but Simm complied.

After a moment, Tolan said, "I'm sure it's a simple oversight. I'll reexamine her once I get into the room."

"She's in SR-three," Simm said. "Without the tox screen results it's hard to rule out any possible organic causes, but judging by what the EMTs told me, I'd say she's presenting all the characteristics of BRP."

Brief Reactive Psychosis was a fairly common disorder brought on by sudden intense stress or psychological trauma. Aggressive behavior and nonsensical phrases were typical indicators. It usually didn't last long, no more than a day or two, but sometimes the symptoms could take up to a month to clear. Anything beyond that and they'd have to start considering Schizophreniform Disorder or even schizophrenia itself.

Unfortunately, without a patient history, they had no way of knowing how long the symptoms had been present.

"You restrain her?"

Simm shook his head. "She hasn't demonstrated any violent or self-destructive behavior since she was admitted. I didn't see any reason to."

"Mistake number two," Blackburn said.

Tolan shot him a glance. Despite what Blackburn might think, he supported Simm's decision. California statute prohibited the use of restraints unless the patient presented an immediate danger to herself or the staff, a law not everyone paid attention to.

But Tolan did. And he was glad Simm had made the right call.

"Thanks, Clayton. Go on home and get some sleep."

"It's early. I've still got an hour or so."

Tolan appreciated the man's dedication, but tried his own hand at bluntness.

"You look like hell," he said, then patted Simm's shoulder. "Now get out of here."

Chapter 8

The corridors of the detention unit were quiet at this time of morning.

That would change soon enough.

After the current roster of patients began to trickle awake and new patients were escorted in, the buzz of activity would rise to almost intolerable levels, making it nearly impossible to think, let alone work.

A colleague of Tolan's had once asked him why he'd left the relative peace and quiet of private practice for the chaos of this place. He couldn't really remember his answer. Something noble, no doubt. Truth be told, he was here for one simple reason:

Penance.

He led Blackburn down a wide, battle-scarred hallway past the windowed doors of the seclusion rooms. There were six rooms in all, each with an adjacent observation booth, each housing one of their more dangerous patients.

As they passed the door to SR-6, Tolan heard a loud pounding sound and turned to see the face of a young man framed in the small rectangle of safety glass in the upper half of the door.

"Hey, Doc, I gotta talk to you."

Bobby Fremont. Twenty-three years old. Suffering from Antisocial Personality Disorder and at the tail end of a manic episode. His voice was muffled through the glass.

Tolan held a finger up to Blackburn, then moved to an intercom mounted near the door and flicked a switch. "What is it, Bobby?"

"Who's the new girl? The one they brought in this morning?"

"That isn't your concern."

"Come on, man, cut me a break here. I've had a stiffy ever since I saw them drag her down the hallway."

Tolan frowned at him. "Sorry they even let you see her, Bobby. They should've closed your shade."

The detention unit was coed only out of necessity. Which sometimes created problems. Especially for guys like Bobby, who was often sexually aggressive.

"Fuck that," Fremont said. "Why you always wanna spoil my fun?"

"That's not what I'm trying to—"

"You fucking with me, Doc? Huh? Is that what you're doing? You start fucking with me, I'll rip your goddamn head off and shit down your throat."

Tolan paused. That was a new one.

"I mean it, asshole. You'll be puking blood all over the goddamn linoleum. And when I'm done with you, I'll stick that bitch six ways to Sunday and she'll love every minute of it."

"Jesus," Blackburn muttered.

Tolan shot him a look, then returned his attention to Fremont. The kid had been in and out of jailhouses and psych wards since he was eleven years old, presenting the typical behavior associated with the disorder: truancy, stealing, vandalism, assault, and more fights than he was able or willing to remember.

The cops, who dealt with him on a regular basis, had brought him here two days earlier for his umpteenth psych

evaluation after he'd beaten a drug dealer almost sense-
less and urinated on his head. Just another day for Bobby.

A sudden thought occurred to Tolan.

This morning's phone call.

*I just wanted to wish you a happy anniversary before I
slit your throat.*

Could the caller have been Bobby? He certainly had
the necessary temperament. But how could he have gotten
hold of a phone? Or, for that matter, Tolan's cell phone
number?

Making a mental note to check with staff, Tolan said,
"Why don't we talk about this in session?"

Fremont slapped a palm against the glass. "Fuck session. Just let me out of this freak factory."

"It's either here or jail, Bobby. You know that."

"Fuck you," Fremont said. "You're a dead man. You
hear me? Don't you ever turn your back on me." He kicked
the door, then disappeared from sight.

Tolan flicked off the intercom and sighed. Aggressive
behavior had kept Fremont from maintaining a job or any
significant social relationships for the better part of his
life. After treating him on and off for the last several
months, Tolan was convinced that, despite claims to the
contrary, Bobby was purposely looking for ways to get
himself back inside.

He suspected it was loneliness more than anything else
that brought him here. The only staff member Fremont
had developed a decent relationship with was Lisa, and
Tolan wouldn't be surprised to discover that she was part
of the allure.

"And I thought *I* had the world's shittiest job," Blackburn said.

Tolan turned. "Do me a favor and keep your comments
to yourself. Especially when I'm talking to a patient."

"Sorry, Doc."

"You keep saying that."

"I've got a couple of exes don't think I say it enough."

"I can only imagine."

Cassie Gerritt, a third-year med school student who moonlighted as an orderly, was stationed inside the observation booth. She was a ruddy-faced kid with an easy, Southern smile, who just happened to be built like a fullback—a physical trait that often came in handy when dealing with some of their more uncooperative patients.

She was seated at a computer, her concentration centered on the glowing monitor, when Tolan and Blackburn stepped into the booth.

She looked up in surprise. "Dr. Tolan. You're up awfully early."

"Nothing like a little Circadian Rhythm Disorder to keep things interesting," he said. "This is Frank Blackburn."

As Cassie and Blackburn exchanged hellos and shook hands, Tolan looked through the one-way mirror into the small room beyond, which, like everything else in the building, was showing its age.

A single fluorescent fixture above the bed did little to illuminate pale green walls that had been scarred by several decades of graffiti. Each year a new coat of paint was slapped on, only to be followed by another layer of desperate and often incoherent messages scratched into the surface by fingernail, pencil, or anything else a patient could manage to get his hands on.

Some of them were written in blood.

Jane Doe Number 314 lay in the fetal position, her back to the glass, her hair still damp from the shower the nursing staff had given her. Her blanket lay at her feet and she was hugging herself, the thin white hospital smock doing little to warm her.

Tolan turned to Cassie. "She's shivering. You might want to turn up the heat in there." One of the few good things the unit had been blessed with was climate-controlled rooms. In theory, at least.

"She isn't reacting to the cold," Cassie said. "It's already set at seventy-eight degrees."

"Oh?"

"Ever since we put her in there, she's been shivering and twitching like she's got bugs in her veins. You ask me, we're looking at an acute case of RLS." Like most med school students, Cassie was always anxious to demonstrate her diagnostic skills, but her accuracy rate left something to be desired.

Blackburn said, "That's that restless leg thing, right?"

She nodded. "It's a neurologic movement disorder. Affects about ten percent of the population."

"I think my first wife had it. Drove me nuts with all her kicking and twitching in the middle of the night. I always told her she was possessed by the Devil. Which pretty much turned out to be true."

They both looked at him and Blackburn shrugged. "Just making conversation."

Tolan returned his gaze to Jane Doe. She was much smaller than he had expected.

Although psychotic rage—if that indeed was what she had experienced—often gave its victims strength beyond their size, the way Blackburn had described her, Tolan had envisioned another Cassie.

An Amazon, not a pixie.

He guessed she was about 5' 1", with a weight count just over 100 lbs.

With the exception of Lisa and, of course, Cassie, it seemed to Tolan that he had always been surrounded by an inordinate amount of petite women: his mother and two sisters, several of the nurses on staff—and Abby, who had often shopped in the junior section of Macy's because the clothes fit her better.

At 6' 2", he had towered over her. To some, their pairing had seemed incongruous, like an old vaudevillian comedy team. But he had loved the compactness of her body, the small, soft curves, and the way it fit so naturally with his.

Adjusting to Lisa's taller, more muscular frame had taken time. And sometimes, like this morning, when they made love, he found himself yearning for, even imagining, those small, soft curves. Then he'd open his eyes, see Lisa staring up at him, and the feeling of finality, the sense of loss that had plagued him for so long, was as devastating as a blow to the chest.

Tolan suddenly realized that Cassie was saying something. A jumble of words flitted by without fully registering on the radar.

"Sorry," he said. "What was that?"

"I hear she's quite a handful. You want me to go in there with you?"

Tolan shook his head. "I'll manage. But stay alert." He turned to Blackburn. "And don't expect much. It may take awhile to get her to trust me."

"Faith, Doc, that's what I've got. I know you won't let me down."

Tolan had no response to that.

Chapter 9

She didn't stir when he entered the room. Showed no indication that she even knew he was there. She had stopped shivering, but her back still faced him, her body pulled into that tight fetal ball.

He grabbed a chair from the corner and sat next to her. As he got in close, staring at her frail, hunched shoulders, an odd feeling washed over him. A feeling of . . . how could he describe it?

Of familiarity.

Which, of course, made no sense. As far as he knew, he'd never seen this woman before in his life. Yet the feeling persisted, like an old memory that weighs on the mind but refuses to surface.

Tolan sat there a moment, watching her, noting the gentle rise and fall of her back as she breathed, wondering what it was that brought that feeling on.

Then, doing his best to push it aside, he said softly, "Good morning."

The shoulders stiffened. He'd startled her. Not what he'd wanted to do, but he pressed on. "Easy now, I just want to talk." He paused. "I'm Dr. Tolan. You think you could tell me your name?"

A sound rose from her small figure, an animal-like whimper. Frightened. In pain. But it wasn't in response to his question. It was an involuntary utterance, as if she were struggling with a nightmare. But he was sure she was wide awake.

She started shivering again, reminding him, oddly enough, of an old dog he'd once had. A black Akita that suffered from Cognitive Dysfunction Syndrome. Canine Alzheimer's. The dog would sometimes shiver uncontrollably, her head low, tail tucked between her legs, as if she'd forgotten who or where she was and couldn't find her way home.

Watching Jane Doe shiver, he remembered Blackburn's insistence that she was a junkie, and wondered if he might be right. Her erratic behavior, coupled with the body spasms, might indicate the beginning stages of withdrawal.

Or maybe, as Simm had suggested, her symptoms were trauma-induced. Severe trauma could produce a number of unpredictable psychological and physical reactions, and this woman had possibly seen or even participated in a brutal murder.

He leaned in closer. "If you can't or don't want to tell me your name," he said, "what do I call you?"

Another whimper. No telling what it meant.

"All right," Tolan said. "No names for now. Let's try something different."

Despite his faith in Simm's examination, he wanted to check her arms for needle marks, hoping he'd be able to avoid too severe a reaction. He thought about calling Cassie into the room, but decided against it. He sensed no threat from this woman. Not even a hint.

"Dr. Simm did a wonderful job of making sure you're physically healthy, but there are still a couple things I need to check. So I'm going to have to touch you. Do you understand?"

No sound at all this time.

She was still hugging herself, elbows tucked inward. He waited a moment, then carefully reached over and took hold of her exposed right hand, which gripped her left shoulder so tightly the knuckles were white.

The touch seemed to set off a spark and she jerked away from him, hugging herself even tighter.

Tolan gave her a moment and she relaxed a bit.

"Let's try one more time," he said. "I promise I won't hurt you."

He was about to reach for her again when a tiny, cracked voice that was barely audible rose from her small frame:

"A lie stands on one leg, the truth on two . . ."

Tolan froze, that wave of familiarity washing over him again. Who was this woman?

"A lie stands on one leg, the truth on two . . ."

She spoke quietly, but the tone and tenor of her voice sliced right through him, exposing a raw nerve.

"Two times four is a lie," she murmured. "Two times four is a lie . . ."

Finally finding his own voice, Tolan said, "Sometimes it seems as if we live in a world full of lies. And lies cause nothing but hurt. Even the small ones." He paused. "Has someone lied to you? Hurt you?"

She spoke again, but it came out so low and soft that he couldn't decipher the words. He wasn't sure if she had responded to his question or had simply repeated the same phrase.

"Talk to me," he said. "Tell me who hurt you."

He reached out again, touching her shoulder, her reaction much less violent this time. She began to move, unfolding her arms, slowly turning toward him.

The wild damp hair fell away from her face as she looked up at him for a brief, lucid moment, her voice soft and full of quiet pain:

"You . . ." she said. "You hurt me."

And in that moment, Tolan felt the hairs on the back of his neck rise. He jumped to his feet, backing away from the bed, and he knew with an unblemished certainty that he had just lost his mind, because the face staring up at him, with its fierce, unflinching eyes—

—was Elizabeth Abagail Tolan.

Abby.

His dead wife.

Chapter 10

Blackburn saw it coming just moments before it actually happened. Pushing his way out of the observation booth, he moved to the seclusion-room door. "Get this thing open. Now!"

Cassie quickly punched in a security code on the keyboard in front of her and, with a faint beep, the lock unlatched.

Blackburn threw the door wide and—

—Psycho Bitch was already midway through her attack, hands going for Tolan's throat. For some inexplicable reason, Tolan just stood there, looking like a virgin hunter about to be sacrificed to a hungry lion.

Blackburn shot across the room and swatted her, hard, right across the face. With a howl, she grabbed her nose and fell to the floor, immediately drawing her body inward, curling into a ball, as she half-squealed, half-whispered the now familiar chant, her words coming out in wet, nasal gasps:

"A lie stands on one leg, the truth on two, a lie stands on one leg, the truth on two . . ."

And now Cassie was there, saying, "Get her on the bed."

They grabbed her limbs, forcing her out of the ball, hoisting her to the mattress as she bucked and twisted, trying to break free.

A moment later, a security guard burst into the room and joined in.

"A lie stands on one leg, the truth on two, a lie stands on one leg, the truth on two . . ."

Nose bleeding, she rocked her head from side to side as Cassie worked with quiet efficiency and buckled her into restraints, wrists and ankles, then pulled a belt across her waist. She continued to thrash, blood flying, until Cassie held her head in place and pulled a strap across her forehead.

"Two times four is a lie, two times four is a lie . . ."

Blackburn thought about Tolan chastising him for calling these people whack jobs. But if a phrase ever described someone accurately, it was that one, because she was about the wackiest whack job he'd ever encountered.

"Two times four is a lie, two times four is a lie, two times four is a lie, two times four is a lie, two times four is a lie . . ."

After a moment, she finally began to calm down, the words gradually dying on her lips.

Blackburn caught his breath, then turned to find Tolan on the floor, his back against the wall, looking about as shaken as a man can get.

Which surprised him. Until this moment, Tolan had come off as a true professional, a guy in control of himself and his patients. Which was pretty much a miracle when you considered what Tolan had been through over the last year. The guy was a rock.

But there was something now that didn't quite fit. Something more to Tolan's demeanor than the sudden surprise of a patient going ape shit. His eyes registered a shock that was far deeper than the situation warranted, as if he had just seen or witnessed an event that Blackburn wasn't privy to.

The image of the old homeless guy came into Blackburn's head. He, too, had had that look when he saw the bitch. Not quite as severe as Tolan's, but he *had* backed away from her with what, at the time, had seemed to be an unwarranted expression of surprise and fear.

Blackburn had just assumed the old guy was off his rocker—so many of the homeless were—but it now appeared that this woman, whoever she was, had some hidden ability to render men powerless. Something in her look or her demeanor or her scent, something Blackburn was unable to see or feel or smell, made them vulnerable to an attack. She was an insect, stinging her victims into submission before she devoured them.

"We okay in here?" the guard asked Cassie.

She nodded and he headed back out the door.

Glancing down at the smear of blood on the back of his hand, Blackburn watched as Cassie used a tissue to swab Psycho Bitch's face and nose. He didn't think he'd broken anything, but she was certainly a mess.

And she was no longer fighting. Just stared at the ceiling as if none of this had happened, looking for all the world like a corpse waiting for the embalmer.

Blackburn wondered if she was too far gone to help him. She was about as cracked as you can get, and no amount of spit and bailing wire would put her back together again. And judging by Tolan's demeanor, he wasn't in any shape to help out.

Blackburn held out a hand to him. "You all right, Doc?"

Tolan ignored the offer. "Her face . . ." he said.

He still looked dazed.

Blackburn frowned, remembering something similar coming out of the old homeless guy's mouth. Looking over at the bitch again, he realized he'd never seen her without blood all over her face.

"Yeah, I guess I banged her up pretty good."

"No," Tolan said, "that's not what I mean. She . . . she looks just like . . ."

Then he paused, letting the words trail off as he dragged himself to his feet. His gaze had fallen on Psycho Bitch, his eyes abruptly coming into focus as the shock that had been clouding them for the last few moments seemed to vanish in an instant. Now they showed relief.

"Doc?"

Tolan shook his head. "Nothing. It's nothing," he said. "I . . . I don't know what happened. She just took me by surprise."

Sensing there was a lot more to it than that, Blackburn was about to respond when his cell phone bleeped. He took it from his coat pocket, checked the screen.

Mats Hansen.

He clicked it on. "I'm kinda in the middle of something here."

"So am I," Mats said. "And you're gonna want to see this."

"What've you got?"

"Not over a cell. You never know who's listening."

"Oh, for crissakes," Blackburn said. "Give."

"No way. This is too hot. This case just took a major left turn. So get your ass over to the lab ASAP."

Then the line went dead.

Mats had always been something of a drama queen, but this was ridiculous.

Blackburn looked at Tolan, who seemed to have almost fully recovered now and was crossing to the bed. When he got there, he stared down at Psycho Bitch with only a trace of hesitation. Whatever had spooked him was gone.

"So what's the prognosis, Doc? Any chance you'll get her to open up?"

Tolan kept staring at her, as if he wasn't quite sure he trusted his eyes. "I don't have an answer for you," he said.

"Or a timetable, for that matter." Then he turned to Blackburn. "But one thing I do know: You owe my colleague an apology."

Blackburn frowned. "How so?"

Tolan nodded to Psycho Bitch's forearms, which were fully displayed under the fluorescent light. "No needle marks."

Blackburn stared at them for a long moment.

In all the excitement, he hadn't noticed them until now. And Tolan was right. There were a few bruises there but nothing else.

What the fuck?

He could've sworn those were junkie arms he'd seen in that passageway. Would've bet a year's salary on it.

Maybe *he* was the one who was high.

"I've got somewhere to be," he said, then gestured to Cassie and crossed to the door. She moved to the keypad mounted next to it and punched in a brief code.

The door beeped and clicked open.

"If anything changes," Blackburn told Tolan, "be sure to give me a call."

He looked at Psycho Bitch's arms again, wondering how the hell he could've been so wrong, the theme to *The Twilight Zone* rolling through his head as he opened the door and left.

Chapter 11

The County Morgue was located in the Government Center just off Victoria Avenue. Blackburn got there in about twenty minutes and found Mats waiting for him in one of the autopsy rooms, the body of Carl Janovic laid out on a stainless-steel table.

It looked like Mats had been busy. The body had been stripped down and prepped for cutting, which was a surprise. The coroner's office rarely moved this quickly. For some reason Janovic's autopsy had been bumped to the top of the list.

What was going on here?

"Any luck with the Jane Doe?" Mats asked.

Blackburn sighed. "She's about half a step away from being a lost cause."

"Where'd you take her? County?"

Blackburn shook his head. "Place is a zoo. I need results, not a Band-Aid."

"Don't tell me you took her to Baycliff?" There was a trace of alarm in his voice.

"Yeah," Blackburn said. "Is that a problem?"

Mats hooked a finger, gesturing for Blackburn to take a closer look at the body. "You tell me."

Putting gloved fingers to Janovic's left ear, he pinched

the lobe and gently pulled on it. The ear flopped back, connected to the head by only a strip of bloody tissue.

Blackburn felt the Snickers bar he'd scarfed down on the way over start to back up a bit.

"I didn't notice this until I got the wig off," Mats said. "Looks like our perp tried to sever the ear. My guess is he was interrupted in the process. Possibly by your Jane Doe."

Blackburn knew what this meant, but wanted it confirmed. "What are you telling me?"

"Exactly what you think," Mats said. "It's Vincent. He's back."

The Snickers bar rolled over a couple of times, then settled with a thud.

Vincent.

Holy Jesus.

The man they called Vincent was a serial perp who had taken the department and the city on a seven-month wild ride. Blackburn had only been peripherally involved in the case, but he'd felt the burn, just like everyone else.

Over the course of those seven months, eight Bayside County residents had been found obscenely butchered, their corpses carved up and rearranged as if the killer was using their body parts as some sort of artistic statement.

Each victim's left ear had been sliced off, nowhere to be found.

When that little detail was leaked to the press, the killer was immediately dubbed Van Gogh, and members of the task force assigned to the case soon started calling him Vincent.

The search for the killer had been extensive, had nearly exhausted the resources of the department, and had caused the early retirement of the task force leader, a borderline alcoholic who had been in over his head from the start.

And they got nothing.

No leads. No suspects. No DNA. No arrest.

The FBI was consulted, but hadn't worked up more than a generic unsub profile that was virtually useless to the investigation.

Then, shortly after he'd taken number eight, Vincent fell off the map and hadn't been heard from since. Several weeks passed, then a year, and as frustrating as the case was, the collective sigh of relief was audible at least three counties over. Wherever he'd gone, they all hoped to hell he wouldn't come back.

Wishful thinking, from the looks of it.

Blackburn stared at the nearly severed ear. If Mats was right, if Vincent was indeed back, then taking a possible witness to Tolan had been a fairly large mistake.

Tolan's wife had been Vincent's eighth victim.

"Tell me you're kidding," Blackburn said. "Tell me you're just having a little fun at my expense."

"Believe me, I wish I could."

"You sure this isn't some kind of half-assed copycat?"

"I'm sure," Mats said.

Putting the ear back in place, he shifted a hand to Janovic's mouth and grabbed hold of his lower lip.

In every homicide, particularly those involving serial murders, investigators try to keep at least one detail out of the press. That detail helps weed out the chaff and send the false confessors packing. The theory being that only the killer would know about it.

In the Van Gogh murders, the killer had left behind a very distinctive calling card that only a select few in the department were aware of. Even Blackburn had been in the dark until recently.

He watched as Mats pulled the lip downward, exposing

the pink flesh inside. There was a tiny mark burned into it with what the medical examiners had determined was a battery-powered cauterizing tool. The kind fishermen use.

Anyone who got e-mail or surfed the Net had seen the mark a thousand times:

;)

Blackburn stared at it.

"Ohhh, fuck," he said. "The shit has just officially hit the fan."

Chapter 12

Tolan wasn't sure what had happened in seclusion room three, but he knew it wasn't something he could easily dismiss.

After leaving Cassie to keep an eye on Jane Doe Number 314, he found Lisa at the nurses' station, signing in for her shift and getting ready for the morning handover. She was wearing her blue scrubs and carrying what looked like a half gallon of coffee in a Starbucks cup. She took one look at him and said, "What's wrong?"

Tolan shook his head. "Nothing, I'm fine."

"You don't look fine."

"I had a long night, remember? Do me a favor and cancel my morning session."

"Michael, what—"

"Just cancel it, okay?"

He immediately realized he'd been too abrupt, so he softened and said, "I'm sorry. Everything's fine, but I'm wrapped up with this new patient and I need some time to think."

Lisa eyed him skeptically, but finally nodded. She had always had the good sense to know when to back off. She squeezed his hand. "Consider it canceled."

"Thanks."

Then he left her there and headed straight to his office.

Self-analysis can sometimes be a dangerous thing, but Tolan knew he needed to sit himself down for a careful review.

He was obviously losing touch with reality. That much was certain.

The face he'd seen, the voice he'd heard, was clearly Abby's, yet the patient in that room just as clearly wasn't. Once he'd gotten to his feet and taken another look at her, he saw a petite, not unattractive young woman who bore only the slightest resemblance to his dead wife.

So why, then, had it seemed so real?

Was it this day? Could the anniversary of Abby's death be having that much of an effect on him?

You. You hurt me.

It was true. He *had* hurt Abby. Many times in the last months of their marriage. But the biggest hurt of all had come in the form of a betrayal. A betrayal she had never even known about.

On the night she died, Tolan was not alone.

When the police called to tell him the tragic news, that she'd been found in her studio, murdered, her body brutally shredded, the shower had been going full blast in the bathroom behind him.

And waiting inside was a woman he'd met only hours before.

He could always make the claim that nothing had happened yet, that no bodily parts had been compromised, no fluids exchanged, but the betrayal of trust had already been committed. And in those last few hours, he had become the kind of man he had always despised.

A cheat. A philanderer. A liar.

You. You hurt me.

He had come to Los Angeles for a business meeting. His book, *What Color Is Your Anger?*, had been a surprise *New York Times* bestseller. Several national television appearances had put him on the network radar. Book signings that usually attracted a crowd of one or two people, suddenly had lines around the block. And celebrities he had known only from their television and movie work were calling to meet him.

It was a pretty heady experience, and he hadn't handled it well. Like so many others assaulted by sudden fame, he had begun to believe the hype and had started to lose touch with what was important to him.

He was, after all, a rising star—George Clooney meets Dr. Phil. At least that's how one talk show host had described him. His network Q-rating among women ages twenty-two to fifty was through the roof and rising. He was the man of the moment. The media's new darling.

In retrospect, it was all pretty ridiculous. His star had been a lot brighter and hotter than it had any right to be and had threatened to burn a hole right through his four-year marriage. He had become difficult to live with and he and Abby had begun fighting on a regular basis.

Vicious fights sometimes. And none more vicious than the one they'd had the night she died.

He had accused her of cheating on him. An accusation she vehemently denied. But the color of his anger was black, as black as an empty soul, and he couldn't be reasoned with.

He had been planning to drive the three hours to Los Angeles the next morning, but left that night instead and drove straight to the Beverly Wilshire Hotel, nearly causing an accident on his way there.

His meeting was scheduled for eleven A.M., an exploratory meet-and-greet at Paramount Pictures' syndication wing, which had been making noise about featuring him in a new daily talk show.

After checking into the hotel, he'd gone straight to the bar, looking to quell his anger with as many drinks as he could manage.

And he managed quite a few.

He was a couple hours into it when a soft voice at his shoulder said, "Aren't you that doctor? The one who wrote the book?"

He turned to find a stunning young woman of about twenty-six standing next to him. She looked vaguely familiar and he was sure he had seen her on television or in the movies. What the tabloids would call a starlet.

"It's Tolan, right? Michael Tolan?"

By then his anger had dissolved into a drunken, formless melancholy. "Right now I'm not sure *who* I am."

The young woman smiled and shook his hand, telling him her name. The warmth of her skin sent a small tremor through him.

"I just love your book," she said. "It's my new bible."

He'd had no real response to that. Was sure that whatever he'd said, it was only semicoherent.

Then she asked if she could buy him dinner.

There were a dozen different rationalizations for his behavior. He could blame it on the trouble in his marriage, or his sudden fame, could point to some typical psychological quirk that drove him, could even cite his newfound belief that his wife was no angel herself—but what was the point? None of it excused him.

Just three days after he and Abby had spent that wonderful afternoon exploring the old hospital grounds, he had discovered what he was capable of.

And he didn't like it.

He and the young woman dined in the hotel restaurant,

Tolan refusing to let her pay for it. They had a nightcap at the bar, then finally parted ways just past midnight, Tolan claiming he had to get some sleep. Truth was, he didn't want to be around her anymore. The temptation was too strong. And he was feeling weak right now. Very weak.

But when he got back to his room, he couldn't sleep. Not a wink.

Instead, he sustained his alcohol buzz by attacking the minibar, knowing full well that he'd pay for this tomorrow, would likely show up at Paramount hungover and smelling of booze.

But he didn't care. He didn't care about anything at that moment. He just sat there, watching lame comedians make lamer jokes on late-night television, feeling more and more sorry for himself with each new bottle he consumed.

Despite her denials, he was almost certain that Abby had cheated on him. With whom, he wasn't sure, but he had found the proof in her purse. Proof that was pretty hard to deny.

So Tolan sat there, drinking his umpteenth bottle from the minibar, the numbers on the clock above the TV swimming before him: 2:48 A.M.

Then there was a knock at the door.

It took him a moment to navigate his way over. He opened it to find his new number-one fan standing there in a hotel bathrobe. A very short hotel bathrobe.

And the legs below it were smooth and tan and finely muscled.

"My shower's broken," she said. "Mind if I use yours?"

Sitting in his office now, Tolan remembered the white noise of that shower, remembered standing near the bed, listening to his cell phone ring not ten minutes after the woman had come to his door. He had finally picked it up, guilt washing over him in sustained, repeated waves, and he had felt like a child caught masturbating in the tub.

Not one of his finer moments.

The caller, a homicide detective named Rossbach, had broken the bad news.

Now, plagued by his memories and the growing sense that he might be losing it, Tolan took a key from his pants pocket, reached down to the bottom desk drawer, and unlocked it. Sliding it open, he pulled out a manila envelope, unfastened it, and poured its contents out onto the desktop.

Abby had been the photographer in the family, had made a living at it, but he had taken a few snapshots of his own, most of them lying in front of him now, waiting to be mounted in a photo album he knew he'd never buy.

After Lisa got into the habit of sleeping over at his house several nights a week, he had brought the photos here to the office. Didn't see any point in contributing to the pain he knew she carried, no matter how hard she tried to hide it. She had been patient with him, suffering in silence as he grieved, but he could see it behind her eyes sometimes, that fear that she was playing second fiddle to a phantom. A memory. The wondering if it would ever change.

He obviously couldn't yet make that promise. But he didn't need to rub her nose in it, either.

Carefully spreading the snapshots out, he stared down at the face of his dead wife and felt his chest tighten.

This was the real Abby, not a hallucination.

And she had been so beautiful.

So fucking beautiful.

The coffee-and-cream skin. The dark, curly hair. The spark in those hazel eyes. That sardonic, half-smile she'd use on Tolan whenever he pointed a camera in her direction. The soft, compact body that she gave to him so completely, so willingly, so free of inhibition.

Had she given it to someone else? It was a question that would never be answered.

She'd had a faint Southern lilt to her voice and a goofy humor that had always made him laugh and amplified her beauty tenfold.

Why had he allowed himself to get so angry with her that night? Why hadn't he believed her?

And why couldn't he let her go?

That, he knew, was what the encounter with Jane Doe had been about. He had allowed his guilt over Abby to get so bad that now—on this anniversary of her death—he was seeing her in the face of his own patient. Instead of getting better, as Lisa had promised, he was worse. Much worse.

In the back of his mind he could hear Abby's voice:

Sleep, Michael.

Sleep will make it all go away.

Staring at the photos a moment longer, he sighed, then gathered them up and put them back in the envelope, returning it to the drawer.

Leaning back, he closed his eyes. Twenty minutes was all he needed. Twenty blissful minutes.

Just as Tolan was starting to drift off, the memory of Abby's smile imprinted on his brain, his cell phone rang.

Shit.

Groaning, he groped for it, put it to his ear. "Yes?"

There was a pause, then:

"Dr. Tolan?"

He opened his eyes, something small and nasty fluttering in his stomach. "Who is this?"

A soft laugh. "You've forgotten me so soon?"

The caller from this morning. The whisperer.

Tolan sat up, keeping his tone low and even. "Look, I know you're trying to frighten me, but I've heard it all before. So why don't we move beyond the theatrics and talk about—"

"Oh, please, Doctor. Fear is such a mundane emotion, don't you think? I really have no desire to scare you or anyone else."

"Then what do you want?"

"It isn't a matter of what I want, but what I intend to do. And I believe I've already told you that. But before you get into a game of twenty questions, let me ask *you* one: Do you have a computer nearby?"

The question threw Tolan. "What?"

"You do know what a computer is, don't you? A pornographer like yourself should be well-versed in the ways of the Internet."

Tolan wasn't sure what he meant by that, but he'd had enough. He wasn't in the mood to play understanding shrink right now.

"Do yourself a favor and get some help," he said.

Then he hung up.

Chapter 13

Tolan sat there, feeling anger rise.

Even if the caller hadn't been trying to frighten him—which was bullshit, of course—he felt frightened nonetheless, and he wasn't sure why. This kind of thing was nothing new.

But despite the low whisper, there was something about the man's voice that rattled him. Something invasive. Primal.

Had he heard it before?

He thought about Bobby Fremont again and wondered if he had somehow smuggled a phone into the hospital. Reaching for the land line, he started dialing the security desk—

—then his cell phone rang again.

Hanging up, he grabbed it and checked caller ID. Nothing.

Feeling a renewed flutter, he paused a moment, then clicked it on.

"You're persistent, I'll give you that much. What do you want?"

"To apologize, Doctor. Calling you a pornographer was out of line, no matter how accurate the term might be."

"That doesn't sound like much of an apology."

"The best I can do, I'm afraid."

"I'll tell you what," Tolan said, softening his voice now, controlling his anger. He could see there was no way out of this. "Why don't you come in here to the hospital and we'll talk."

Another laugh. "I'm not a big fan of psychotherapy."

"Few people are. But something's obviously bothering you and acting out is never the solution."

"Thanks for the two-bit analysis, Doctor, but let's try to keep this as uncomplicated as possible. Just answer my question."

Tolan was at a loss. Wasn't sure what the caller was referring to. Then it hit him. "About the computer?"

"You *are* listening after all."

Tolan sighed. "Then, yes, I do have one. A laptop, sitting right here in front of me."

"Are you connected to the Internet?"

"Yes." Where was this going?

"Open your favorite search engine and do a search on the name Han van Meegeren."

Tolan frowned. "Who?"

"Han van Meegeren," the caller said, then spelled it out for him. "Go ahead, I'll wait."

He thought about hanging up again, but curiosity had gotten ahold of him, and he hesitated only a moment before flipping open his laptop. Hitting a button to take it out of hibernation, he waited for his wireless card to find the connection, then called up his Google screen, typed in the name, and jabbed the return button.

The screen blossomed with the familiar blue typeface listing dozens of websites.

Scanning the site summaries, he saw that the main theme of each centered around the subject of art forgery. Apparently van Meegeren was an infamous practitioner of the craft.

"As you can see," the caller said, "good old Han was

quite the faker. If you get a chance to explore further, you'll find that the Dutch authorities once arrested him for collaborating with the Nazis. They traced a painting in Hermann Göring's collection to him and threatened to charge him with treason."

"How unfortunate," Tolan said, thinking again of the sleep he needed. "What does this have to do with me?"

"Patience," the caller said. "Your bedside manner is severely lacking."

"It's been a bad morning. Get to the point, if you have one."

"Oh, I have one. One I'm sure you'll find quite interesting. But back to van Meegeren for a moment. The painting in question was a work supposedly done by Johannes Vermeer in the 1600s, but it turned out that van Meegeren himself had painted it. He was a forger, not a traitor."

"That seems to be the general theme here, but again—*what* does it have to do with me?"

"I think you already know, Doctor, but let's move on to another website, shall we?"

This was getting ridiculous. He'd let it go on far too long.

As if sensing his hesitation, the caller said: "Don't worry, we're almost done. Just indulge me this one last time. If this next website doesn't satisfy your curiosity, feel free to hang up on me again."

He was toying with Tolan, but the hook was securely in place now. Tolan waited for him to give him the website address, then typed it in.

"Keep in mind," the caller said, "that this is a one-time-only URL. I'm running it on an anonymous server that can't be traced back to me."

This gave Tolan pause. "Where are you sending me?"

"The simple press of a key will tell you."

True enough, he thought, and hit the enter key. A

moment later, what filled the page made him rise out of his chair involuntarily and back away from the computer. He dropped his phone to the desk as if it were contaminated.

"Dr. Tolan?"

He stared at the screen.

Photographs. A dozen or more. But nothing like the photos of Abby he had just been looking through.

Each one featured a brutally dismembered body. A killer's knife had carved its way through flesh and bone, severing limbs, mutilating them, leaving pools of coagulating blood. The parts had then been rearranged in a kind of sick mosaic. A cubist nightmare.

Tolan wondered if these were crime scene photos that the caller had somehow managed to pilfer from an evidence locker. Such a find might trigger a fantasy and fuel the building of this website. Yet, despite the subject matter, there was an artistic quality to the photographs, a sense of form and composition that no crime scene photographer was likely to bother with. Or care about.

"Dr. Tolan?"

Choking back a wad of bile, he picked up the phone. His hand was shaking. "Who the fuck *are* you?"

"This is my abstract collection. Quite remarkable, don't you think? Notice the way I used texture to enhance the line, and the subtle contrast of bone against flesh."

Tolan glanced at his land line. Was there a way to conference this call and somehow get Blackburn involved? He didn't think so.

Staring at the computer screen, he sat down again, then quickly jabbed Ctrl+P, sending the pages to his printer. When he *did* contact Blackburn, he wanted evidence to show him.

"Dr. Tolan?"

The printer whirred behind him and he felt his whole

body tighten, as if he'd been caught doing something unseemly. He swallowed, nearly choking on his response. "What?"

"One last question: Do you know what's missing from this collection?"

"Other than your sanity?"

Another soft laugh. "Nice. I'll have to remember that one." The caller paused. "I worked very hard to achieve this level of perfection, Doctor. Many artists simply rely on luck and instinct to create their work, but this collection took careful planning and execution. Gacy, Gein, BTK, Dahmer—they were all amateurs. Paint-by-number wannabes, every one of them. But I ask you again: Do you know what's missing?"

"I have no earthly idea," Tolan told him, but the moment he said it, it hit him like a brick to the side of the head, and he wondered why he hadn't put it together the instant he'd seen these photos.

Vincent.

He was talking to Vincent.

A wave of nausea swept over him with such ferocity that he immediately leaned toward his waste basket, struggling to keep from throwing up. He hovered over it, not realizing that he'd put the phone down again until he heard the tinny voice on the line.

"Doctor?" A pause. "Dr. Tolan?"

Tolan waited for the nausea to ease up, then righted himself and picked up the phone. "You fucking monster."

"I take it you now understand what I'm talking about. But for the sake of clarity, I'll spell it out for you."

"Shut up," Tolan said.

"If you click the link at the bottom of the page—"

"Shut the fuck up."

"—you'll see it for yourself. What I consider one of the most egregious cases of forgery I've ever encountered."

"If you don't shut up, I'll—"

"What?" the caller said. "What will you do, Doctor? Turn me into the police? Call my mother and have her spank me? Just click the link. You know you want to."

What he wanted to do was throw his phone against the wall, but for some unfathomable reason he didn't. The caller was right.

Despite his rage, and the nausea continuing to crawl through his stomach, he grabbed the mouse, scrolled down to the bottom of the page and saw the underlined blue link waiting for him:

<u>Abby Tolan</u>

"I went to a lot of trouble to procure the photos behind that link, Doctor. Had to hack straight into the OCPD crime scene database to get them. But whether or not you click it is unimportant to me. The work is substandard. Crude." He paused as if taking a moment to calm his own anger. "Your dear departed wife isn't in the collection above for one simple reason: She was never part of it."

Tolan just stared at the link, unable to respond, his finger frozen above the mouse.

"She's a forgery. A fake. A vile pornographer's talentless approximation of my work. And I don't like that, Doctor. I don't appreciate being credited for such obvious hackery—if you'll excuse the pun."

"What are you trying to tell me, you sick son of a bitch?"

"The police got it wrong. The police, the papers, everyone. I didn't kill your wife. But I think you know that, don't you? You and Han van Meegeren have something in common." Another pause. Tolan could almost feel the rage transmitted through the line. "And when I get you alone," the caller finally said, "you'll find out what true artistry is."

Then the line clicked.

Chapter 14

If Solomon had a flaw—and he'd be the first to admit he had more than a few—it was his inability to let something go.

All through breakfast he sat across from a grizzled old Vietnam vet named Red, only half listening to the old fool, his mind rolling back over the morning's events.

"So there I am," Red was saying, "sitting in the middle of a bathhouse in Patpong, this sexy thing standing buck naked in front of me, soaping herself up for one of them special Thai massages?"

"Uh-huh," Solomon murmured.

"And get this: I'm just getting my clothes off, Mr. Johnson standing at full attention, and this cute little Betty frowns, shakes her head, says, 'No go. Too big.' You believe that? Like riding my dick is the most heinous crime anybody ever asked her to contemplate."

This, of course, was only an approximation of what Red had really said, a story Solomon had heard at least a dozen times since he met the man, Red usually half in the bag when he told it. Solomon wasn't sure if Red was expecting some kind of response, but he just nodded and threw him another "uh-huh" as if he was actually listening.

What he was really doing was thinking about Myra.

Beginning to have doubts about what he'd seen, thinking he may have let sixty-eight years' worth of backwater superstition cloud his judgment. After all, the lighting in that ambulance wasn't all that great, right? Maybe he'd been mistaken and it *was* Myra after all. His Myra. All that dirt and blood on her face. Maybe he'd been done in by a trick of the eyes.

He sure hoped so.

"Tell me something," he said, interrupting his table mate's running monologue.

Red didn't seem to mind. He'd been talking with his mouth full and took a quick swallow. "Yeah?"

"Somebody goes Section Eight on the street, gets picked up by the cops, where do they take 'em?"

Red frowned, took another bite. "How long you lived here, you don't know that?"

"I wouldn't be askin' if I did."

Solomon had seen the cops grab quite a few crazies off the street, had heard the usual bullshit about where they might be headed, but didn't really pay much attention. Wasn't his business.

Red looked at him a moment as if trying to decide if he was for real. Then he said, "You got two choices; the psych ward at County or, if they're full up, they ship you up top the hill."

"Up top what hill?"

"Pepper Mountain, my man. Headcase Hotel. Up on the mesa? Half the squatters down at the riverbed have checked in at one time or another. It's like a goddamn five-star compared to County."

Headcase Hotel.

Solomon remembered hearing the name, something about folks trying to get themselves locked up there on purpose, just so they could get a hot bath and a decent meal. But he'd never been curious enough to fill in the blanks. Had never known it was located up on Pepper Mountain Mesa, just above Baycliff, a little oceanside community about five miles northwest of the city. All he knew about the area was that a bunch of rich folks had beach houses there.

He wondered if you could see those houses from atop the mesa, and found himself smiling at the thought of all those loonies looking down on Bayside Drive. It undoubtedly made a few of the blue bloods squirm.

He wondered, too, about Myra. Wondered which one of the nut houses they took her to. He was convinced now that he'd overreacted this morning when he shoulda kept his cool. He'd been nervous was all, that big cop and people in their pj's staring at him as he climbed into the back of that ambulance. Maybe he shoulda just followed Clarence's lead and stayed the hell away from it.

Too late now.

Drums or no drums, he knew he had to take action. Either to help a friend, or—if his old eyes *hadn't* been seeing things after all—to warn the poor sonofabitch who got in her way.

Only problem was, where had they taken her? County or HH? It was a coin toss. And there were no guarantees he'd be able to track her down even if he knew.

But in his time on this planet, one thing Solomon had learned—and learned the hard way—was that you can't win the game if you don't bother to roll the bones. And he was just superstitious enough to think that, one way or another, The Rhythm would set him on the right path.

So all through the rest of breakfast he formulated a plan. Not much of one, but he didn't have all that much to work with.

Looking at the glass of watery orange juice in front of him, he gulped it down, then got up to ask for another. They were pretty generous with the liquid around here and he figured he'd better start loading up the ammunition.

Forty minutes later, Solomon St. Fort took a long arcing piss onto the hood of an Ocean City Police cruiser, shouting, "Make it stop, Mama! Please make it stop!" and hoped that after they finished beating on him, they'd take him exactly where he needed to go.

Chapter 15

Blackburn knew he was about to lose his case. Had known it the moment he saw that winking smiley-face emoticon burned into Janovic's lower lip. The return of Vincent Van Gogh was not the kind of thing the department left to a single Special Victims investigator. Or a squad room full of them, for that matter.

The return of Vincent Van Gogh required the reassembly of the task force, and once that happened—which was bound to be any moment now—Blackburn would be lucky if he was asked to go for coffee.

He had half-heartedly tried to convince Mats to keep the revelation under wraps for a while. But Mats wasn't about to commit career suicide for Blackburn. Why should he? Mats was a company man, and Blackburn was fairly certain he'd already made the call, igniting a chain reaction that had quickly reached the residents of the fourth floor. It was only a matter of time before Blackburn got the official word.

Down here on Earth, the Special Victims squad room was nearly as quiet as the morgue.

Half the squad was either out on calls or late coming in, and Jenny, the support clerk, had been on maternity leave for at least a month. Blackburn figured they'd get around to replacing her about the time they found him a new partner.

A bulging black plastic bag was waiting for him on his desk top. He eyed it dubiously, then turned to Fred De Mello, who sat slumped at a nearby desk, staring at a computer screen, looking in dire need of either a cup of coffee or colonic hydrotherapy. Blackburn wasn't sure which.

De Mello was a twenty-year veteran who had long ago decided he'd chosen the wrong career path. His skills in the field, even on a good day, were just a hair above lackluster. But he could work the computer databases and phone like nobody Blackburn had ever seen. He was the go-to guy when it came to working up a victim profile. Which was why Blackburn had dragged him out of bed and tossed him the baton on Janovic.

Blackburn gestured to the bag. "Any idea where this came from?"

De Mello glanced forlornly toward a corner of the squad room, where a fresh pot of coffee was brewing. "Paramedic brought it in. Said he found it on the floor of his rig."

"And I should care why?"

"He thought some old derelict might've dropped it while you were all wrestling around with your Jane Doe." De Mello paused, assessing Blackburn with what passed for a wry smile. "Didn't know you were into group gropes."

If anyone else had made this comment, Blackburn would have replied with a pithy little zinger of his own, but trading quips with De Mello was about as much fun as shoveling cement. The man's sense of humor was as flat as hammered cow shit.

Besides, Blackburn wasn't in the best of moods right now. He needed a cigarette in the worst way. Ignoring the comment, he said, "You making any progress on my victim?"

"Getting there."

"Crime techs tell me they found a Palm Pilot." Normally, Blackburn himself would have given the apartment a thorough search, but he'd been distracted by Psycho Bitch.

Not that it mattered. He wasn't one of those bullshit touchy-feely television detectives who had to walk through a crime scene trying to channel the killer. All that counted was the evidence, and the techs were more than capable of collecting it.

The initial interviews of Janovic's neighbors, conducted by the first responders, had been a bust. None of them really knew or paid much attention to the guy, some just referring to him as the "fag in 5C"—a rumor about his lifestyle that had been circulated courtesy of the apartment complex manager. None of them had been awake at the time of the murder, none of them heard or saw anything unusual and, possibly worst of all, none of them had a clue who any of Janovic's friends were.

He kept to himself, they said. And so did they.

This attitude had always slayed Blackburn. As a kid, he'd known his neighbors three houses up on either side. They'd all get together on weekends, hanging out like one big happy family. Nowadays, you take one look at your neighbor and you're likely to get a shotgun waved in your face. It just wasn't right.

The Palm Pilot in question had been found in Janovic's nightstand drawer, and was bagged along with everything else worth bagging. Hopefully it would give them something to work with, like names and phone numbers. And an appointment calendar.

"It's a top-of-the-line model," De Mello said. "But the goddamn thing is password protected. I sent it up to Billy."

Billy Warren was their resident computer wiz.

"I ran Janovic's name through the system," De Mello went on. "Guy's a real piece of work."

"Oh?"

"Been in and out of custody since he was thirteen."

"What charges?"

"Drugs, mostly. Some petty theft. And two counts of prostitution."

Blackburn frowned. "So how'd he wind up living at a place like the Fontana Arms? It ain't the Taj Mahal, but the monthly's gotta be pretty stiff."

"Good question. Guy doesn't make that kinda coin giving blowjobs on The Avenue. Maybe he's got a sugar daddy. I'll take a look at his financials."

De Mello glanced again toward the coffeemaker, saw that the pot was finally ready and waiting, and rose to make its acquaintance. "How'd it go with your witness?"

"Don't ask," Blackburn said, figuring there was no point telling him about Tolan's meltdown. Instead, he returned his attention to the plastic bag, unfastened the twisty tie, and pulled open the bag.

The stench hit him before he knew what he was dealing with: urine, a hint of feces, an amalgamation of street smells so strong it made him gag.

"Jesus," De Mello said. "What do you got in there? A body?"

Blackburn ignored him again, reaching inside to pull out a wad of clothes. Dirt-caked jeans, ratty T-shirt, faded Army jacket.

In a corner of his brain he saw the old homeless guy, a bundle of clothing tucked under one arm as he climbed into the ambulance to get a closer look at Psycho Bitch. Blackburn hadn't thought anything of it at the time, but now he had to wonder.

Were they hers?

They looked about the right size.

Maybe the old guy hadn't been a nutcase after all. Maybe he'd been telling the truth. She was a friend of his. But why, then, had he spooked when he saw her, ranting on about her face not matching her body? And why, for that matter, had she attacked him?

Weird. Very weird.

Of course, it probably wasn't any weirder than disappearing needle tracks. Blackburn still couldn't figure that one out. This case was making about as much sense as a foreign film without subtitles.

Maybe he'd be better off without it.

He was about to stuff the clothes back in the bag when he noticed something poking out of the right rear pocket of the jeans. Looked like a folded piece of paper.

Retrieving a pair of tweezers from his desk drawer, he carefully pulled out the paper, dropped it on his desk top, then gingerly used the tweezers and the eraser end of a pencil to unfold it.

It was a battered page from a magazine.

The top left corner said *BOMBSHELL,* which Blackburn immediately recognized as one of those men's magazines aimed at horny young males. The cover was usually graced by a scantily clad, marginally famous TV star showing off her new boob job.

The page in front of him featured a rundown of the latest and greatest gadgets for the man on the move: cell phones, iPod clones, and a watch that spoke the time in a sexy digital voice.

It was all pretty dated. At least three or four years old, which, by current technology standards, was ancient history. He doubted the page had been saved because of this.

Using the tweezers again, he flipped it over, surprised by what he saw.

It was a woman. Petite. Curvaceous. Wearing a barely there yellow bikini and smiling precociously for the camera. Cool green eyes that said, without apology, "Let's fuck."

She was holding a bottle of men's cologne. Something called Raw, which was apparently like catnip to the ladies. One drop could get you into some serious trouble—the kind of trouble most red-blooded American males welcome.

Including Blackburn.

The woman looked only vaguely familiar, but what struck him about the photo was the tiny Hello Kitty tattoo on her left shoulder.

Just like Psycho Bitch.

Was it her?

Was this what had once been beneath all the blood and grime?

The eye color was off, but that could be faked. And except for her size and, frankly, her tits—which were the best money could buy—Blackburn had a tough time reconciling this photograph with the woman he'd taken to Baycliff. But he'd seen the street do some pretty nasty things to people.

He stared at that tattoo and felt a twinge of excitement. This was the first possible lead he had to Jane's identity. Something to latch on to. Something that might help to get her to open up and tell them what had happened last night.

Something that might lead them straight to Vincent.

Except for one small problem.

He was about to lose this case.

Wasn't that always the way? Just when you get a break, they yank the reins away from you.

Maybe he should take a cue from De Mello. Content to be a bench warmer, a glorified research hound. Drink your coffee, eat your danish, and get involved only when it's absolutely necessary.

But Blackburn wasn't cut that way. He'd grown up in a family full of competitors, scrambling for attention. The Blackburn engine simply didn't run without high-performance fuel.

As he stared at the photo, a voice called out, "Hey, Frankie boy, heads up."

He looked up just in time to see something hurtling toward him. Caught it just short of being beaned in the forehead:

A bag of carrot sticks.

What the hell?

Leaning against the squad room doorway was Kat Pendergast, a crooked smile on her face.

Blackburn glanced at the carrots. "What's this about?"

"Your oral fixation. Remember?"

It took him a moment before it came back to him. When it did, he allowed himself a smile. "The important thing is that *you* remembered."

"Just doing my part. I know what it's like to kick a nasty habit."

Blackburn was about to ask her *How nasty?* when he realized De Mello was staring at them from the middle of the room, coffee cup in hand, a dazed look on his face. Just the hint of sexual tension had stopped him in his tracks. Blackburn was willing to bet the guy hadn't been laid in years.

He showed De Mello the bag. "Your mouth's hanging open, Fred. You want a carrot?"

De Mello snapped out of it and indicated the danish he held in his other hand. "Uh, I'm good."

"You might want to get that coffee and danish to go," Pendergast told him. "I was sent to corral you guys. Fourth floor."

Uh-oh, Blackburn thought. Here it comes.

De Mello looked pained. The coffee didn't seem to be doing the trick, so maybe he *did* need that colonic after all. "Both of us?"

"Anyone involved with the Janovic case," Pendergast said. "You're working background, right?"

"Yeah, but—"

"They want us all. On the double. Got some major shit going down."

Major shit, indeed, Blackburn thought, then watched Pendergast turn on her heels and head toward the elevators.

Damn, she looked good in that uniform.

Chapter 16

They were in the elevator, headed to the fourth floor, when Blackburn's cell phone bleeped. He dug it out and checked the screen.

Tolan.

Christ. Great timing.

He clicked it on. "Hey, Doc, I'm gonna have to get back to you."

"We need to talk. Now."

"I'm at the station house, about to go into a meeting."

"This is a little more important than a meeting."

That sounded ominous. "What's going on?"

"Not over the phone," Tolan said, sounding like Mats. Another drama queen. "Meet me here in forty minutes."

"Is it Jane? You get her to talk?"

"No. This doesn't have anything to do with her."

"Then what's the urgency?"

"Forty minutes," Tolan said, and hung up.

Blackburn closed his phone, wondering what the hell that was all about. Had somebody told Tolan about Vincent? Not likely. So what had gotten the guy so keyed up and why was he being so cryptic about it?

It seemed to Blackburn that just about everyone on this godforsaken planet took the most circuitous route possible to get to the point.

Whatever happened to the direct approach?

He was pondering this question when he realized Kat was staring at him. "Bad news?"

"My doctor," Blackburn said. "Wants me to cut down on my carrot intake."

She grinned, then the doors opened and the three of them stepped off the elevator, making the short walk to the fourth-floor conference room.

Kat's partner, Dave Hogan, was waiting outside the door.

Kat nodded to him. "They call you in yet?"

"Just finished up," Hogan said. "You could cut the tension in that room with a friggin' bolo knife."

"Who's in there?" De Mello asked, a nervous edge to his voice.

"The chief, assistant chief, a bunch of bigwigs, and about a half dozen members of the task force. I don't think I need to tell you how huge this is."

"Task force?" De Mello said, looking lost. "What the hell's going on?"

Hogan and Pendergast eyed him as if he were on crack, not realizing, of course, that Blackburn hadn't gotten around to telling him about Vincent. Blackburn, being the bastard he was, thought about letting him stew awhile longer, then decided to be charitable.

But before he could get a word out of his mouth, the conference-room door opened. The chief's executive assistant—an attractive young thing in gray slacks and a white blouse that did little to hide her curves—stuck her head out. "Detective Blackburn? They're ready for you."

Blackburn exchanged looks with the others, then followed her inside.

The conference room was filled to capacity, the oblong table jammed with bodies.

As Hogan had said, Chief Escalante was there, sitting at the head of the table.

The rest of the room was occupied by various and sundry departmental brass and high-muckety-mucks, along with the six members of the task force itself, including Homicide stars Ron Worsley, Jerry Rossbach, and—

Shit.

Blackburn almost froze when he saw her. Felt his feet get heavy as he stepped through the conference-room doorway.

Just to his left, at about the middle of the table, sat Sue Carmody, her blond Republican hair pulled into a tight ponytail, her face taut with displeasure at the sight of him.

He could only imagine what *his* looked like.

Carmody's presence here meant only one thing: She'd been assigned to the task force. The lead detective had retired, either Worsley or Rossbach had taken his place—

—and Carmody had been bumped into the empty slot.

Wonderful. Just wonderful.

So not only was Blackburn about to lose his case, he'd have to turn it over to Goldilocks. Whoever she was sleeping with obviously had major muscle in the department.

Maybe it was the big man himself.

He glanced at Escalante, looking for some hint of silent communication between the two. The guy normally had about two layers of gloss and hairspray coating his perfectly coiffed head, but right now he looked like a man who needed that cup of coffee De Mello was nursing outside. The news of Vincent's return was not the kind of thing you wanted to wake up to.

If he and Carmody were bumping uglies, there was no indication of it in this room.

Escalante waved Blackburn to an empty chair at the near end of the table. "Have a seat, Detective."

Blackburn did as he was told.

"As you may have guessed, word of Vincent Van Gogh's reentry into our lives is not being taken lightly. As soon as I got the call, I ordered the reassembly of the task force, with a few new additions."

A few? Blackburn thought, glancing around the room. Who else had been tagged?

"I don't know if this latest victim is merely an anomaly or the start of another spree," Escalante went on, "but I want this sonofabitch stopped cold. I understand we may have a witness on tap?"

"That's still to be determined," Blackburn said. "At this point, all we know is that she was present at the scene."

He gave them an abbreviated rundown of the morning's events, leaving out the incident with Tolan, but making it clear that Jane wouldn't be easy to crack.

"What made you take her to Baycliff? Don't we usually go to County with this kind of thing?"

"No offense to the doctors at County, but I've had some previous experience with Tolan, and they're minor leaguers compared to him. The woman is clearly disturbed and I needed the best. I doubt many people here would argue there's anyone better. Not in this half of the country at least."

"That may be true, but the man's wife was one of Vincent's victims, for godsakes. You do realize this is the one-year anniversary of her murder."

Surprised, Blackburn glanced at his watch. November 15th. Jesus. He hadn't even thought of that.

Now Rossbach spoke up. "Considering the conflict of interest, we'd better get her transferred out of there as soon as possible."

"My thinking exactly," Escalante said.

"Has anyone asked Dr. Tolan how he feels about this?"

All eyes turned to Sue Carmody. Her question was directed at the entire group, but Blackburn knew it was meant for him. Bitch.

"I haven't had a chance to tell him," he said. "We're meeting as soon as I'm done here."

"What I'm suggesting is that a conflict of interest doesn't necessarily preclude Dr. Tolan from working with us on this. Maybe he'd rather stay on board."

Rossbach snorted. "He'd have to be a friggin' masochist."

"Well, I've worked with him too," Carmody said. "Probably more than anyone here. And he once told me that the reason he left private practice and took the job at Baycliff was *because* of what happened to his wife."

"How so?" Escalante asked.

"He said he wanted to get dirty. Spent too many years listening to neurotics complain about their cheating wives and their overbearing mothers, when what he really should be doing is trying to *stop* people like Vincent before they get started. Said he wanted something good to come from his wife's murder. I can't think of anything better than catching her killer."

The chief assistant district attorney cleared his throat and said, "You're forgetting the legal implications. If any of this winds up in court, a defense attorney'll have a field day. He could impeach Tolan in about two seconds flat."

Carmody shook her head. "I'm not so sure about that. Tolan has a solid reputation. Renowned therapist. Best-selling author."

"That was *before* his wife was murdered."

"He's done some pretty remarkable work since then. I've seen it firsthand. And ask any of the ADAs who have called him as a witness. He's pretty spectacular on the stand. Conflict or not, putting Tolan in a witness chair would likely work to our advantage no matter what some overpaid defense attorney throws at him."

Several heads around the table nodded, but Rossbach didn't seem convinced. "I still think it's a bad idea. Besides, we don't want to put all our eggs in this one basket. What if this woman never opens up? What then?"

Escalante frowned. "Nobody's suggesting we put limits on the investigation. I want every possible avenue explored. That's what you're here for. But this woman could very well be our only tangible link to Vincent, and I think it behooves us to pursue this angle vigorously." He looked at Carmody. "Detective, I want you and Blackburn to follow up on this."

Say what?

Carmody looked just as shocked as Blackburn felt. "Sir?"

"You two were partners before you transferred to Homicide, right?"

"Yes, but—"

"Then it makes sense to partner up again. We need all the help we can get on this. Does that work for you, Detective Blackburn?"

A couple of thoughts raced through Blackburn's head. It was obvious now that Carmody *wasn't* boinking Escalante. It was equally obvious that *he*, Frank Blackburn, was one of the few new additions to the task force that Escalante had mentioned.

He hadn't lost his case after all.

As distasteful as working with a hormonal basket bunny like Carmody might be, if the alternative meant being left out in the cold, he'd gladly take one in the gonads for the department. Besides, being up close and personal again with Miss Wonder Butt's wonder butt was not entirely objectionable.

"Detective Blackburn? Do you have any problem with that?"

"Uh," Blackburn said, feeling the heat of Carmody's

gaze on him. He was afraid to look directly at her. "No problem at all."

"Good," Escalante said. "I want the two of you to talk to Tolan and try to determine if this conflict is more a hindrance than a help. If you still think he's the man for the job, then get him back to work on that witness right away. I want to know exactly what she saw."

Easier said than done, Blackburn thought.

"Did Detective De Mello come up with you?"

Blackburn nodded. "He's right outside."

"I understand he's one of our best background analysts."

"And resident lard ass," Ron Worsley murmured. The first words he'd spoken since Blackburn entered the room.

Scattered laughter broke out, but abruptly ended when Escalante shot the offenders a look. He turned his gaze on Blackburn again. "Tell De Mello he's part of the team. And, lard ass or not, I expect you all to utilize him fully and without remark. Understood?"

Guilty nods around the table.

"Loud and clear," Blackburn said.

He still didn't look at Carmody. He could feel her outrage from ten feet away.

Chapter 17

They spent the next several minutes slicing up the investigative pie, Blackburn still reeling from his double dose of luck—good and bad. The task force was split into five two-man field teams. Each team would put the magnifying glass to two of the prior murders, starting from scratch, sifting through the murder books, reinterviewing witnesses, while Blackburn and Carmody concentrated on Janovic and Jane Doe.

After the meeting, Blackburn quickly briefed De Mello, who took the news with a predictable lack of enthusiasm but promised to step up his efforts on the victim's background and push Billy on cracking the Palm Pilot.

Blackburn told him about the *BOMBSHELL* magazine page sitting on his desk. "Get the ad agency's name from the fragrance manufacturer and find out who the model is. I can't be a hundred percent sure it's our gal, but I like the odds."

He was thinking about those odds as he headed for the stairs to the parking lot. Just as he reached the stairwell door, Carmody caught up to him.

Oh, goody.

"*You're* in a hurry." She was still struggling to contain her rage and he suddenly felt as if he was standing too close to a hornet's nest.

"I'm meeting with Tolan, remember?"

"Aren't you forgetting something?"

Blackburn studied her. "And that would be?"

"Your partner," she said, without even a hint of humor.

He eyed her dully, then opened the door and waved her past him. "After you."

They were quiet as they descended the steps, Blackburn silently cursing Escalante. When they reached the ground-floor landing, Carmody gestured him to a halt. Her frown was so deep, the muscles in her jaw had to be screaming in agony.

"Let's get this out in the open right now," she said. "If we're going to be working together again, I think we need some ground rules."

"If?" Blackburn said. "Where in Escalante's little speech did you hear an 'if'?"

"Don't start, Frank. This is exactly the kind of thing that drives me crazy and you know it."

"What I know is that we're stuck together whether we like it or not. So let's just make the best of it, okay?"

"Fine," Carmody said. "But if you make one crack about my ass or any other part of my anatomy, I swear to God I'll file papers against you so fast you won't know which way is up."

Blackburn stifled a smile, but Carmody caught it.

"What?" she barked. "What's so funny?"

"Do you ever stop and listen to yourself?"

"What do you mean?"

"You just said 'crack about my ass.' Even you've gotta admit that's pretty fuckin' hilarious."

Carmody's face hardened. "You're emotionally retarded, you know that?"

"I've been accused of much worse. But tell me something. If you despise me so goddamn much . . ." He hesitated.

"What?"

"Why the hell did you sleep with me?"

The question was a surprise. Even for Blackburn, who wasn't quite sure why he'd asked it.

A renewed spark of anger lit Carmody's eyes—a look Blackburn knew all too well. If he pushed much harder, the nest would burst and there'd be hell to pay.

"I mean it, Frank. Don't fuck with me. I did you a favor transferring to Homicide without making a fuss. But if you start getting cute again, I will not hesitate to take you down."

"You didn't answer the question."

"And I'm not going to," she said. "We made a mistake. One I regret and you just can't seem to let go of. But as far as I'm concerned, that whole conversation is permanently off the table."

Ouch.

"All right, all right," Blackburn said. "Don't get your pretty little panties in a wad. I'm about as happy as you are about this situation, but I promise to behave."

"I wish I could believe you."

"If wishes were horses, beggars would ride."

"What the hell does that mean?"

"My mother used to say it. Mostly around Christmas and birthdays. What it means is that you don't always get what you want. But I'm making you a promise to be a good little soldier. And in return for that promise, I'm asking you to do me just one favor."

She studied him dubiously. "What?"

"Loosen the fuck up."

Chapter 18

Shortly after he got off the phone with Blackburn, there was a knock at Tolan's door. He jerked in surprise, then immediately felt foolish for allowing it to startle him.

He wasn't normally the jumpy type. But then this situation wasn't exactly normal, was it?

There was no mistaking Vincent's threat.

He wanted Tolan dead.

And when someone as skilled and dangerous as Vincent Van Gogh wants you dead, well . . . It's usually a matter of where and when.

Tolan stared at the link at the bottom of his computer screen.

ABBY TOLAN.

He thought again of the night the police had called him. The shower running behind him, a naked stranger waiting, the sudden shame he'd felt soak into his bones as his cell phone rang.

You. You hurt me.

He hadn't been asked to identify the body. That's how bad it was. The killing had been so brutal, so unrelenting, that they'd been forced to confirm Abby's identity through dental records. She had been found in her studio darkroom, her body in pieces and burned by photo chemicals.

Tolan had never seen the crime scene photos. Hadn't

wanted to. Yet when Vincent had directed him to that link, which he knew would lead him straight to the horror in Abby's darkroom, he had to admit that he'd been tempted to look.

Only sheer willpower kept him from clicking it.

Another short knock snapped him out of his thoughts. Then the door opened and Lisa stuck her head in.

Tolan immediately closed his laptop.

"You've been in here half the morning," she said. "Some of your patients are getting anxious. Especially Bobby Fremont."

"Bobby's always anxious. I really wish you'd be careful around him."

"He's not going to hurt me. I'm the only friend he has in this place. And he wants to know why you canceled group."

"What did you tell him?"

"That you'd explain at this afternoon's session."

Tolan nodded. "Assuming there is one."

She frowned at him. "What's going on, Michael?"

"I'm expecting Detective Blackburn here within the hour. Can you make sure he gets buzzed in with a minimum of fuss?"

Lisa stepped inside now and closed the door behind her. "Goddamn it, Michael, quit avoiding my questions."

"I'm not avoiding any—"

"Ever since I started my shift you've been acting strange. Is it this new patient?"

"You've seen her?"

"No, I've been busy. Is there a reason I should?"

Tolan shook his head. "This has nothing to do with her anyway."

"Then what is it?"

He wasn't sure why he was holding back. He hadn't told her about Vincent's earlier call because he'd wanted to protect her. Keep her from worrying. But that excuse seemed silly now. She was a grown-up, for godsakes, the head nurse at a respected psychiatric unit, and a bigger part of his life than he deserved. If anyone did the protecting, it was her.

Still, he was reluctant to tell her. Not just about the calls, but about Jane Doe Number 314 and everything that had happened this morning. Lisa was the only light in his world right now and he didn't want any clouds in that particular sky.

"It's nothing," he said. "I'm just a little on edge, is all. Got a couple of crank calls."

"Crank calls? From who? What did they say?"

"Nothing you need to worry about."

Her face hardened now and he knew he'd just said the wrong thing. But he couldn't stop himself. "It was probably just some ex-patient trying to irritate me. It's really not that big of a deal."

She stared at him, stone-faced. "No big deal, huh?"

"Less than that," he said. "An annoyance."

He could see she wasn't buying it. "So I guess I'm an annoyance too, is that it?"

"Come on, Lisa, that isn't fair."

"Fair? I just want you to be straight with me, Michael."

She was right. If it had been Abby standing there, he wouldn't have hesitated to tell her the truth. Still, he felt the need to delay the inevitable.

"I'm sorry," he said. "I'll fill you in at lunch. I promise."

She stood there a moment, saying nothing, then opened the door. She was about to step outside when she stopped. "Tell me something, Michael. Do you love me? I mean, do you really care about me?"

Oh, Christ, Tolan thought. Not this, not now. "You know I do."

"That's the thing," she said. "I don't. You *make* love to

me, you're very good at that. But sometimes I wonder what's going on in that head of yours. Especially when you're holding something back."

He said nothing.

"I'm not here to judge you. I've told you that a hundred times. But if this thing we've got going isn't working for you—"

"Lisa, stop. I'm sorry, but I can't deal with this right now. I'll tell you everything at lunch."

She looked stung. "I guess that answers my question."

She turned, went outside.

"Lisa, wait."

Then she closed the door.

So much for that cloudless sky.

He didn't know how long he sat there, brooding over the morning's events, but it had begun to stir something inside of him. Something dark. Got him thinking about the true source of his guilt, the one thing about those last moments with Abby that he hadn't yet shared with anyone. Not even Lisa.

Probably never would.

Closing his eyes, he tried to will it away, to relegate it to the periphery of his brain where it always sat, like some crouching beast. But it was too late. Damage done.

He needed a distraction.

Taking the pages from the printer tray, he folded them twice, then stood and shoved them into his back pocket. The only thing he could think to do now was to get back to work. Quickly make his rounds, then check in on Jane.

When Tolan and Lisa were undergrads at UCLA, one of their housemates remarked that most shrinks are crazier than their patients.

Maybe there was some truth to that.

Chapter 19

Cassie was in the observation booth, fiddling with the controls on the computer cam. There were two small video cameras mounted in the seclusion room, broadcasting a wide angle and overhead view. Tolan had had them installed shortly after he took over as director, thinking that the more eyes they kept on their problem patients, the better off they'd be.

He looked at the computer screen. Jane wasn't moving. Stared blankly at the ceiling. "Any changes?"

"Not much," Cassie said. "She stopped twitching, that's about it. Oh, and she was singing for a while there."

"Singing?"

"Some kind of nursery rhyme, I think. I couldn't really make it out."

Singing was good. A form of communication beyond the few words she'd spoken before and after her break. Although, at this point, Tolan couldn't be sure how much of that was real and how much was a product of his sleep-starved imagination.

A large part of his job involved observation and interpretation. But if you couldn't rely on the accuracy of your own senses, you were in serious trouble.

"I'm going in," he said. "Feel free to join me this time."

Cassie slid off her stool and they moved outside to the seclusion-room door. Tolan keyed in the security code, then the lock unlatched with a faint beep and a moment later, they were standing over Jane.

Her eyes were closed now.

"Let's get these things off her," Tolan said, indicating the restraints.

"You sure you want to do that?"

"Yes. They're more a hindrance than a help. We can always slap them back on if we absolutely have to."

"You're the boss," Cassie said.

He knew she thought he was being reckless, but she went to work without any further comment.

As she unbuckled the restraints, Tolan watched for Jane's reaction. Her catatonia seemed to have deepened. She gave no indication she even knew what was happening.

A small clot of blood clogged her left nostril—a remnant of Blackburn's backhand.

Tolan moved to the toilet and sink in a corner of the room, took a paper towel from the dispenser, and wet it with warm water.

Moving back to the bed, he said to Jane, "Easy now, I'm just going to wipe your nose a bit."

No response.

No reaction at all.

Sensing it was safe to proceed, he carefully dabbed at the clot, doing his best to clear her nostril.

As he worked, she opened her eyes again.

She was, he now realized, quite beautiful. And as he took a closer look at those eyes, he was surprised by what he saw. Something he hadn't noticed during their last encounter.

He turned to Cassie. "Did you read Simm's workup on her?"

Cassie was down by Jane's feet, unbuckling the last of the restraints. "Yeah, it was pretty thorough."

He thought back to his conversation with Simm and Blackburn. "I could've sworn he said she suffered from heterochromia."

"Right," Cassie said. "Green and brown."

Tolan frowned, then took a penlight from his breast pocket and shone it in Jane's eyes. She shifted her focus toward Tolan, squinting against the intrusion.

So there was life in there after all.

He killed the light, stared at her. She stopped squinting, but seemed to be looking right through him.

There was no sign of heterochromia at all. No corneal damage whatsoever.

Both of her eyes were brown.

Hazel, to be more precise.

What the hell was going on here?

First, Blackburn had insisted he'd seen, to use his words, an armload of smack tracks. Yet there were none. Then Clayton Simm had said the patient had a clear case of heterochromia. Also wrong.

Adding his own lapse of judgment to the mix, Tolan wondered how three competent men could be so obviously mistaken about what they'd seen. What were they dealing with here? Some kind of human chameleon?

The intercom came to life behind him. "Dr. Tolan?"

The voice belonged to Martinez, one of the unit's security guards.

Tolan turned, seeing his reflection in the two-way glass. Despite the circles under his eyes, he looked a lot better than he felt. "What is it?"

"Detective Blackburn is here."

So soon? The last forty minutes seemed like five. But time has a way of getting away from you when you're in the middle of a breakdown.

"Have him wait in the staff lounge. I'll be there in a minute."

Returning his attention to Jane, he stared into those vacant hazel eyes. Was this another hallucination?

"Do me a favor," he said to Cassie, then gestured to Jane. "Take a look at her eyes and tell me what color they are."

Cassie did as she was told, furrowed her brow.

"That's weird. They're both brown. Looks like Clayton screwed up."

Tolan said nothing.

With Cassie's confirmation, he immediately felt better about his momentary lapse this morning, because it was obvious now what had triggered it.

Jane's eyes reminded him of . . .

—scratch that.

They *looked* just like Abby's.

Chapter 20

He was surprised to find that Blackburn wasn't alone. Detective Sue Carmody, Miss Anal-Retentive herself, stood near the soda machine, eyes brightening as he entered the room.

Tolan looked at the two of them and immediately sensed tension. This was not a happy couple.

"Detective Carmody," he said. "I thought you and Frank parted ways."

"Only in an ideal world," Blackburn muttered.

Carmody shot him a look, then offered Tolan a telegenic smile and shook his hand. "It's good to see you again, Doctor. Did Frank tell you how Sarah's doing?"

Sarah was the rape victim they'd brought to him several months ago. A frail fourteen-year-old who was not only able to describe and identify her attacker, but had testified against him at trial, never once taking her eyes off the man. Brave girl.

"We haven't had much time to catch up."

"Her mother says the psychologist you recommended is a godsend. Her therapy's going great and she's thriving in school. She was chosen to be part of the county's academic decathlon."

"That's good to hear," he said. And it was. The last he'd seen the girl was at trial. But this line of conversation was so far off subject that he felt annoyed. They weren't here for a trip down memory lane, and he wanted to get to the meat of the matter.

Apparently Blackburn felt the same. Throwing Carmody a sidelong glance, he said, "Now that we've got that fascinating bit of news out of the way, let's concentrate on the here and now." He looked at Tolan. "Seems this case has developed a little wrinkle you should know about."

"Which is?"

"Let's get your news out of the way first. You sounded pretty shook up over the phone."

Shook up couldn't begin to describe how he felt. He was a new recruit waiting for dawn to bring him his first taste of battle.

He gestured them toward a nearby door, then opened it and led them outside to a small open courtyard that held three patio tables shaded by maple trees. It was a beautiful place to escape from the drab hospital confines, but was rarely occupied at this time of day and would afford them some privacy.

Closing the door behind them, he gestured toward one of the tables. They all sat, the two detectives waiting patiently as Tolan gathered himself.

He decided not to waste any time getting to the point.

"It's Vincent," he said. "He's back."

Blackburn and Carmody exchanged looks.

"How did you know that?" Carmody asked. "Did someone from the department call you?"

"No," Tolan said, a little thrown by the question. "*He* did."

Carmody's face went blank for a moment, as if she hadn't quite heard him right. She glanced at Blackburn, whose expression mirrored hers. "*Vincent* called you? Vincent Van Gogh?"

Tolan nodded. "Twice. On my cell phone. This morning, around three A.M., then again, a little over an hour ago. I don't know how he got my number."

Blackburn's eyes narrowed. "And you didn't feel the need to tell me about this before?"

"I didn't know who I was dealing with. Thought it might be one of my old patients."

"What made you change your mind?"

"These," he said, then took the folded pages from his back pocket and handed them across the table to Blackburn. "I got them from Vincent's website."

Blackburn and Carmody exchanged another look. "His what?"

"You heard me." He gestured to the pages. "He calls it his abstract collection."

Blackburn unfolded and slowly leafed through them, his expression darkening. "Jesus H. Christ . . ."

"I don't get it," Carmody said. "Why would he call *you*? What did he want?"

"It seems I've upset him."

"Upset him? How?"

Tolan paused, remembering the threat as if Vincent were whispering in his ear at that very moment.

"He thinks I killed my wife."

THREE

The Artist Presently Known as Vincent

Chapter 21

He couldn't remember her name.

The day itself was fresh in his mind, imprinted there, and he found himself thinking about it almost as often as a normal man thinks about sex.

But then he wasn't normal. He knew that. Had known it since he was five years old, chasing spiders across the front porch of his parents' small house in Carsonville, using his father's shoe to smack them dead, feeling the thrill of excitment when that tiny round body popped against the wood, spewing gooey yellow spider guts. Gooey yellow spider guts that, to the one they called Vincent, tasted just like candy.

The family kitten came next. His sister's kitten, to be more precise. Little more than a rodent, really, a stray she had picked up on her way home from school one day, an annoying piece of gray fuzz and sharp nails that crawled up his pantleg one time too many.

He was nine then, and had already killed and eaten his share of insects—a secret he kept to himself, much like the boy down the street who picked his nose and ate his boogers. He had stayed home sick from school and was reading a comic book in bed when the fur ball climbed up onto the blanket, purring furiously.

He couldn't tell you what possessed him to reach for

his baseball glove, but he did, and quietly slipped it on, smothering the pathetic little creature right where it sat.

He took it into the backyard then, and using his father's rusty hacksaw, cut it into several pieces, which he scattered in the woods.

His grandmother had once told him that, as a child, living on an egg ranch in Oklahoma, it was her job to destroy the chickens when they were past their prime. She would step on the chicken's neck, then yank its body, ripping its head from its torso.

The chicken, unaware that its head was missing, would shake and shimmy and flap its wings until it drained of blood and finally died. Then it was off for a good plucking and a place on the Sunday dinner table.

This had always been one of Vincent's favorite stories. Especially the ripping part. He had tried several times in his short life to duplicate the event, using whatever stray animal he might come across.

But the truth was, killing animals bored him. Seemed like some true crime story cliché that had never really given him that kick to the psyche he craved. And by the time he was fourteen, Vincent began looking for a new thrill. A real thrill.

So he killed his first human.

Ten years old, she was a cute little blonde with freckles on her nose, wearing a pink and green Care Bear T-shirt.

But try as he might, he just couldn't remember her name.

Nancy? Natalie?

Neither one sounded right.

Naomi? No. Strike that one off the list too.

As much as this bothered Vincent, he didn't suppose it mattered. Despite this small failure, the moment itself was still etched in his mind. The words they spoke, the path they took, the look of spoiled innocence on her young face.

It's true what they say.

You never forget your first time.

"Where are we going?" she asked.

"I told you," Vincent said. "We're gonna get ice cream."

"Out here?"

They were walking through the woods about a block and half from Vincent's house, Vincent trying to hide his giddiness, wondering if anyone had seen them take the pathway into the trees.

He didn't think so.

Tightening his grip on the chunk of rock in his pocket, he said, "I had to hide it. My mom doesn't like me eating sweet stuff. Especially ice cream."

"Why not?"

"I'm diabetic. Have to take shots every day."

"Eww," the little girl said. "I don't like shots. Does it hurt?"

"Not anymore."

"How come?"

"You get used to it."

They were nearing the spot now, the small clearing where Vincent had dug a hole. "We're almost there," he told her. "What's your favorite flavor?"

"Mint and chip. What's yours?"

"Same thing. I even brought some cones."

"Really?"

Vincent nodded. "Sugar cones. Just like Baskin-Robbins."

The little girl smiled at him then, and he could see that she was jazzed, her dim little mind probably filled with the image of a double-decker cone, too stupid to realize that a carton of ice cream wouldn't last ten minutes out here in the woods before the heat and an army of ants got to it.

They walked through the last cluster of trees into the clearing and the little girl frowned, pointing at his handiwork.

"Look," she said, stopping in her tracks. "Somebody dug a hole. You think it was a coyote?"

"Could be," Vincent said.

"I don't like coyotes."

"Why not?"

"My dad says they ate Melody."

"Who's Melody?"

"My cat. She disappeared last month."

"Oh?" Vincent said. "What did she look like?"

"Orange and white, with stripes and a little black patch by her nose."

Vincent smiled and brought the rock out of his pocket, feeling his heart start to thump inside his chest.

"I think I remember her," he said.

It had been an unsatisfying kill. Probably because the girl had been too stupid to know what was coming, and the reaction was not quite what Vincent had anticipated. She had merely stared at him with a confused look on her face, said "Ow," then dropped to the ground like an empty sack.

He had thought about trying to step on her neck, but considering her size, that would have been impractical. Instead, he hit her several more times with the rock until she was finally dead. Watching her eyes go dim had given him a small charge—made him come in his pants as a matter of fact—but it was all too abrupt. Too rushed.

The real satisfaction had been in the aftermath of the

deed. Not only had he looked at her smashed head and thought, how beautiful, but later, when the police and fire department and his neighbors all gathered together to search for the missing girl, he had felt for the first time as if he were something special.

He remembered traipsing through the woods with his buddy Larry and some of the other neighborhood kids, calling out her name, knowing that he had a secret, and wanting desperately to tell them what it was.

But Vincent wasn't stupid. Although he knew in his heart that what he'd done was not wrong—she was a moronic kid who deserved to die—he was smart enough to also know that the people around him would never understand.

How could they? Their vision was blurred by the rules of society. Rules that did not apply to someone like Vincent.

He was, after all, an artist. And an artist who follows any rigid set of rules could not really call himself an artist at all.

As his namesake once said, "Nature always begins by resisting the artist, but he who really takes it seriously does not allow that resistance to put him off his stride."

Wise words, those.

Words of a genius.

Not that any of this went through Vincent's mind at fourteen. He'd been more of an instinctual being then. And his instincts were very good indeed.

The greatest satisfaction from that first kill came a few hours later, when the dogs finally found the girl's body. The look of horror on the faces of his neighbors, the tears, the cries of anguish—all of it caused by *him*, his handiwork—had sent such a pleasing jolt through his body that he nearly came in his pants again right then and there.

It was a high that had lasted for days. Weeks, in fact. A memory that he still cherished, even now, all these years—and bodies—later.

If only he could remember her goddamn name.

Vincent had lost track of the number of people he'd killed since then. So many of them had been taken before he'd reached his own stride as an artist, when he was little more than an apprentice to the craft, when quantity seemed more important than quality. He could not claim the astronomical body count of, say, Herman Mudgett. But he had reached double digits a while ago.

The majority of them had been done when he was still a teenager. Every spring break, every summer, every three-day weekend, he'd jump into his prized vintage 280ZX and drive to a new town, trolling for subjects.

He had no particular preferences in those days, had not yet learned to plan and categorize his work. His choice of subjects was random, based on circumstance and opportunity.

That changed during his college and grad-school years, when he learned to slow down, be more selective. His workload at school gave him little time for outside activities, so he limited himself to one or two a year, leaning toward young coeds, using the techniques of Ted Bundy to lure them, techniques he gradually refined and reshaped to make his own.

One he remembered quite fondly was a redheaded Oakland girl he'd picked up hitchhiking on the highway. She had turned to hooking, she told him, to help pay her school tuition.

The story was bullshit, of course, but he'd invited her to climb inside.

After they pulled into the far end of a department store parking lot, the redhead hitched up her skirt, yanked the crotch of her panties aside and straddled him, working her hips as if she were churning butter.

"Oh, yeah, baby. That feels real good."

Just as they were both getting into it, Vincent put his thumbs against her throat and squeezed.

The startled look on her face had been precious. She began to struggle then, thrashing about in the small car, trying to pull herself off him, hammering at him with her fists. But he jammed his pelvis upward and squeezed a little harder until her windpipe gave out and she finally slumped forward, slack and lifeless.

Then he came.

And as she lay there against him, he spotted a little brown spider crawling along the edge of the car door. Elated, he smacked it dead and popped it into his mouth, savoring its sweet nectar.

Leaving the redhead in the car, he went into the department store and bought a hacksaw and the biggest, baddest hunting blade he could find. Then he took her to the nearby woods, cut her into a dozen pieces, and arranged them on the ground in several different configurations, creating what could only be classified as works of art.

He wished he'd had a camera then. Something to help him capture the moment. He had grabbed his art pad from the trunk and made a few sketches, leaving blood stains on the paper—but drawing had never been his strong suit. Like his namesake, he was less interested in the sketch itself than the color: broad strokes that expressed mood and emotion.

And a simple drawing could never capture that.

Vincent *did* have a camera now. An eight megapixel piece of perfection that crystallized his work with such clarity that you almost felt as if you were *there*.

He had bought it two years ago, shortly before he came

to Ocean City, and paid top dollar for it, too. By then, he felt as if he had finally come into his own as an artist, creating true masterpieces in blood. Work that screamed out to be photographed, captured for eternity, remembered.

Then, a little over a year ago, he had begun in earnest to create his abstract collection. After the first, a young bartender named Trudy Dewhurst, he had been struck by a moment of inspiration—a sudden desire to honor his favorite painter.

He had sliced away Trudy's left ear.

The work itself was more reminiscent of Picasso or Cézanne or even Gleizes. But it was Van Gogh who had always inspired him with his bold use of color, the detailed brush strokes.

His genius.

His madness.

His refusal to compromise.

Taking Trudy's ear had been Vincent's way of paying homage to his hero. And the mark he left inside her lower lip—the little smiley face—was a wink and a nod to the police. His special little fuck-you.

This, however, had all been spoiled by Dr. Michael Tolan.

Seven new works completed and still going strong— and this impostor, this fraud, this charlatan, this . . . this cretin . . . had destroyed everything Vincent had worked for.

When he first heard about Abby Tolan's murder, saw the reporter on TV attributing her death to him, he had thought he might actually have a heart attack. His chest tightened, his head tingled, and each breath he drew was constricted by rage. He'd wanted to run to his apartment balcony and howl at the moon.

But he restrained himself. Struggled to regain his usual cool.

He couldn't quite believe what they were saying, yet there it was in the newspaper the next morning, in bold black typeface:

VAN GOGH TAKES EIGHTH VICTIM

The words seemed to burn his retinas, as if someone had used his cauterizing tool on his eyes.

What they didn't understand—what they could never understand—was that Vincent's subjects were not *victims* at all. To be a victim, you must be victimized—exploited in some way. But Vincent's subjects were, in fact, revered. He treasured them. Just as any artist treasures the canvas he paints, the colors he mixes, the brushes he wields.

They weren't victims, but tools, as important to him as his camera and hacksaw and knife. They were a means to an end.

And the end always justified the means.

As for his eighth subject—a laughable count when you considered all of his previous work—Vincent hadn't even chosen one yet. He'd had a number of possibilities in mind, certainly, but none of them had been Abby Tolan.

Even if he'd known the woman existed, it wouldn't have mattered.

The papers said she photographed celebrities for a living, had seen her work published in *Rolling Stone* and *Newsweek*, had shown it at some of the most prestigious galleries in the country. And the samples they'd printed had been superb, inspired.

The New Times ran a profile of her a week after the murder, a fairly morbid piece called "A Study in Darkness" that featured several photos she'd taken just days before her death. Haunting shots of the crumbling ruins near Baycliff Hospital. Black-and-white studies of a once majestic structure, of its charred and dilapidated hallways, a communal shower full of moldy, broken tile, a shock therapy table with frayed wrist and ankle straps.

Those shots in particular had touched Vincent. Reminded him of a part of his childhood when the adults around him had decided that they knew more about what was going on inside his head than he did.

The last person Vincent would ever dream of killing was the woman who had created those photographs. She was an artist. And there were already too few of them in the world.

Yet Tolan, who had no interest whatsoever in artistic integrity, had simply wanted the woman dead.

Tolan had used Vincent. Had used his work in a most hateful way. Had snuffed out the life of a beautiful, talented woman, sliced off her ear, then had somehow found out about his little *fuck-you*—all in a pathetic attempt to cover for his crime.

The police investigators' failure to see the vast artistic differences between so-called *victim* number eight and the seven works of genius that preceded her was not surprising to Vincent. Police are pedestrian animals, lacking the sophisticated nature one needs to appreciate fine art.

He had considered sending a letter to the newspaper, pointing out the obvious forgery and expressing his condolences for the unnecessary loss of life. But that would only make him sound like a whiny crybaby.

And Vincent was not a crybaby.

Instead, he got away from Ocean City for a while. Traveled north to see his mother.

But while he was there, he had started drinking again, and one night, found himself in the middle of a bar fight. Someone was stabbed—a minor injury, it turned out—but the blade had been Vincent's, and the police who arrested him and the judge who heard the case did not take kindly to the use of weapons. Vincent was sentenced to alcohol rehabilitation and several months on an honor farm.

Those months, however, had turned out to be a blessing in disguise. Had given him perspective.

He knew now what it was he needed to do. Had thought of a way to turn this travesty of justice around. It would be a private victory, but a victory nonetheless. One that would allow him to reclaim his artistic integrity.

A month after he was released, he headed back to Ocean City—anxious to begin hunting his prey.

For that's exactly what Dr. Michael Tolan was to him now.

Prey.

Chapter 22

"This is huge," Carmody said, after Tolan finished telling his story. Clearly excited, she leafed through the website pages for what must have been the fourth or fifth time since Blackburn had handed them to her. "We need to let Rossbach know about this."

A moment later she had her cell phone in hand and was punching speed dial.

Blackburn looked annoyed. "You wanna take that somewhere else? Me and the doc need to chat."

Carmody shot him a look, but didn't argue. Rising quickly from the table, she went inside.

When she was gone, Blackburn sighed. "And to think I almost had her baby."

Tolan didn't know if he was expected to laugh, but he was in no mood for Blackburn's jokes.

Blackburn didn't seem to notice. "Pardon me for being a little slow on the uptake, but let me get this straight. What this all boils down to is a guy on the phone accusing you of being some kind of third-rate copycat."

"Pretty much."

"You have any idea why he'd think that?"

"Isn't it obvious?"

"Not to me, no."

"You know as well as I do that when a wife is murdered, the husband is usually the prime suspect."

Blackburn shook his head. "Not when there are clear signs of a serial perp."

"But what if they were faked? What if this van Meegeren analogy is true?"

Blackburn frowned. "Are you trying to tell me something?"

"I'm just looking at the possibilities. Vincent was pretty adamant. Said the police and the papers got it wrong."

"And maybe he was just fucking with you."

"Maybe. But if Vincent didn't kill my wife, then the question remains—"

"Hold on, now," Blackburn said, raising a hand for emphasis. "Let's not forget we're talking about a nut job. No offense, but that's what he is. And calling you up and accusing you of murder is probably just the kind of thing he gets off on."

What Blackburn said made sense, of course, but then he hadn't been the one to talk to Vincent, to feel his outrage.

"I deal with this stuff every day, Detective. I think I know when someone is telling the truth."

"And I respect that, Doc, but the fact remains that your wife wasn't killed by a copycat."

"How can you be so sure?"

"Copycats always get something wrong. Some tiny detail. And your wife's murder was textbook Vincent. If it hadn't been, you would've had the department so far up your ass you'd be farting donuts."

Tolan said nothing.

"So unless you want to confess," Blackburn continued, "we gotta assume the guy's playing you. He's already victimized you once. Now he's getting a charge out of doing it again." He paused. "Providing, of course, it actually was Vincent who called you."

This surprised Tolan. "What are you saying?"

"You yourself said it might've been one of your patients. A whispery voice making threats on a telephone line doesn't prove much of anything."

"You're forgetting the website," Tolan said. "The photos."

Blackburn shrugged. "You can download all kinds of shit off the Internet these days. No telling where they came from. For all I know, it's just some guy getting creative with Photoshop."

Tolan stared at him. "Why the resistance, Detective? You don't believe me?"

"On the contrary, Doc. I'm pretty sure it *was* Vincent who called you—mostly because I don't believe in coincidences. But unlike my so-called partner in there, who likes to jump straight to Defcon One, I tend to want to digest things a bit before I go off half-cocked."

Something he'd said caught Tolan's attention. "What coincidence?"

"Huh?"

"You said you don't believe in coincidences. What coincidence?"

Blackburn looked at him. "Remember that little wrinkle I mentioned earlier?"

Tolan nodded.

"The body we found this morning. The one who's got your new patient all in a tizzy? We have every reason to believe he's Vincent's latest victim."

Tolan felt a chill rush through him. Was this another one of Blackburn's jokes? "I thought you said that was just a stabbing."

"It pretty much was."

"I don't understand, then. Was he sliced up like the others?"

Blackburn shook his head. "The perp was interrupted before he could get that far."

"Then how do you know it was Vincent?"

"The details," Blackburn said. "It's all in the details."

Blackburn spent the next several minutes explaining those details, telling Tolan about the medical examiner's findings, the reassembly of the task force, and the belief that Jane Doe Number 314 could well be the key to finally catching Vincent Van Gogh.

As Blackburn spoke, Tolan began to feel light-headed. This was all coming at him too fast.

"Keep in mind, Doc, that what I'm telling you is strictly confidential. But I figure the more you know, the better you'll be able to get her to open up. Unfortunately, we may have a problem in that area."

"I've been saying that all along."

"Not with the witness. With you. Not everybody on the task force is as enthusiastic about your involvement as me and Carmody."

Tolan wasn't surprised. "They're worried about my objectivity."

"Or lack thereof."

He was right, it was a valid concern. Tolan now had a personal stake in the case and if it went to trial, any defense attorney worth his salt would claim that he had somehow manipulated or coached the witness.

"So the question is," Blackburn said, "*can* you be objective about this?"

Tolan wasn't sure he knew the answer. Objectivity had not been his strong suit this morning. Far from it.

He thought of Jane and those brown eyes that looked just like Abby's and wondered what they'd seen. Even if he *could* set aside his feelings, would he ever be able to break through the seemingly impenetrable wall she'd built?

Before he could respond, the door opened and Carmody stepped back onto the patio. "Rossbach's sending a tech team up." She looked at Tolan. "Do you have any objection to phone taps?"

"None at all."

"What about your office line?"

"Considering the circumstances, I'm sure the administration will be happy to cooperate."

"Good," she said, then turned to Blackburn. "Rossbach says they're going to hit up all the victims' families, see if Vincent made any more phone calls. And there's been a change of plans: He wants the witness transferred to County."

Blackburn looked surprised. "I thought we all agreed to give the doc a shot at this."

"That was before they knew about the calls. He says there's too much at stake."

"Rossbach's a douche," Blackburn said.

"He's also right. And what he says goes." She looked at Tolan again. "I'm sorry it has to be like this, but—"

"Wait a minute, wait." Tolan raised his hands in protest. Despite any conflicts, he knew he couldn't let Jane out of this hospital. Not now. "I think I may have a solution. A compromise."

"What kind of compromise?"

He was thinking on his feet at this point and had no idea if what he was about to propose would fly, but it was worth a shot. "The problem isn't with Baycliff but with me, right?"

"Right," Carmody said.

"So what if we keep her here, but I turn her care over to another therapist?"

Blackburn snorted. "That pretty much defeats the whole purpose of me bringing her here in the first place."

"I understand that," he said. "But I can still serve as a consultant. Make suggestions on how best to approach her, without being accused of trying to manipulate her."

Blackburn thought about it a moment. "Head shrinking by proxy. I like that, Doc. I'd rather have *some* of you than none at all."

"Besides," Tolan continued, "if Jane saw Vincent stab that man in his apartment, what's to stop him from coming after her, too?"

"Don't think we haven't thought of that," Carmody said.

"He's right," Blackburn told her. "We keep her here, we won't have to spread ourselves so thin."

Carmody ignored him, addressing Tolan. "Who do you have in mind to take your place?"

Tolan considered the question. Baycliff had several excellent doctors on staff, including the four of them here in the detention unit. Kessler and Edmunds rotated shifts, Simm worked graveyard and, as supervisor, Tolan was a floater—although he usually worked the day shift when the place was jumping.

Both Kessler and Edmunds were competent, even above-average clinicians. But in the time he'd been here, Simm had proven to be a true asset to the team. Tireless, dedicated, instincts that rivaled some of the best practitioners Tolan had known.

"Clayton Simm," he said.

Blackburn scoffed. "The guy you want me to apologize to?"

"He's one of the best I've seen." Tolan didn't mention the botched heterochromia diagnosis, but it had been a bad morning for all of them and he still had complete confidence in the man. "More important, he listens to me."

Blackburn nodded, turned to Carmody. "What do you think?"

"I think if we do this, *you're* the one who's running it past Rossbach."

"No problem," Blackburn said. "We both speak douche."

Chapter 23

"I'd appreciate it, ma'am, if you could answer a question for me."

The woman looked up from her paperwork, waiting for Solomon to continue. She had the face of somebody who wished she were on a beach somewhere, soaking up some sun, rather than stuck behind this desk, dealing with the likes of him. It was the kind of face you'd find at the DMV or the Social Services office. Pinched and unhappy. And very, very tired. A look Solomon had seen a thousand times in his life.

He tried his best smile on her. "You probably see just about everyone comes in here, right?"

"Is that the question?"

"Pardon me?"

"You said you wanted to ask me a question. Was that it, or are you gonna waste my time with a lot of mindless chitchat?"

She went back to her paperwork and Solomon felt his smile falter. You work in a warehouse like County General, you're bound to be a bit surly, but this one was downright nasty.

The way he figured it, nobody was chaining her to this desk.

He decided to cut straight to the heart of the matter. "I'm lookin' for a friend of mine. I think the police mighta brought her here earlier this morning."

She looked up at him again. "A friend of yours." It wasn't a question, just a flat, disinterested statement with a touch of weariness thrown in for good measure. "And who would that friend be? Abe Lincoln? The tooth fairy? Somebody from your home planet?"

Wondering what had crawled up this woman's ass and died, Solomon said, "Her name is Myra. And you'd remember her, because all she had on was a blanket and a lot of blood."

The woman scowled. "We don't discuss our patients."

"You see," Solomon went on, "the reason I ask is because she's got some health issues I think the doctors need to know about."

"They're doctors. They'll figure it out."

"Maybe so, but what if she goes into insulin shock before they get to her?" It was a lie, of course, but bound to provoke a response.

"She's diabetic?"

Solomon nodded. "She don't get proper treatment, she could die."

"I could think of worse things," the woman muttered, then returned her attention to her task.

"So that's it? You don't give a damn?"

"No, Mr.—" She glanced at the top of the page in front of her. "—St. Fort, I don't."

"What kinda nurse are you?"

She glared at him. "First off, I'm not a nurse. I run the emergency intake desk. The one you're sitting in front of right now. Second, I'm tired of seeing people like you take a free ride off the backs of hard-working people like me. And third, I especially don't give a damn because I've never seen this woman in a blanket you're talking about, and I figure she's either already dead or just a figment of your alcohol-soaked imagination."

This lady was mad at the world. Give her ten minutes with Katrina or a couple days down at the river bottom, maybe she'd realize just how good she had it.

But no matter. Solomon had found out what he needed to know. He'd lost the coin toss. Myra wasn't here. Now all he had to do was figure out a way to get himself up to Headcase Hotel.

"Just so you know, ma'am, people like me ain't no different from people like you. We've just had some bad breaks, is all."

She glanced at the page again.

"It says here you urinated on a police car. Was that a bad break?"

Solomon said nothing.

She gave him a nasty little smile, then looked past his shoulder and gestured with two fingers. "You can uncuff him now. The orderlies will take him from here."

One of the cops who'd arrested him came over then and told him to stand up.

"When do I get to see Dr. Clarence?"

The woman behind the desk frowned. "Who?"

"Dr. Clarence," Solomon said. "He's been my doctor for what? Three years now? Every time I come to Baycliff he takes good care of me."

"Look around, Mr. St. Fort. This isn't Baycliff, it's County General."

Solomon squinted at her. "What're you talking about? I told this fool. I'm supposed to go to Baycliff and see Dr. Clarence."

"You didn't tell me shit," the cop said. He was about to take the cuffs off, but Solomon jerked away from him.

"Somebody call Dr. Clarence. I need to see him right now. He's gotta take care of me."

"Easy," the cop said.

But Solomon didn't listen to him. He started thrashing now, twisting away from his grasp. "Get me Dr. Clarence, goddamn it! Where's Dr. Clarence?"

The woman behind the desk looked sharply at the cop. "You might've mentioned he was already under some-body else's care."

"How the hell was I supposed to know?"

Solomon kept thrashing, shouting out for Dr. Clarence. An orderly came over and grabbed him by the arms.

"She's hurting me, Mama! Make her stop hurting me!"

The woman behind the desk stood up, her face redden-ing. "You shut up."

"Make her stop! Make her stop!"

The woman was glaring at the cop now. "You think I'm going to sit here and do all this paperwork just so we can transfer him out in a couple hours?"

"What do you want *me* to do about it?" the cop said.

"What do you think? Get him the hell out of here. Now. Take him up to Baycliff to see his precious Dr. Clarence."

"I'm not a goddamn taxi service."

"Then throw him back on the street, for all I care."

"You're County General, for crissakes. You can't just turn him away like that."

"Oh?" the woman said. "Watch me."

She grabbed the paperwork in front of her and uncere-moniously ripped it in half, flashing her nasty little smile again. "Sorry, Officer, we're full up this morning. You'll have to take him somewhere else."

"What'd you just do there, little Miss Hard Worker? You rip up my note to Dr. Clarence? Was that my note to Dr. Clarence?"

The woman kept her gaze on the cop. "Get him out. Now."

And as the cop scowled at her and roughly grabbed hold of Solomon, Solomon bit back his own smile.

The Rhythm never lets you down.

Chapter 24

It was closing in on noon when the caravan of police technicians took the winding road up to Baycliff Psychiatric. A special communications truck was parked near the ambulance bay, just outside Tolan's office, his land line rigged with recording and tracing equipment.

The signal from his cell phone, Sue Carmody explained, would be picked up at a cellular switching station. And if Vincent was using one to make his calls, current technology allowed them to track his whereabouts within a three-hundred-foot radius.

There was a palpable, almost desperate excitement in the air. A hope that this might be it. An actual shot at catching a serial killer.

But Tolan didn't share the excitement. As much as he appreciated the effort, it was, he thought, a waste of time.

Vincent was no dummy. He knew that Tolan would go straight to the police. There wouldn't be anymore phone calls. And despite what Blackburn had said, Tolan knew that Vincent wasn't playing games with him. Not about this.

Not about Abby.

You. You hurt me.

As he stood near his office doorway, watching a

technician test his land line, Tolan thought back to that night again, to the fight he'd had with Abby.

It had all started with a stick of gum.

Craving a sugar fix, Tolan had been searching through her purse, looking for the pack of Doublemint she always kept in there—when he found something else. Something entirely out of place.

A small blue box.

The words on the label were still imprinted on his brain: Lifestyles Sheer Pleasure. Three-pack.

A box of condoms.

A box of condoms that had been opened.

And two of them were missing.

At first, Tolan couldn't quite believe what he was seeing. Had even checked to make sure it was Abby's purse. But the gesture was pointless. He knew it was hers, the one she carried wherever she went. And as he began to understand what this meant, what that open blue box signified, surprise gave way to hurt, then anger, then . . .

Then . . .

Then what, Michael? Keep going.

One of the police technicians coughed, bringing Tolan back to the present as dread blossomed inside him like a malignant growth.

But it wasn't Vincent's threat that weighed on him now. It was that simple, dark truth he had kept hidden away for over a year. A simple truth that Vincent's phone calls and this morning's events had brought screaming back to the surface.

Tolan had a blank spot.

A gap in his memory.

Was missing time from that night.

You. You hurt me.

Abby had been coming out of the bathroom when he confronted her, waving the open box in her face.

"What the hell is this?"

He remembered her startled expression when she realized what he was holding. The fading smile. The puzzled frown. "Where did you get that?"

"Where do you think?" He indicated her purse.

She just stood there a moment, then shook her head. "You're kidding me, right? Those aren't mine."

But he wasn't kidding. And when she realized that, her expression immediately changed. Hurt. Guilt. Fear? He wasn't sure which.

"Who is he?" Tolan demanded.

"There's no one, Michael. You know I wouldn't—"

"—a client of yours? That guitar guy? You take him in for a little darkroom quickie?"

Abby just stared at him. "Is this what we've come to?"

But Tolan didn't let up. He asked her again, and then again, growing more and more agitated. And despite her denials, despite her insistence that she would never betray him like that, every uncertainty Tolan had about their marriage, every doubt, every concern, coalesced into a rage so all-consuming that his whole body began to shake.

He had shouted at her then and, stunned by his behavior, she had given it right back—

—until he finally crossed the line. Called her a name he knew would cut her to the bone.

You. Fucking. Whore.

That was when Abby slapped him. Right across the face. Tears in her eyes.

Then . . . nothing.

That slap was the last thing Tolan remembered until a honking horn on the 101 jolted him back to consciousness. He had drifted out of his lane and immediately cut the wheel, righting himself.

It had taken him a moment to catch his bearings. He was alone, headed south toward Los Angeles.

What the hell?

He glanced at the dashboard clock. Two hours had passed. Two hours that seemed like two seconds.

And as the realization that he had just emerged from some kind of mental fog began to register, he wondered if he should call her.

What had happened in those last two hours? How had he wound up here?

He dialed her cell phone, but she didn't answer. After two rings it went straight to voice mail. And as he waited for the beep, he wondered what he should say to her.

Then the vision of that blue box filled his head and, despite his confusion, he realized he didn't want to say *anything* to her. He was still angry. Still hurt by what she'd done. So he simply left a quick message telling her he was close to L.A. and would call her back in the morning. Then he hung up. Whatever had happened after that slap would eventually come back to him and he'd deal with it then.

But it hadn't come back. Not that night. Not the next morning. Not ever.

Not even after the 3:00 A.M. phone call that changed his life.

And no one had asked him about it either. Not Lisa. Not Ned, his ex-partner and therapist. Not the police.

The detectives had questioned him, yes, but never as a suspect. Abby was, after all, the victim of a high-profile serial killer. It was right there in the details. They were more interested to know if Tolan had ever noticed anyone hanging around the house or near Abby's studio. Or if she had ever complained of unusual or threatening phone calls or encounters with strangers.

When asked what time he had last seen her, he had

used his arrival at the hotel as a marker and merely subtracted three hours.

He hadn't told them about what he'd found in her purse. Or the fight. Or his blinding anger. He hadn't told them because it didn't matter. They had known from the very beginning who her killer was—and Tolan had believed it too.

Or had he?

He had always carried a small measure of doubt about that night. An uneasiness. And maybe that was why he'd had so much trouble sleeping over the last year. Maybe that was the true source of his grief. His guilt.

Was Vincent right? Justified in his outrage?

Could he, Michael Tolan, have killed his own wife?

Impossible. He had been angry that night, yes, angrier than he'd ever been before—an anger so debilitating it had caused some sort of cognitive misfire. But he had never been a violent man. Would never raise a finger against anyone, let alone Abby. He had loved her too much.

His anger had been a momentary aberration, is all, brought on by the sudden fear that she had betrayed him. And yes, he had shouted at her, had called her a whore—an inexcusable insult considering her past—but to think that he could cut her up so savagely, was so far beyond imagining that he almost laughed.

Almost.

Because Tolan knew full well that people often delude themselves about what they're capable of doing. History has proven time and again that, being the savage animals we are, our instinct for violence often gets the better of us.

That anyone can cross that line. Anyone.

And the trigger is usually something mundane. Something simple and unexpected.

Like an open box of condoms.

Chapter 25

Blackburn hated circuses, and the scene at the detention unit was quickly turning into one.

Carmody had already shifted into Advance Man mode, working the phone until a crew of dancing bears arrived, all carrying the dim hope that a killer would behave in a way that was contrary to human logic.

Blackburn stood in the observation booth adjacent to Psycho Bitch's room. Someone had taken her out of her restraints—big mistake—and she was curled up in that fetal ball she seemed to love so much, using only a fraction of the real estate on her hospital bed.

The orderly, Cassie, sat behind the computer, dutifully watching over her.

Tolan's wonder boy, Clayton Simm, had yet to make an appearance. Tolan had called him at least twice and gotten his machine.

So they were in a holding pattern for the moment. And as much as Blackburn hated circuses, he absolutely despised holding patterns.

He was debating the pros and cons of a frontal lobotomy—could probably get one right down the hall—when the vestibule door opened and a tall, well-toned female in hospital scrubs stepped into the booth.

Yowza.

"Cassie, why don't you take a break?"

The orderly looked up at her and smiled. "Thanks. I could use a smoke."

So could I, Blackburn thought. He didn't figure there was ever an easy time to quit, but it seemed he'd picked the worst one possible. He thought about that bag of carrots on his desk and wished he had one right now to chew on. Pendergast had been right. It was an oral fixation. He needed something in his mouth—which, when he considered the implication, didn't say much for his masculinity.

But the woman in scrubs did. She was hotter than a goddamn firecracker.

As Cassie left the booth, Scrubs turned to him and offered a hand to shake. "Detective Blackburn, right?"

"So they tell me," he said, as he shook it.

"I'm Lisa Paymer, director of the EDU nursing staff. You probably don't remember me, but we met when you were here a few months ago."

Ahh. He'd thought she looked familiar.

"I must've been preoccupied," he said, "because you'd be awfully hard to forget."

The remark went over with a resounding thud. She wasn't biting. She wasn't even swimming in the same pond.

"We see a lot of uniformed officers around here," she said stiffly, "but very few detectives. Especially so many all at once. Our patients are getting pretty upset with you people traipsing up and down the . . ."

She paused, her gaze now fixed on Psycho Bitch.

"My God . . ."

"What?"

"I read her workup, but this is the first time I've seen her. I didn't realize . . ."

"Realize what? You know her?"

She thought about that for a moment, then shook her

head. "No, but she reminds me of someone." She shifted her gaze to Blackburn. "Is this all because of her?"

"Part of it," Blackburn said. "The rest you'll have to get from Doc Tolan."

"That's the problem. He isn't talking."

"He doesn't exactly strike me as the shy type, so he must have a good reason."

She looked again at Psycho Bitch. "I can see that. But I'm concerned about him. He said something about crank phone calls. Is he in some kind of trouble?"

Blackburn assessed her. "I take it the two of you have more than a professional relationship?"

She nodded.

Well, well, Blackburn thought. The doc wasn't doing so bad after all. Dipping your pen in the company inkwell is always an iffy proposition—as Blackburn knew too well—but if you've gotta break office protocol, you might as well go for the gold.

"He worries about me," she said. "So he won't tell me what's going on. I'm hoping you will."

Uh-oh. No way was Blackburn getting in the middle of that. And he sure as hell wasn't going to tell her about Vincent.

"I think this is where I say, sorry, ma'am, police business."

"Which means?"

"That it's none of yours."

She didn't like that response. There was a momentary flash of anger in her eyes, then she softened. Blackburn got the feeling she did that a lot. Kept her anger bottled up. Controlled. She reminded him of his second wife, who'd always had a kind of Stepford quality about her, until the facade finally cracked. He still had a scar on his scalp as a souvenir.

"I've been a psychiatric nurse for over fifteen years,

Detective. I worked at County General, for godsakes, and that's about the worst of the worst. So I think I can handle whatever bad news you people are hiding."

Blackburn shook his head. "Sorry, ma'am, but I've got nothing to tell you. I'm sure the doc'll clue you in when the time is right."

And speaking of timing, that's when the door opened again and Tolan stepped into the booth, obviously surprised to see them. He paused in the doorway, his gaze shifting from one to the other.

"Am I interrupting something?"

"I was just leaving," Lisa said. She glanced in at Psycho Bitch again, then stared pointedly at Tolan. "Don't forget our lunch date." She turned to Blackburn. "Nice to see you again."

Nice to see you, too, Blackburn thought.

Then she was gone.

Tolan watched after her, looking a lot like a naughty kindergartner who had just been scolded by his teacher. Maybe there was a spanking in his future.

"If you want to hang on to that one," Blackburn said, "you'd better start communicating with her. And soon."

"With all due respect, Detective, you're probably the last person in the world I'd ask for relationship advice."

"Good point," Blackburn said.

Chapter 26

Vincent almost had to laugh.

He had been sitting here for quite some time now, watching the activity around the hospital, the arrival of the unmarked police van, the scurry of technicians.

All because of him, of course.

All because of his genius.

How funny that they didn't even know just how close he was. Close enough to touch.

It was a scene he'd witnessed dozens of times in his life. Almost routine at this point, but he still enjoyed the spectacle as much as he had after that first kill, so many years ago.

Little ice cream girl.

Oddly enough, one of the detectives reminded him of her. The one with the pale yellow hair.

Unlike the little ice cream girl, however, this one kept it pulled back into a tight ponytail. And there was a sense of intelligence about her. No-nonsense. Always in control.

He liked that. Liked it a lot.

But he had always liked watching the police. The concern laced with excitement. The sense of purpose. As if they might catch him this time.

Oh, they'd catch him, all right.

Sooner than they expected.

And before long, Vincent Van Gogh would be retired to the local history books, the newspaper archives, the memories of the family members who had been touched by his artistry. Blessed by his genius.

Then somewhere, in another town, another state—possibly even another country—Vincent would be reborn. Wiser for the mistakes he'd made. Stronger.

A greater talent than he had ever hoped to be.

Who knows what they'd call him then.

"Your girlfriend says our gal here reminds her of someone. Any idea who that might be?"

Tolan ignored the question. Seemed lost in his own thoughts as he stood at the computer, keying through the notations on-screen.

Blackburn tried another one. "So when do I get the bad news, Doc? Are we wasting our time?"

Tolan looked up. "Hard to say. The tox screen came back negative for drugs or alcohol, so we can rule out any organic disorders."

Blackburn again thought about those missing smack tracks and decided that, along with the lobotomy, he might order up some LASIK surgery.

"If she's suffering from BRP," Tolan continued, "the prognosis is good, but we may simply have to wait it out."

"You can't give her a shot or something?"

"Neuroleptics are a wonderful tool, but unlike most of my colleagues, I usually hold off awhile before I go there."

"This isn't your usual situation."

"True," Tolan said. "But I'm supposed to be hands off, remember? Let's see how Clayton feels about it. He just called, by the way. He was sound asleep when I—"

"Spare me the play-by-play. What's his ETA?"

"He said he needed about three gallons of coffee and a shower first."

"Which means he'll get here when he gets here, right?"

"Right," Tolan said.

Blackburn sighed again. More waiting. This Simm guy decides to take a leisurely shower and in the meantime, only God knew what Vincent was up to.

"Hopefully, by the time he arrives," Blackburn said, "I'll have some fresh ammunition for you."

"What kind of ammunition?"

He nodded to Psycho Bitch. "Her identity."

He told Tolan about the magazine ad. De Mello had already contacted the design company who'd handled the layout. Turned out they'd used customized clip art for the bikini model and Photoshopped the bottle in her hand. The company who sold them the clip was busy trying to locate the photographer who had taken it. De Mello was pretty sure he'd have a name before lunch was over.

"Excellent," Tolan said. "Might help us track down her medical hist—"

A sound from the intercom cut him off. A guttural moan that came from the room beyond the glass.

Psycho Bitch was stirring now. She began muttering something incomprehensible, then surprised them both by starting to hum.

"That's something new," Blackburn said.

"Cassie told me she was singing earlier. Some kind of nursery rhyme."

They listened a moment, and Blackburn noticed that the doc was frowning now, as if trying to recognize the tune. He started to say something, but Tolan held up a hand, silencing him.

Then, in a timid, childlike voice, Psycho Bitch began to sing:

Mama got trouble
Mama got sin
Mama got bills to pay again.

Blackburn saw Tolan visibly stiffen, eyes widening almost imperceptibly.

Daddy got money
Daddy got cars
Mama gonna take him on a trip to Mars.

"Jesus Christ," Tolan said.

"What?"

Psycho Bitch kept singing, repeating the words, and Tolan suddenly had that same stunned look on his face that he'd had earlier this morning, right after she attacked him.

"What, Doc? What's going on?"

It seemed to take Tolan a full thirty seconds to respond, Psycho Bitch continuing to serenade them.

Mama got trouble
Mama got sin
Mama got bills to pay again.

"That song," he said, his voice cracking.

"What about it?"

"My wife . . ." He turned, looking straight at Blackburn. "This is impossible. . . ."

"What, Doc? What?"

"That's Abby's song."

Chapter 27

She used to sing it to him in bed.

She'd trace her fingers along his abdomen, along his "happy trail," as she called it. Walk them upward toward his stomach and on up to his chest, singing:

> *Mama got trouble*
> *Mama got sin*
> *Mama got bills to pay again.*

Then she'd bring her hand back down, grabbing hold of him, gently tugging at him, letting him grow against her palm. When he was ready, she'd climb on top and guide him into her.

> *Daddy got money*
> *Daddy got cars*
> *Mama gonna take him on a trip to Mars.*

He'd stare up into that beautiful face, all of her concentration centered on her task, her hips moving to find just the right spot, the one that made her eyes close and her jaw go slack, a small moan escaping between her lips.

Mama got trouble
Mama got sin
Mama got bills to pay again.

The first time she sang it to him, he'd asked her where it came from.

"Me," she'd said with a small laugh. "My first stab at creativity. Write about what you know. Isn't that what they tell you?"

He wasn't sure what she meant by that.

"It's a hopscotch song. My friend Tandi and I used to play in the alley behind our apartment house, while our mothers were working."

"Working?"

"My mother was a prostitute."

She said it without hesitation, as if she'd said something as innocuous as *My mother was a grocery store clerk*. But there was a faraway look in her eyes. A kind of sadness there that Tolan found both heartbreaking and alluring.

He got up on his elbows then. "And you made up that song about her?"

Abby nodded.

"How old were you?"

"Nine or ten, I guess. But there weren't any secrets in our house. The details may have been a little vague, but I knew exactly what my mother did for a living."

Tolan didn't know what to say.

"By the time I was sixteen," she continued, "I figured I'd be following in her footsteps. Then one of her Johns left his camera behind and I latched on to it and never let go."

Tolan kept looking at her, wondering how to ask his next question. Wondering if he *should* ask it.

Then her faraway look abruptly disappeared. "Would it bother you if I said yes?"

"To what?"

"To the question you're afraid to ask. Would it bother you?"

She looked so beautiful. So . . . fragile. His gut tightened at the thought of another man touching that flawless skin, kissing those full lips.

"It wouldn't thrill me," he said.

Then her eyes clouded and he immediately regretted the words. Although she was still a mystery to him, he felt privileged to be spending time with her. To have her in his bed. And it honestly didn't matter to him what she might have done in the past. He loved her, unconditionally. Had loved her, he realized, since the moment he walked into her studio, looking only to get a photograph taken for his new book jacket.

"No," he said quickly. "It wouldn't bother me at all. Nothing about you could ever bother me."

If only that had turned out to be true.

"Abby's song?" Blackburn said. "What the hell are you talking about?"

But Tolan barely heard him. The floor was tilting beneath him and he had to grab on to the computer console to steady himself. This wasn't happening.

Mama got trouble
Mama got sin
Mama got bills to pay again.

He was hearing things. Had to be. There was no possible way this woman could know that song.

"Doc, what the fuck is going on?"

Tolan glanced through the glass at her, then quickly moved to the seclusion-room door.

"Wait a minute," Blackburn said.

Tolan ignored him. Punching in the security code, he threw open the door and stepped inside. Her voice was clearer now, no longer distorted by the intercom, and the sound of it knocked his equilibrium even further off-balance.

Daddy got money
Daddy got cars
Mama gonna take him on a trip to Mars.

That was Abby's voice, all right. No mistake about it.
The room swayed. How was this possible? How?
Tolan staggered over to the bed, wanting to get a look at her again, to see that face, even though he was sure he was hallucinating.

He felt a hand grabbing his shoulder—Blackburn—but he shrugged it off and kept going, moving to the side of the bed.

Jane was hugging herself tightly, rocking gently as she continued to sing.

Mama got trouble
Mom got sin

He grabbed her now, the words dying on her lips as he forced her to turn in his direction. And as her wild hair fell away from her face, he saw those hazel eyes again, Abby's eyes, staring up at him as they had before. But this time looking directly at him. Full of pain.

But it wasn't just Abby's *eyes* he saw. Those were her cheekbones, too, and maybe even her nose. It was a face that seemed to be at war with itself, as if she were some kind of shapeshifter in the middle of a transformation. The skin undulated, her bone structure subtly changing right there before him.

Oh, my fucking God . . .

Then she said, in a small, plaintive voice, "Why, Michael . . . Why . . . ?"

And the sound of it, the sound of his name, brought tears to his eyes. Filled him with an incongruous mix of joy and bewilderment and horror—

—a horror that deepened when his gaze dropped to the left side of her face.

And what he saw there—or *didn't* see—sent him spiraling out of control, certain now that he had indeed lost his mind. He was as much a candidate for admission to this hospital as anyone the police had ever brought through those front doors.

The woman who had Abby's eyes, Abby's nose, Abby's cheekbones, and what would surely soon be Abby's chin . . .

. . . was missing her left ear.

Chapter 28

It wasn't just the room that was swaying now, but the whole goddamn world. Tolan stumbled away from Jane or Abby or whoever the hell she was, and turned, only to find Blackburn staring at him with a quizzical look on his face, saying something to him.

But all Tolan saw was a moving mouth. Heard nothing but the beating of his own heart, an accelerating *tha-thump* reverberating inside his head.

He had to get out of here. Had to get away from this woman and this cop and this room and this hospital. Had to find some place to be alone for a while, to clear his mind.

He launched himself past Blackburn and through the open door into a corridor filled with staff and patients—a security guard crossing toward him; an orderly escorting an elderly man toward the shower room; a nurse pushing a medicine cart; Bobby Fremont, framed in his windowed doorway, shouting angrily at Tolan as he flew past.

Tolan ignored them all, continuing down the hallway and around the corner until he reached a private access door. Fumbling his key card from his pocket, he quickly beeped himself out.

Then he was outside, sucking in fresh air, taking in

gulps of it as if he'd been holding his breath underwater for the last several minutes. But he couldn't seem to get enough, couldn't fill his lungs, and he didn't slow down, kept moving around the side of the building to the main walkway and on toward the staff parking lot.

The thumping in his head had started to subside now, only to be replaced by the sound of the rustling pepper trees, which seemed to be watching him, whispering their disapproval.

Then he was in the lot, found his car, unlocked the door, threw it open. But he didn't get inside, just stood there a moment, using the doorframe for support, still trying to breathe.

He was, he knew, smack in the middle of a full-born panic attack. He had to relax, talk himself down, to release the toxins that had invaded his mind. But he still couldn't breathe.

Easy now, a voice said, and he realized it was Abby talking to him. *You're fine, Michael, you're gonna be fine. Try to slow your breathing, take long deep breaths.*

Tolan tried, but he couldn't do it. Couldn't seem to get enough air.

Talk, Abby said. *Say something. If you can talk, you can breathe.*

It was a common technique for dealing with patients suffering a panic attack. Get them talking. But Tolan had never thought it would be used on him.

He said the first thing that came to mind:

"A lie stands on one leg, the truth on two."

He didn't know why that phrase had suddenly popped into his head, but there it was.

"A lie stands on one leg, the truth on two."

He thought about the significance of the words. Had he been living a lie this past year? Was that why he seemed to have lost his balance? Why he was suddenly plagued by these hallucinations?

"A lie stands on one leg, the truth on two."

The irony, of course, was that Abby had given him the book that contained those words. *Poor Richard's Almanac.*

Poor Richard, indeed. Poor Abby.

Poor Michael.

Putting his hands on his stomach, he said the words again, feeling the rhythm of his breathing, each new breath now slower than the last, his panic finally, thankfully, subsiding.

Feeling foolish and ashamed, he climbed into his car, sank deep into the driver's seat.

He half expected Lisa or Blackburn or someone with a butterfly net to show up, but several minutes went by and no one did. He was alone out here. Just as he'd wanted to be. Alone with his thoughts, his worries, his dread.

His madness?

He knew he should march right back into that hospital and tell them both what was going on. Tell Blackburn about his missing time, that they needed to look more closely at Abby's murder, because he couldn't make any guarantees about his own culpability.

This woman, this Jane Doe, had made him see that. Her resemblance to Abby had opened a Pandora's box of emotions. Emotions he could no longer contain. And in trying to suppress them this past year, he had developed his own psychosis.

The psychosis of a guilty man?

But he didn't get up. Didn't march into the hospital. Didn't tell anyone about the time he'd lost, or the delusions that plagued him.

Instead, he simply leaned back in his seat, closed his eyes.

But the moment he did, a whispery voice said:

"Hello, Dr. Tolan."

And before he could react, the sting of a needle touched his neck and he was suddenly falling backward down a long, dark hole.

FOUR

The Man Who Wasn't There

Chapter 29

Solomon felt it the moment they started up the winding road toward Headcase Hotel. It was only a vague feeling at first, but the closer they got, the stronger it grew.

Trouble.

There was trouble here.

A definite break in The Rhythm.

The two cops were talking football in the front seat, the driver every once in a while glancing at Solomon in the rearview mirror, giving him the cop scowl. This was the one who had started to beat on him once they left County General. Told Solomon he'd blown it, the way he'd acted up with the intake lady, calling him a liar and whatnot. Said that once they got to Baycliff he was gonna tell the doctors that Solomon was a violent sex offender. See how that worked out for him.

Solomon didn't really care.

Not about that, at least.

But this trouble he sensed, this break in The Rhythm—it was worrisome, to say the least.

On the one hand it told him what he'd needed to know. That the woman he called Myra was here.

But on the other hand, it also told him that what he'd most feared this morning might very well be true. That she wasn't quite the Myra he knew. She might not even be Myra at all by now.

The car rounded a curve and Solomon saw the hospital up ahead, a cluster of drab old buildings that could just as easily have been a college or an old-town office complex. As they pulled into the parking lot, he noticed a small forest of pepper trees beyond the main walkway.

Solomon felt a strange vibe coming from those trees. Like there was something alive back there. Something dangerous.

Trouble.

It was bound to get worse before it got any better.

It always did.

Chapter 30

Two meltdowns in one morning.

That had to be a record.

Tolan was obviously a guy with some very serious psychological issues and Blackburn wished he'd never brought Psycho Bitch here in the first place.

After Tolan fled, Blackburn had turned to her, trying to figure out what it was about this woman that triggered such a strong reaction from the guy. But she had already resumed her previous position—knees up, head tucked to her chest, as she whispered the same mindless chant:

"Two times four is a lie, two times four is a lie . . ."

Had she said Tolan's name earlier?

She'd spoken to him, he knew that much. Said something soft and low, and Blackburn had thought he'd heard her say "Michael." But he couldn't be sure. Couldn't be sure of anything at this point.

"Two times four is a lie, two times four is a lie . . ."

Who was this woman?

Did Tolan know her?

What power did she have over him?

After locking her in the room, Blackburn had turned to an orderly crossing the hall.

"You see which way Doc Tolan went?"

The orderly pointed. "Around the corner."

He was about to start in that direction when his phone bleeped. He dug it out, flipped it open.

De Mello.

He thumbed a button. "Hey, Fred, you get the name of that model yet?"

"Still waiting for a callback," De Mello said. "But I've got the cell phone records you asked for. Where do you want me to fax them?"

Tolan had given them permission to pull his cell records in hopes they'd be able to trace Vincent's calls. It was a long shot, but they had to try.

Blackburn remembered seeing one of those printer/fax combos in Tolan's office when the techs were wiring it up. That was as good a place as any. Besides, maybe that was where Tolan had gone.

"Give me a couple minutes," he said. "I'll call you back with a number."

Five minutes later he was standing in Tolan's office—no sign of the doc in evidence—waiting for the fax machine to kick into gear. After a moment, it rang, picked up, then the printer started whirring, slowly pushing out the list of cell phone calls.

As Blackburn waited, something caught his eye.

Tolan's bottom desk drawer. Hanging open.

Inside was a manila envelope labeled in black marker: ABBY.

Blackburn knew he should let it go, that it was none of his business, but curiosity got the better of him. Reaching into the drawer, he pulled out the envelope, then raised the flap and saw that it was filled with photographs. Dozens of them.

He took out a handful and sifted through them. Shots of Abby Tolan.

She'd been a beautiful woman. Stunning, in fact. He had only seen the autopsy photos and the single portrait in the murder book, but looking at these, he now understood why both Tolan and Nurse Lisa had reacted to the witness the way they had. The resemblance was close. Close enough to dredge up a lot of grief.

He was about to return them when he noticed something odd about some of the photos inside the envelope. Pulling out another stack, he laid them on the desktop and looked down at them in stunned surprise.

What the hell?

A slow chill ran through Blackburn as the fax machine behind him beeped, telling him his transmission was ready.

He found Carmody in the communications van, micromanaging as usual, making sure the audio techs weren't asleep at the wheel.

"We've got problems," he said. "Major problems."

"What's wrong?"

"Tolan took off, for one."

Carmody looked alarmed. "Why? What happened?"

"That's what I'm trying to figure out. The witness starts singing and he goes ballistic. One of the nurses saw him crossing toward the parking lot and now his car's gone."

"Damn it," Carmody said, climbing out of the van. "We need to find him. If Vincent somehow—"

"Forget Vincent." Blackburn gestured to the van. "This is a waste of time. All of it."

"What are you talking about?"

Blackburn sighed. "You hungry?"

"Not particularly."

"Well, I shouldn't be either, but I am, and there's something I gotta show you. Let's go get lunch."

They got trays in the hospital cafeteria, Blackburn filling his plate with slop that looked barely edible. But he was used to barely edible, so he happily scooped it on and looked forward to hammering it down.

Carmody stuck to fresh greens. No dressing.

Typical.

He could see that she was about ready to burst. Agitated by his delaying tactics. To her credit, however, she kept her impatience in check for once, giving Blackburn some slack.

He knew it wouldn't last long. But he'd needed a few moments to think about how he was going to frame this. Tell her what he now suspected.

"So here's the thing," he said, once they'd settled at a table. "Ever since I brought Psycho Bitch here, I—"

"Who?"

He eyed her patiently. "The witness."

Carmody gave him that look she was so good at. The one that said he was a politically incorrect, misogynistic idiot. "Psycho Bitch?"

He shrugged. "I call 'em like I see 'em."

She shook her head, stabbed a bite of salad. "You're a sad man, Frank. Got the sensitivity of a snail."

"Yeah? You didn't seem to mind so much when I spent the night at your apartment."

Her expression froze. "Don't even go there."

Blackburn was about to do just that, and then some, but caught himself. It seemed that whenever he got around Carmody for any extended length of time, he let himself get sucked into some weird vortex where he actually gave a shit what she thought of him. Like he was some pimply-faced teenager trying to get the prom queen to take notice.

He looked at her a moment, noting that she was wearing less makeup these days, and that she still wore those tiny ruby earrings her father had given her when she was fifteen. Her birthstone. He wasn't sure why he remembered that particular tidbit about her life, but it made him uncomfortable to know that he did.

He cleared his throat. "Right. Back to Tolan."

"I'm losing my patience."

As if she ever had any.

"The thing is," Blackburn said, "once I get hold of something, it's hard for me to let go. You know that. And I can't stop thinking about what Psycho—Jane Doe keeps saying."

"Which is?"

"Two times four is a lie."

Carmody blinked at him. "What?"

"Two times four is a lie. She says it over and over. At first I thought it was just a buncha nut-case nonsense, but now I'm not so sure."

"Okay," Carmody said. "I'm curious. Tell me why I should care."

"Think about it. Two times four. Four multiplied by two. What does that equal?"

"Eight."

"Exactly. And how many victims have we attributed to Vincent?"

Carmody hesitated. "Eight," she said.

"Right again. But now the circus is in town based solely on the strength of a couple of phone calls. Phone calls accusing Tolan of being a copycat. Of murdering his wife. Which, if true, would mean that Vincent's victim count is only seven."

"If true?"

"Two times four is a lie."

He waited for Carmody to process this, but wasn't surprised when she balked. "You expect me to believe that this woman somehow knows how many people Vincent has really killed?"

"No, but maybe she knows that Tolan's wife wasn't one of them."

Carmody stared at him. "You think Tolan killed his wife."

"Just like Vincent said."

She clearly wasn't buying. Seemed amused, in fact. "That's pretty wild, Frank. Tell me another one."

"Don't be so quick to dismiss me, okay?"

"There's a flaw in your logic. If Tolan killed his wife, why would he bother telling us about Vincent's phone calls in the first place? Wouldn't he want to keep that to himself?"

Blackburn waited a moment, then said, "What if I told you those phone calls are complete bullshit? That he made it all up?"

"That's ludicrous. Why would he do that?"

Blackburn shrugged. "Why else? Guilt."

"Oh, for Christ's sake, Frank, if you brought me here to spew this nonsense—"

"Just let me finish, okay?"

Carmody glared at him. "This had better be good."

They said nothing for a moment, launching into an impromptu staring contest, Blackburn trying to decide if he wanted to put a fist in her face or simply lean across the table and plant a kiss on her lips.

That would certainly catch her off guard.

"How many times," he said, breaking away from the stare, "have you gotten a perp in the interrogation room, he's denying and denying—didn't know the girl, wasn't near the place—but you get the sense he's holding back. And you know he wants to tell you about it, keeps steering the conversation in a direction that makes you think he might want to confess."

"And you think that's Tolan?"

"Like I said, what if the phone calls from Vincent

weren't real? What if that web page he showed us was a fake? What would that tell you?"

"That he has some very serious mental health issues. But you're making an assumption that isn't backed up by the facts."

"Isn't it?" Blackburn dipped his hand into his coat pocket and brought out the list of cell phone calls. "Right after Tolan pulled his disappearing act, I got a call from De Mello. He faxed me this."

He unfolded it and laid it on the table in front of her.

"Tolan says Vincent called him around three this morning, then again about an hour before we got here. Notice anything missing?"

Carmody scanned the sheet. "Here's one right here. A little after three A.M."

"Yeah, that's me, calling about Jane." He pointed to the next entry. "And this one is Tolan calling me, right before I went into the meeting with Escalante." He paused. "There's no activity in between."

Carmody frowned. "What about his home and office lines?"

"We don't have the records yet, but he specifically said Vincent called him on his cell phone, remember?"

She remembered, all right. Blackburn could see it in her face.

"I don't believe this. He lied to us."

"That he did," Blackburn said, leaning back in his chair. "Right to our fucking faces."

Chapter 31

Lisa had been to the parking lot three times in the last half hour and still no sign of him. His parking space was empty.

She took her cell phone out, dialed his number. It rang several times, then his voice mail answered. Beeped.

"Michael," she said, "it's me again. Where are you? We were supposed to have lunch, remember? Call me when you get this."

She hung up, feeling hurt and angry.

Wanted to wring his neck.

She knew these crank phone calls, or whatever they were, had rattled him. But she suspected the patient in SR-3 was the real reason for his behavior. Had known it the moment she saw her curled up on the bed—that same petite, fragile frame as Abby's. The same wild dark hair.

Lisa hadn't been able to see the patient's face, but wouldn't be surprised if there was a resemblance there, too. Enough to get to Michael.

And the timing couldn't be worse.

Why did she have to show up today of all days?

Lisa had seen Michael in a lot of different moods over the last year, but he'd never been so distant, so reluctant to communicate as he was today. And she hated it when he kept things from her. Hated the wondering and the worrying.

All she wanted in this world was to take care of him. He'd been through so much and she wanted to make it right again. To make him see *her* for once, instead of Abby.

And just when she thought he was making progress, this woman—this street person—comes along and ruins it.

Each time Lisa had been out here, she'd hoped to see Michael's Lexus coming back up the hill. But all she'd found was a sea of parked cars, glinting in the sunlight. No sign of human activity, except during her last trip, when a couple of police officers escorted an old black man toward the EDU.

The old man had smiled at her as they passed, a knowing twinkle in his eyes. "You look like a woman in search of a lost soul," he'd said.

And as surprised as Lisa had been, she couldn't dispute his words.

Michael *was*, in effect, just that. A lost soul.

Her lost soul.

"But why?" Carmody said, staring down at the list again. "Why would he do that? He had to know we'd find out. He gave us permission to pull these records, for godsakes."

Blackburn nodded. "I told you. He's just like that perp who wants to confess, but can't quite bring himself to do it. So he has some make-believe phantom do it for him."

Carmody shook her head. "I don't know, Frank. Making up phone calls is pretty crazy, and throwing together that website is even crazier, but none of it means he killed his wife. Maybe he's just an attention whore, like that idiot who confessed to killing JonBenet Ramsey."

"Maybe."

"And what about Janovic?" she said.

"What about him?"

"Even if we entertain the notion that Tolan had something to do with his wife's death, how does Janovic fit into the equation? Is his murder just a coincidence? Did Vincent kill him? Or is that Tolan playing copycat too?"

Blackburn hesitated. "I haven't figured that part out yet."

"Surprise, surprise."

"But you know me and coincidences. Maybe he was after Jane, and Janovic got in the way."

"That doesn't make any sense," Carmody said. "From what you've told me, it sounds like the killer was *interrupted* by Jane. And why would Tolan kill his wife, wait a whole year, then go after some street whore?"

"Like I said, maybe she isn't just a street whore. Maybe she knows Tolan. She might even be related to him."

"Related? How?"

"I don't know, but she looks a lot like the wife. Maybe they're cousins or something. Sisters. When she started singing, he immediately recognized the tune, like it was an old family favorite or something. I thought he was gonna crap his pants."

"You're forgetting something," Carmody said.

"What?"

"The burn marks. The smiley face. How could Tolan know about that?"

And there it was. The same old stumbling block.

"Maybe it got leaked somehow."

Carmody shook her head. "No way. The task force kept that one under tight lock and key."

"Try telling that to the idiots who prosecuted O.J. They'd laugh in your face."

She stared at him. "Come on, Frank, I'm hearing a lot of 'maybes' but no concrete proof. One of the few things I've always admired about you is that when it comes to cases, you never jump to conclusions. You always follow the best evidence."

"You're right," Blackburn said.

And she was. Left-handed compliment or not. He had never been the type to finger a suspect then look for evidence to back it up, ignoring all to the contrary. He had always looked to the facts of a case to point him *toward* a suspect.

But when a storm comes along and you get hit by a bolt of lightning, it tends to jangle the brain, mix things up. And these cell phone records and Tolan's bizarre behavior had certainly seeded the clouds.

Not to mention the photographs he'd found in Tolan's office.

"He did it," Blackburn said. "Two times four is a lie."

"The babbling of a sick woman. It means nothing."

"She saw something, Sue. I don't know what it was, but now we've got Tolan in the middle of a meltdown, caught in a complete fabrication. It's all connected somehow. It's gotta be." He paused. "And then there's these."

Reaching into his pocket again, he pulled out the second stack of snapshots he'd taken from the envelope in Tolan's desk drawer. Shoving his tray aside, he laid them out in front of her.

Six photos. Each a shot of Abby Tolan. At the beach. The park. On the street. Standing in her gallery. And she was smiling for the camera. A radiant smile.

But in every single photo, there was one thing missing.

Carmody stared down at them, the color draining from her face. "My God . . ."

My God, indeed, Blackburn thought.

Someone had gone through them, one by one—

—and cut out Abby Tolan's eyes.

"Tell me now the sonofabitch didn't kill her."

Chapter 32

He couldn't move his arms and legs.

He had awakened to near darkness, lying on his back, on a table of some kind, slanted slightly toward the floor, his wrists and ankles strapped down.

Four-point restraints.

A small patch of light bled in through a crack in the wall, giving him just enough illumination to get a sense of his surroundings. He was in a windowless room that smelled of mold and burned wood and plaster.

The ornate light fixture mounted on the blackened ceiling above him was cracked and broken, with missing bulbs. Whatever this place was, it had been abandoned decades ago.

The old hospital? He couldn't be sure.

The drug he had been given still sluiced through his veins, slowing his thought processes, but its effects were starting to wear off.

Something was stuck to the sides of his head, to his temples—pieces of tape, perhaps. But as his brain began to clear, he realized it wasn't just tape . . . but disposable electrodes.

What exactly was going on here?

If he had to guess—and he supposed that was all he

could do—he'd say he had been prepped for some kind of sleep study.

Which made no sense. He wasn't at Baycliff, wasn't even in a fully functioning structure as far as he could tell. There were no doctors here, no technicians, no hospital staff at all. He was alone. Alone with the darkness and the faint, muffled hum of a motor.

A generator of some kind?

He couldn't be sure. But the sound was familiar to him. Much like the rumble of the ten-gallon trifuel his parents had used to power their cabin near Arrowhead Springs so many years ago.

He didn't often think about those days. The months they'd spent up in the mountains, away from the rest of the world, as his mother tried to deal with one of her many "episodes." She had become cruel and unmanageable, and his father had been at his wit's end trying to look after her. Tolan didn't find out until years later that she had been suffering from Dissociative Identity Disorder, but he was certain that her illness was what had spurred him to become a psychiatrist.

He heard another sound. The squeak of rusty wheels. Then a door creaked open, muted sunlight momentarily slicing through the room, giving him a glimpse of charred furniture and broken glass cabinets.

A figure was silhouetted in the doorway. Judging by the size, it was a man, and he was pushing a cart, a cart loaded with a small, boxy piece of machinery. Hard to tell in the dim light, but it looked like an ECT instrument.

Fear blossomed in Tolan's stomach.

A moment later, the door closed again, returning the room to near darkness. Then a whispery voice said:

"You're awake, I see."

Vincent.

"What's going on? Why did you bring me here?"

There was movement, the squeak of wheels again. The cart being repositioned.

"When I was a boy," Vincent said, "I suffered occasional bouts of depression. My mother and father, being the concerned parents they were, brought me to a hospital very much like this one used to be. To a doctor just like you."

A penlight flicked on, shining directly in Tolan's eyes. He squinted.

"The doctor felt I was in need of a quick fix. That medication would take much too long to kick in. So he prescribed six rounds of bilateral electroconvulsive therapy. And twice a week, for three long weeks, a very attractive young nurse marched me into a room like this one and strapped me down to a table just like the one you currently occupy."

The fear in Tolan's belly spread through him like a virus.

"Unfortunately," Vincent continued, "rather than prescribe the usual anesthesia and muscle relaxers associated with the treatment, the doctor decided to administer it drug-free."

"That's barbaric," Tolan said.

"Yes, I thought so. But I was only fourteen years old at the time. What say did I have in the matter?"

Despite the whisper, the voice sounded familiar to Tolan. But he couldn't place it. Wished he could see the man's face—not that it would do him any good.

Vincent redirected the penlight to the side of Tolan's head. Leaning forward, he attached a wire to the right electrode, then shifted the light and attached another to the left.

"What about your parents?" Tolan asked.

"They were wonderful people, but not very sophisticated. They trusted the doctor. And why shouldn't they have? He assured them that electroshock was safe and effective."

Most people believed that ECT had been discontinued by the psychiatric community, but nothing could be further from the truth. Close to 100,000 people a year received the treatment.

"It usually *is* safe," Tolan said.

"That's up for debate. But it certainly doesn't help when your doctor's a sadist. And there's no arguing about what it does to your memory."

He was right. Studies had shown that electroconvulsive therapy caused short-term memory loss. People undergoing ECT had difficulty remembering events just prior to and during treatment.

Vincent turned away and Tolan felt a slight tug on the wires.

"What are you going to do?"

"That's a silly question, don't you think?"

Tolan heard the flick of switches, and panic rose in his chest. "You can't."

"I don't think you're really in a position to stop me, Doctor. Just think of yourself as a fourteen-year-old boy."

Tolan tried to protest, but before he could get the words out, a rubber bite bar was shoved into his mouth and secured by a strap around his head.

Tolan tossed from side to side, using his tongue to try to push it out, but it was no use. The strap tightened, lodging it in place.

"Just a little precaution. I don't want you biting your tongue off."

An ECT instrument typically put out as much power as a wall jack, sending an electrical current through the patient's brain. Tolan had never been a recipient of electroconvulsive therapy, had never administered it himself, but he knew that in the wrong hands, and without anesthesia, it could not only be painful and dangerous—it could kill you.

"What dosage do you think we should start with?" Vincent asked. "Too high will knock you out—and we don't want that. Too low and we've defeated the purpose of the treatment in the first place."

Tolan jerked his arms upward, straining against the restraints, trying to break the straps. But it was no use.

"Let's start at two hundred fifty volts and work our way upward."

Another switch was flipped and a faint whir filled Tolan's ears.

Jesus Christ, he thought. Jesus fucking Christ. He's going to do it. He's going to—

Pain shot through Tolan's skull, a piercing, hot blade of fire that expanded and spread throughout his body. A bone-cracking pain, worse than anything he could remember. He bucked involuntarily against it, squeezing his eyes shut, clamping his jaw down so hard on the bite bar that he thought his teeth might break, a muffled scream working its way between them.

Then it was done. Over.

And the relief was sweet. So fucking sweet.

Vincent reached down, loosened the strap, and pulled the bite bar free, letting Tolan spit away the foam that had gathered in the corners of his mouth. Then a wave of nausea swept over him, and for a moment he felt as if he might throw up.

"Jesus," he said.

"I'm afraid Jesus won't help you," Vincent told him. "But an answer to my question will."

". . . What question?"

"You have to understand that I've always tried to be a

fair man. I believe in due process. Innocent until proven guilty and all that."

Tolan didn't know how to respond.

"And while I'm reasonably certain of your guilt, I think it would be unfair to continue with the plans I've laid out for you, until I hear your confession." He paused. "So tell me, Doctor. Are you ready to confess?"

". . . you can't do this," Tolan croaked.

"Oh, I can and I will. Let's ramp it up a bit, shall we?"

He shoved the bite bar back into Tolan's mouth, tightened the strap, then flipped a switch and—

Pain shot through Tolan's skull, vibrating through his body with such intensity that, for a moment, he thought he might burst apart. It was like sticking your nose in a light socket. And what popped into his head was the image of a cartoon wolf, his body lit up like a thousand-watt bulb, Bugs Bunny gripping the throw switch.

Then it was gone. Mercifully gone.

The bite bar came out again. Followed by another wave of nausea. More spitting. Bile stung his throat.

"Are you ready to confess? Or shall I kick it up another notch?"

"No . . ." Tolan said. "Please . . ." He could barely breathe. "Stop . . ."

"I have to hear the words, Doctor."

Tolan thought about that last night with Abby. About his accusation. The slap. The blackout.

He shook his head. "I didn't kill her. I couldn't have. I loved her."

"Oh, please, Doctor. The I-loved-her defense? Surely you can come up with something more convincing than that. Unless, of course, you aren't entirely convinced yourself."

"I could never hurt her. I've never hurt anybody."

"Oh, really? Are you sure about that?"

"Yes . . ."

"What about Anna Marie Colson?"

Tolan felt another jolt go through him, but this one had nothing to do with the ECT machine.

"You didn't think anyone knew about her, did you?"

Anna Marie Colson was a young coed Tolan had briefly dated back during his pre-med days at UCLA. One of his housemates. She had, in fact, broken his post-adolescent heart by hooking up with a law student and never looking back. Several months later, both Anna and her new boyfriend were killed in a street robbery gone wrong.

"She was mugged," Tolan said.

"But they never found her attacker, did they? And I think the police were quite interested in you for a while there, weren't they?"

"No, you've got it wrong, you've got it—"

The bite bar was shoved back in, the strap tightened, a switch flipped and—

Pain radiated through Tolan's body a third time—the worst jolt yet—forcing him to buck and shiver, arching his back, bending his toes. His bones felt as if they might crack, his head ready to explode. And just when he thought he'd faint dead away, it stopped.

Then the nausea was back with a vengeance and he retched against the bite bar. Vincent quickly removed it and grabbed Tolan's head, turning it to the side. Tolan retched again, spewing thick threads of saliva onto the table.

He was going to die.

Felt it coming.

Another jolt and he'd be gone.

He spit again, trying to evacuate the fluid from his mouth. Normally, atropine would have been administered to reduce the secretions, but there was nothing normal about this situation at all. He felt like a fugitive from *One Flew Over the Cuckoo's Nest.*

"No more," he croaked.

"Then I take it you're ready to confess?"

Tolan said nothing. If he denied killing Abby, it would only be more of the same.

"Don't try my patience, Doctor."

Tolan remained silent. Maybe Vincent knew something about him that he couldn't or didn't want to see. Maybe Vincent had some killer radar that let him know when he'd met one of his own kind.

Tolan couldn't, with any certainty, say whether or not he had killed Abby. He simply couldn't remember. But what difference did that make to Vincent? Vincent only wanted to hear one thing.

And anything was better than this. Anything.

Vincent grabbed the bite bar again and was about to reinsert it when Tolan shook his head, warning him away.

"All right," he said. "All right. I confess. If that's what you want to hear, I confess."

The penlight shone directly in his eyes. "Not very convincing, Doctor. Say it."

"I just di—"

"*Say* it, or I swear to God I'll fry your fucking brain."

Tolan closed his eyes against the light, tried to catch his breath. Then, after a long moment, he said, "I killed my wife. I killed Abby. We fought that night and, God have mercy on me, I killed her."

Vincent leaned in close to his ear. "Thank you, Doctor."

Then, without warning, a needle stabbed Tolan's neck and he once again disappeared down the rabbit hole.

Chapter 33

Solomon sat cuffed to a chair just inside the security cage.
The chair, in turn, was bolted to the floor.

He'd been waiting here awhile now, watching the nurses
and security guards go about their business, listening too,
hoping he might hear something about Myra.

When the cops dropped him off, the angry one, the one
who'd beat on him, had said to the guard, "Watch your
pecker with this one."

"Don't you worry," the guard had said. "He tries anything, he'll be pulling back a bloody stump."

"It isn't his hands you gotta worry about."

They'd both gotten a good chuckle over that, the guard
saying, "Yeah, well, I'd threaten to knock his teeth out,
but he probably doesn't have any."

They laughed again, and after that touching moment of
male bonding, the cops were gone, leaving Solomon to
wonder what kind of men wanted to treat people like that.
He had his share of problems, sure, but he'd always tried to
treat others with respect. Even the cops.

Even after one of them had killed Henry.

He could see the lobby doors from here, and on out past
them to the walkway leading to the parking lot. Saw that
pretty nurse go out there a couple more times, scanning
the lot, looking for someone.

He'd noticed her name tag when the cops had pushed him past her. Could only remember the first name: Lisa. Saw she was a director of some kind. A woman in charge.

She didn't seem all that in charge right now. Kinda worried-looking. And he'd sensed a storm inside her. The Rhythm off balance. Struggling.

Solomon couldn't really tell you why, but he knew she was the one he needed to talk to. To tell about Myra.

So he sat there, quiet, waiting. Didn't have much choice in the matter.

After a while she came back through the lobby doors and the guard buzzed her into the security cage. She looked distracted, but he tried to get her attention anyway.

"Excuse me, ma'am."

The guard was talking to her now and she hadn't heard him.

"Ma'am? Excuse me."

She turned, looking over at Solomon. "Yes, sir?"

"I need to talk to you."

She smiled then, but it was a polite smile, not a happy one. "Let me guess. You found my lost soul?"

He thought for a moment she might be mocking him, but she didn't seem the type.

"Still workin' on it," he said. "Can't do much chained to this chair."

"You shouldn't have to wait much longer. The intake clerk will process you, then we'll get you into the showers and find you a bunk."

"I got somethin' I need to tell you. Somethin' important."

"Don't worry," she said. "As soon as you're processed you'll be assigned a doctor."

Solomon shook his head. "No, no doctors. You. It's about the woman the police brought in here early this morning. My friend Myra. Little bitty thing."

This caught her off guard. She came over to him then. "You know her?"

"That's just it," Solomon said. "That's what I want to talk to you about. But it's hard to explain, sittin' out here in the open like this."

She looked at him for a long moment as if trying to decide what to make of him. But Solomon could see that her curiosity was piqued.

"Let the intake clerk process you," she said. "Then I'll come find you."

"Thank you, ma'am. I appreciate that."

She nodded to him, then started down the hall, stopping to talk to a nurse, pointing in his direction as she spoke, throwing another smile his way.

Watching her, Solomon knew he'd made the right choice. Despite the smile, he still sensed that storm inside her. Something bothering her. Weighing on her mind.

She glanced out toward the parking lot and Solomon wondered what she was looking for out there.

Wondered if she'd ever find it.

Chapter 34

They put out an alert on Tolan, had the patrol units out looking for his black Lexus. A unit was dispatched to his home, but came up empty.

The other members of the task force had been apprised of his deception and sudden disappearance, and after an impromptu telephone conference, Rossbach made a command decision. They would now take a two-pronged approach to this investigation. The task force would continue working the previous victims and the Janovic case on the assumption that Vincent was indeed back in action, while Blackburn took a closer look at Tolan.

"I think it's a dead end," Rossbach said. "There's no way we sprung a leak, I can tell you that. But Tolan's behavior is just fucked-up enough to raise a lot of questions. So find him, sit him down, and get him talking."

"Will do," Blackburn said.

"Oh, and Frank? Just so you know, since you're the bonehead who took our only witness to Dr. Dementia, you're the goat on this. Understand? We get any blowback, you're the goddamn goat."

Blackburn wouldn't expect anything less.

They considered finally transferring Jane Doe to County, but were told that County had had an unusually busy morning and didn't have a bed to spare. At this point, nobody was expecting much out of her anyway, so they left her where she was, posting a uniformed officer right outside her room with specific instructions that, should Tolan return, he be immediately detained and not allowed inside.

Carmody agreed to stay behind to question staff and wait for Clayton Simm, still a no-show. Blackburn had gotten his number from admin and called him at home, only to wake him from a sound sleep.

"What the hell, Doc? You should've been here an hour ago."

Simm seemed befuddled. "Who is this?"

"Frank Blackburn. We met this morning, remember?"

Simm's voice hardened. He obviously wasn't a fan. "Right," he said. "What's this about?"

"Tolan didn't tell you?"

"Tell me what? What's going on?"

Christ, Blackburn thought, that sonofabitch Tolan had never even called the guy. A lie stands on one leg, all right. And Tolan had long ago reached the tipping point.

Blackburn filled Simm in, explained the conflict of interest, but remained purposely sketchy with the details. He and Carmody had decided to keep the recent revelations about Tolan under wraps. All Simm needed to know was that they had a witness they wanted answers from.

Sounding as groggy as a two-year-old past midnight, Simm agreed to get there as soon as he possibly could.

No telling when that would be. He was Carmody's problem now.

After they hung up, Blackburn decided to catch a ride back to headquarters with the audio-tech boys, leaving the sedan in the lot for Sue to use.

Before they left, he took one last look in on Jane, wishing he could shake her a few times and get her talking. But he had a feeling the cocoon she'd wrapped herself in was like a Kevlar vest.

Not meant to be penetrated.

Chapter 35

When Blackburn got to the station house, De Mello was playing his iPod so loud you could make out the tune from all the way across the squad room.

Sympathy for the Devil.

It was a wonder the guy still had eardrums.

His attention was centered on his computer screen, fingers ripping through the keys. Around him lay the remnants of a serious junk food overload. Candy and cupcake wrappers, an empty liter of soda, and a half-eaten Hostess apple pie. And, of course, coffee. Always coffee.

When Blackburn started his way, De Mello shut off the music. "Just the man I want to see."

"You finally get a name for our witness?"

"Not yet. But things are popping here since we last spoke. Got two new items of interest."

"Let's have 'em," Blackburn said.

De Mello slipped his headphones off and tossed them aside. "First, I've got Janovic's bank statements. He definitely had a steady source of income."

"Yeah? What'd you find?"

De Mello punched a key and an electronic bank record popped up on the computer screen. Using the mouse, he highlighted a handful of entries.

"He's been making regular deposits over the last several months," De Mello said. "Always the same amount. Always cash. But he's got no visible means of support."

Blackburn stared at the screen. "Two grand a month. Drug money?"

De Mello shook his head. "I checked with narcotics and they say he was strictly a consumer. And to bring in that kind of cash, he'd have to sell a lot of crack. Or suck a lot of dick."

"Maybe it isn't how many, but whose."

"Extortion?"

"Steady deposits," Blackburn said. "Always the same amount. Makes sense to me."

He thought about what Mats had said at the crime scene. That Janovic knew his attacker. Blackmail was a pretty strong motive for murder.

The question was, who was Janovic blackmailing and why? Was there a way to connect Tolan to this?

They could try checking Tolan's bank records for any steady withdrawals, but there was no way they'd ever get a warrant at this point in the game. Not without something stronger than a bunch of defaced photographs and a couple of bogus phone calls. Blackburn had already dropped off the copies of the website pages to the crime scene techs for closer examination, but figured Tolan had simply faked them to bolster his story. Attempts to connect with the actual site had ended with a 404 Page Not Found error.

"What else've you got?" Blackburn asked.

"Janovic didn't have a home phone," De Mello said. "So I went through his cell records and compiled a list of possible friends to look at. But unlike the rest of America, he didn't seem to spend much time on the phone."

"So what did he use? Smoke signals?"

"His favorite means of communication was the Internet. Some email, but mostly instant messages. Which leads me to the second item."

De Mello dug around in the mess on his desk until he found a LifeDrive Palm Pilot. "Billy's a wiz. Cracked this thing in record time." He flicked it on, then handed it to Blackburn. "It's got a wireless connection, and since Janovic didn't have a computer, I figure he did his web browsing and instant messaging with this."

"What am I looking for?"

"Check out the folder labeled BUNK BUDDIES."

"You gotta be kidding me."

Blackburn pulled out the Palm Pilot's stylus and began clicking through the menus until he found the folder in question. Another click brought up a list of what looked like code names.

"Notice all the asterisks?" De Mello said. "I'm guessing it's a rating system of some kind. Take a look at the fourth one down."

"DickMan229. Three stars. What about it?"

"It's obviously an online nickname. So I tried Googling the words Bunk Buddies and found a small social networking website."

"A what?" Blackburn had spent probably an entire fifteen minutes of his life on the Internet. Had found the place too impersonal, completely devoid of conversational nuance. Make a simple sarcastic quip and it was likely to be interpreted as a declaration of war.

"It's a virtual community," De Mello said. "A kind of gathering place where people with common interests make online friends, like Facebook and MySpace. Only Bunk Buddies is regional and caters to the local underground gay crowd. People looking to hook up."

Blackburn risked asking the obvious. "I take it Janovic was part of this thing?"

De Mello nodded, then hit a few computer keys and a web page blossomed on his screen, showing a photo of Carl Janovic in full drag, listed as Carly921. Except for the hint of a five o'clock shadow, he didn't look half bad. If Blackburn were blind drunk and suicidal, he might mistake him for Carmody.

In a box next to the photograph was a list of Janovic's likes and dislikes, favorite bands, movies, books. It was all pretty innocuous.

"So what's this have to do with DickMan229?"

"Take a look." De Mello scrolled down to a section of the page that read CARLY'S BUNKMATES, which featured several thumbnail photographs. Men in various degrees of undress. He highlighted one of them, a shirtless guy who looked to be in his late twenties. Dick-Man229.

"If you click here," De Mello said, wielding the mouse, "you go straight to an instant messaging system—Pillow Chat. I hot-synced the Palm Pilot and downloaded this log to the computer."

He clicked a tab, changing to another screen. A text log popped up, showing an exchange between Carly921 and DickMan229. Blackburn read it. Or at least tried to.

```
CARLY921: hey b hru
DICKMAN229: iash
CARLY921: u up for some i&i
DICKMAN229: waw
CARLY921: 2nite spst
DICKMAN229: btwbo
```

Blackburn scratched his head. "What the fuck is this? Morse code?"

De Mello grinned. "Close. It's chat speak. They're setting up a date."

Blackburn was dumbfounded and didn't bother to hide it.

"Let me translate," De Mello said, then pointed to each entry as he spoke:

"Hey, babe. How are you?

"I am so horny.

"You up for some intercourse and inebriation?

"Where and when?

"Tonight. Same place, same time.

"Be there with bells on."

Blackburn stared at the screen, suddenly regretting that the computer had ever been invented. Hell, that human beings had ever been invented.

"When did all this take place?"

"Three nights ago, around eleven P.M."

"I assume you've already figured out who this Dick-Man character is?"

"That I have," De Mello said. "And this is where it gets interesting."

He hit another key and an arrest report came up on screen, showing a mug shot of the same shirtless guy.

"He's a street hustler by the name of Todd Hastert. Popped a few times for soliciting and for crystal meth possession."

"Another charmer," Blackburn said.

"Thing is, up until about a year ago he was legit. Worked in the M.E.'s office as a morgue attendant. Got eighty-sixed when he failed a piss test."

A small alarm went off in Blackburn's head. Morgue attendants routinely prepped bodies for postmortem examination. Which meant Hastert might have been privy to all kinds of information, including autopsy reports. Only a handful of people at the time had known the secret details of the Van Gogh murders, and one of those people was the medical examiner. If you were looking for a leak, Todd Hastert might be a good place to start.

"Tell me you've got a line on this guy."

De Mello reached over to the Palm Pilot in Blackburn's hand and stabbed the name DickMan229 with his fingernail. An address came up on the small screen.

"Your wish is my command."

Chapter 36

Carmody had questioned three nurses, two orderlies, and one of the security guards, and none of them had even the remotest idea where Tolan might have gone.

They uniformly described the doctor as a good guy, a great boss, always accessible, always ready with a kind word. He overextended himself sometimes, sure, tended to wear himself out, but they'd never known him to suffer any significant lapses of judgment.

Until now, Carmody thought.

But if you're going to suffer a lapse, you might as well do it on a grand scale. And Tolan had certainly managed that.

Why, she wondered, had he made up such an elaborate story?

He had to know he'd be caught.

Carmody had always thought of him as a direct, no-nonsense kind of guy. So why the hoax? Was Frank right? Was this simply Tolan's roundabout way of unburdening himself of a year's worth of guilt?

It was, after all, the anniversary of his wife's murder. Had the significance of the day shaken something loose?

As she questioned the EDU staff, the defaced snap-shots of Abby Tolan kept playing like a slide show in her mind. She wasn't entirely convinced of Frank's theory, but those photos had certainly lent credence to it.

The symbolism was clear.

A "good guy" doesn't cut his wife's eyeballs out.

So maybe Frank's instincts were correct.

One thing Carmody had learned about Frank Blackburn, in the short time they were partnered up, was that despite his unrelenting, annoying demeanor, his instincts had always been pretty accurate. She had to give him that much.

She just wished that that was *all* she had given him.

There's nothing worse, she thought, than knowing you've slept with a guy who annoys the crap out of you. A guy whose every political, social, and moral belief is the exact opposite of your own.

Carmody thought about that night a lot more than she should. The night of their big mistake.

They had gone to The Elbow Room for a celebratory drink after their success with the Sarah Murphy case—another scumbag rapist in the bucket and headed to trial—and they'd both been pretty giddy over their success.

Frank was dropping her off at her apartment when her own worthless instincts reared up. Made her lean across the seat and kiss him. It was a surprise to them both and she couldn't to this day tell you why she'd done it. But she had. And it was a great kiss. Better than it should have been.

It wasn't long before they were inside her apartment, inside her bedroom, throwing their clothes off, clinging to each other like two lonely, desperate strangers.

The funny thing was, neither of them was particularly lonely *or* desperate, but something about that night made it seem that way, and being naked with Frank was neither awkward nor embarrassing.

He laid her across her bed and peppered her with soft kisses, lingering in all the right places, using his tongue and his fingers so skillfully that he brought her close to the edge faster than any man she had ever been with.

She didn't know what she had expected when she'd kissed him in the car, but it certainly wasn't this. Nothing about his demeanor had ever hinted that he could be so attentive to a woman, so loving.

And when he entered her, slowly pushing himself inside, teasing her, making her wait for that first, exquisite thrust, she felt the rush coming on, stronger than ever before. As he finally pushed himself deep, moaning in her ear as if this was the most wonderful thing he had ever felt in his life, as if *she* were the most wonderful thing—

—she came.

And not for the last time that night.

Then, three hours before the sun rose the next day, Carmody had been lying next to him in her bed, listening to him breathe, wondering what the hell she had just done and how she was going to get out of it. Sleeping with your partner is never a good idea. Ever. Under any circumstances.

Carmody liked to think of herself as a reasonably intelligent woman, someone who weighed the pros and cons of every move she made before she actually made it. Yet that night, all reason had abandoned her and now she had to pay the consequences.

She'd had no desire to be in a relationship with Frank. And she knew that irrevocable damage had been done to the partnership. When Frank awoke, slipping back to his usual, sarcastic, annoyingly alpha male persona, she'd decided right then and there to put her papers in for a transfer to Homicide.

It was a move that had hurt him. She knew that. Had made him even more insufferably male, acting as if he couldn't have cared less about the transfer, that he was, in fact, happy to get rid of her. But most men are so ridiculously easy to read. So obvious about their wants and desires and their fears, and she knew that Frank had been severely stung by her decision. And in those last couple weeks together, they became increasingly hostile to each other, a hostility that lingered to this day.

A hostility she often regretted, but couldn't quite release.

Carmody approached the nurses' station, hoping to page the head nurse, whom Frank had mentioned was Tolan's girlfriend. She was halfway to the counter when her cell phone rang.

Pulling it out, she glanced at the screen, saw only the words INCOMING CALL.

Flicking it on, she said, "Sue Carmody."

Silence on the line.

Well, not silence exactly. She could hear someone breathing.

"Hello?"

No response. Just the breathing.

She was about to say something, when the line clicked. Assuming it was a wrong number, she continued toward the nurses' station, glancing past the EDU security cage toward the lobby doors.

Although the parking lot was some distance away, she could plainly see that there was a car parked in Dr. Tolan's slot. It looked like his black Lexus.

And there was someone behind the wheel.

She turned then, heading toward the doors, when her phone rang again.

She immediately clicked it on. "Sue Carmody."

Silence. More breathing.

She stared out at the Lexus.

"Dr. Tolan?"

No response.

Carmody moved through the security cage and out toward the lobby doors. "Dr. Tolan, is this you?"

Another moment of silence, then a choked voice said, "I killed my wife. I killed Abby. We fought that night and God have mercy on me, I killed her."

Then the line clicked.

Carmody froze. Holy crap.

Looking toward the lot, she saw the Lexus starting to back out of the parking space.

Move, Sue, *move*. Don't let him get away.

Slamming through the lobby doors, she tore down the walkway. The Lexus was pulling out now, rolling toward the exit.

Carmody tucked her cell phone into a pocket and sprinted to Frank's sedan, which was parked in one of the slots reserved for police personnel. Unlocking it, she threw open the driver's door and jumped behind the wheel.

The Lexus was already headed down the hill, disappearing from sight.

Jamming the key into the ignition, she started the car, gunned the engine, then rocketed out of the parking space, picking up speed as she pulled out of the lot onto Baycliff Drive, which wound down through the mountains toward the 101.

As she drove around the first curve, she saw the Lexus again, but it had turned off the main drag onto a narrow access road that disappeared behind an outcropping of rocks.

Where the hell was he going?

Spinning her wheel, she rolled after him, reaching for the radio mic as she drove, flicking the call button.

"Dispatch, this is unit two-nineteen, in pursuit of POI Michael Tolan, driving a black Lexus, headed east on an access road just off Baycliff Drive."

She waited for a response and got none.

"Dispatch?"

Nothing. Glancing down at the radio, she realized it had been switched off.

Sonofabitch.

She flicked a knob, but nothing happened. The thing was dead.

Goddamn it, Frank.

He'd forgotten to test it before checking the car out of the police garage. Either that, or someone had tampered with it in the hospital lot.

Tolan?

The Lexus was disappearing around a curve, moving deeper into the mountains. Carmody drove past an unlocked security gate marked NO TRESSPASSING and realized that this was an access road that led to the old hospital.

Why was Tolan going there?

She picked up speed again, took the curve, and saw the Lexus up ahead. Digging out her cell phone, she was about to put it to her ear when she noticed the NO SERVICE icon flashing on her screen.

Shit.

The mountains must be blocking the signal.

Dropping the phone to the seat next to her, she thought about turning back, waiting until she could get some backup out here, but was afraid she might be wrong about where Tolan was headed. What if there was another road that took him down the hill and away from the old hospital? And without a radio there was no way to head him off.

Then again the man had just confessed to murdering his wife, and the last thing she should be doing was going after him alone. That was a Blackburn move, and she was no Frank Blackburn.

The Lexus disappeared around another curve.

Making her decision, Carmody punched the pedal and sped after it. As she rounded the curve, she saw it pull through another gate.

Up ahead, beyond a thick cluster of pepper trees, sat the dark monstrosity that had once been Baycliff Hospital. It was a massive old structure, half burned to the ground, but still imposing, its dark doorways and broken windows like malevolent eyes.

Carmody pulled to the side of the road and waited as the Lexus momentarily disappeared behind the cluster of trees. A moment later it was in view again, pulling to a stop in front of the building.

No one got out.

The driver just sat there.

I killed my wife. I killed Abby. God have mercy on me.

Thinking she might be about to witness a suicide, Carmody put the sedan in gear, then drove through the gate, rounding the short curve that wound through the cluster of trees. When she emerged on the other side, she discovered that the driver's door of the Lexus was now hanging open, the seat empty.

Shit.

Pulling to a stop behind it, she killed the engine and climbed out, taking her Glock from the holster she kept clipped at the small of her back. She glanced around. No sign of him.

"Dr. Tolan?"

She moved past his car toward the building, staring at the black hole that had once been the main entrance, wondering if he'd gone inside. If he had, she wasn't about to follow. She may have been stupid enough to come this far alone, but she wasn't *that* stupid.

She kept her Glock raised. "Dr. Tolan?"

No response. No sign of him.

Then her phone bleeped. She turned, realizing she'd left it on the passenger seat. And it was working again, no longer stuck in a dead zone.

Moving to the car, she leaned in and snatched it up, flicking it on. "Hello?"

Silence. Only the sound of breathing.

"Dr. Tolan? Is that you?"

She looked toward the building again. It towered above her like a set from an old horror movie, and she half expected a snarling, ravenous ghoul to come tearing out of that black entranceway, its teeth bared.

"Dr. Tolan, where are you?"

The silence continued a moment, then a soft voice said, "Right behind you."

And when Carmody turned, she was struck in the chest by twin Tazer darts, the sudden shock of electricity knocking her straight to the ground.

Chapter 37

They had put Solomon in what the orderly called the Day Room. A bunch of bolted-down tables and chairs facing a large wire-mesh window that overlooked the ocean.

Solomon had been right. Standing at the window, he could see houses way down there along the coastline, little two-bedroom beach homes right up against the sand, waves lapping at their back porches.

The Day Room was full of loonies. Some of them sat in chairs, quietly babbling, while others milled about, looking as if they weren't quite sure what to do with themselves. A stack of game boxes sat untouched on a shelf in the corner. Parcheesi. Checkers. Monopoly. Another shelf held old paperback books and magazines.

A television, mounted high on the wall behind a cage, was set to a channel showing a weeping young couple who seemed to be offering some kind of confession to a talk-show host. Some of the folks watching wept along with them.

A woman in a blue robe kept circling the room, holding an open book in front of her and pretending to read as she quietly sang "Moon River." The book was upside down.

Every once in a while an old coot stuck in a wheelchair

would cry out, "Help me, Jimmy! Help me!" but nobody paid much attention to him. Not the orderlies, not even the guard sitting behind a nearby desk.

Solomon had seen some pretty crazy things on the street, but this place topped them all. He sure wished that nurse lady would show up like she promised. He needed somebody sane to talk to.

He kept looking around for Myra, but didn't see her. Figured they probably considered her too dangerous to leave her in here. Put her in her own box, just in case she got feisty.

"Mr. St. Fort?"

He turned from the window, saw the nurse lady, Lisa, coming toward him, a smile on her pretty face.

He gave her one of his own. "Afternoon, ma'am."

"Sorry I took so long to get back to you. I usually spend my day running around like a chicken with its head cut off."

Solomon jerked his thumb in the direction of the parking lot. "You ever find what you were looking for out there?"

Her eyes clouded and Solomon knew he'd just poked a sore spot.

"Not yet," she said. "Why don't you come with me? We can go someplace that isn't so noisy."

She gestured to the guard, then turned and started away. Solomon followed her.

She took him to a small, windowless room. Exam table in the middle, covered with a wide sheet of paper. She invited Solomon to sit on the table, while she pulled up a stool next to it.

"You wanted to tell me about your friend," she said. "I have to admit I'm pretty curious about her myself."

"Where you keepin' her?"

"Don't worry, she's being cared for. We've put her in her own room and she's under constant observation."

"You got any idea why the police brought her here?"

The nurse lady frowned and shook her head. "I was hoping you could tell me. They're keeping it on a need-to-know basis. And apparently they don't think I need to know."

"Aren't you a supervisor or something?"

She nodded. "So they tell me."

"Then why wouldn't you need to know?"

"I'm afraid you'd have to ask one of the detectives in charge. They're a pretty tight-lipped bunch. I've read her chart, but there's not a whole lot there."

"I was on the street when they picked her up," Solomon said. "Heard the cops talking about her."

"And?"

"They said she tried to stab a guy with a pair of scissors. Some cab driver, over on The Avenue."

The nurse lady's eyes widened slightly. Just enough to tell Solomon she was surprised and definitely interested.

"But what I have to tell you," he said, "won't be in a police report, and it won't be on any chart. I don't want you thinkin' I'm crazy, but what that woman is going through has its roots in the heart of the Vieux Carre."

"The what?"

"The French Quarter. New Orleans. Down in the dark alleyways and behind private doors. You won't hear too many people talkin' about it, because those who know tend to keep it to themselves, keep it in the family. Most of the locals have never even heard of it."

He looked at her a moment, wondering how deep into this he should get. Then he said, "You can call it a religion, a lifestyle, a crazy man's superstition—doesn't matter. *La manière du rythme* is what it is and ain't nobody on this good earth can deny it."

"*La manière . . .* what?"

"The way of The Rhythm."

She frowned now. As if she had just been confronted by someone trying to hand her a copy of *The Watchtower*. He was taking her into foreign territory and her first instinct was to retreat.

Most people who knew about The Rhythm were born into it, like Solomon, so it never took any real convincing. But outsiders were different. Had a natural tendency to be skeptical. He'd tried telling Clarence about it once and Clarence had just looked at him and said, "What the fuck you been smokin', man?"

But if Solomon was right, if he'd judged this woman accurately, once she got past those initial instincts, she'd be receptive to what he had to tell her.

Weighing his words, he said, "People who believe, people who *know*, know that the way of The Rhythm is like a heartbeat. Keeps us alive. And life is all about balance and timing."

"That's true no matter what religion you practice."

Solomon nodded. "Action and reaction. Everything we do, every move we make is countered by another move. It's the world's way of gettin' itself back in sync."

"Like karma," she said.

Solomon shook his head. "Karma's different. That's all about people being mindful of what they do. Be good and get good in return. Do bad, get bad back."

"Then I don't understand."

"The Rhythm don't give a shit what you do, just so long as everything's in balance. And when it ain't, it'll do anything it has to to correct it."

"What does any of this have to do with your friend?"

"Her being here ain't no accident," Solomon told her. "She's here because The Rhythm wants her here. Wants us all here, to balance things out."

"What things?"

"I'm not sure. But the woman you've got in that room isn't who you think she is. She's what we call *un emprunteuse*."

"A what?"

"*Un emprunteuse*. A borrower. One of the children of the drum."

Another frown. Solomon knew he was treading on dangerous ground here. Had just crossed that invisible line that most people don't want to cross. But to her credit, the nurse lady didn't laugh or get up and throw him out. She'd probably heard wilder stories in her day.

"Are you a Christian woman?"

She shrugged. "More or less."

"Then you probably believe that when people die, they become spirits, right? That the soul travels on."

"I suppose so."

"Well, sometimes, when a person dies before her time, when her death throws off the beat, messes up the rhythm, she finds herself kinda trapped in the middle of nowhere, lookin' for a way to make things right. And one of those ways is to borrow a little time among the living."

"And you think that's what your friend has done?"

"If I'm right about this, the woman in that room ain't my friend," Solomon said. "Not anymore, at least."

"I don't understand."

"Oh, she might look a little like Myra. Got some of the same marks and features, but Myra's just the vessel. Somebody else has got ahold of her body, and she's changing."

A pause. "Changing how?"

"Her eye color, maybe. Nose not quite as big as it once was, fingers thinner, shoulders wider. She's slowly taking on the form of the borrower. And the migration ain't an easy thing. There's a lot of pain involved. Takes hours.

Sometimes days. All depends on how accommodating your host is, and how familiar the borrower is with the ways of The Rhythm."

She gave him a bemused look. "Wouldn't your friend have something to say about all this?"

"That's what I'm telling you," Solomon said. "The only way a borrower can take over is if the host is either too weak to resist or just plain dead. But just because we're dead, don't mean we ain't still attached to our bodies. Some of us can get pretty possessive about it. So the borrower's got a better chance at success if she knows the host. Got permission to come aboard, so to speak."

"I don't suppose you know who this so-called borrower might be?"

There was a minute trace of sarcasm in her voice now, and he could see that he'd misjudged her. That she was merely tolerating him. Giving him a chance to speak his peace before she tossed him back in with the rest of the loonies.

Solomon couldn't really blame her. This was pretty nutty stuff to an outsider. But when you thought about it, it wasn't any crazier than the beliefs of any other culture or religion. If you're born into it, you believe. If not, you either laugh or start dialing the mental health hotline.

"No," Solomon said, refusing to give in. "I'm afraid I don't know who she is. But somebody in this hospital does. You take her out of that box, parade her around for a while, and I guarantee somebody'll recognize her."

The nurse lady stiffened. Had he struck a chord?

Hard to say.

She gave him a curt smile and stood up. "This is a fascinating story, Mr. St. Fort, it really is. But I have a lot of work to do. Why don't we get you back to the Day Room now?"

"That's it? That's all you want to know?"

"I think I've heard enough. Maybe we can talk more later."

He knew she was only humoring him. Mentally, she had just made a big red check mark next to his name and he had a feeling he'd soon be on a regiment of antipsychotic drugs. But he also sensed by that last reaction that what he'd said wasn't completely lost on her. She seemed a bit rattled. Unnerved.

She started to turn toward the door and he grabbed her wrist. "Hold on, now, hold on."

Her face hardened. "Please let me go."

He immediately released her. "I know what I'm telling you sounds crazy. I don't blame you for thinkin' I'm just like the rest of these poor folk, but whoever took Myra's body didn't come here to play patty-cake."

"Then why *is* she here?"

"Hard to say, but she knows somebody. Somebody in this hospital. And she wants to communicate." He paused. "Maybe more than that."

"And she winds up here just by coincidence?"

Solomon shook his head. "You aren't paying attention. There ain't no coincidences. That's The Rhythm doin' what it does. Makin' sure all the pieces come together at the right time, in the right place."

Another curt smile. No warmth. Not even tolerance this time. "Enjoy your stay, Mr. St. Fort."

She turned to leave again and Solomon grabbed her arm a second time. "Listen to me. I don't know what happened to the woman who's taking over Myra's body, I don't know if she had an accident or if somebody killed her, but—"

"Let *go* of me," the nurse lady said, pulling her arm free. Then she threw open the door and shouted, "Security!"

"You've gotta listen to me. Let me have some time with her. If it ain't too late, I might be able to reverse the change. Get Myra back before anything bad happens."

"Security!"

A split second after the word left her mouth, a big guy in a uniform showed up, looking ready to bust some heads.

"Get him out of here."

"Yes, ma'am."

The guard grabbed Solomon by the shoulders, pushing him toward the door.

But Solomon resisted, turning toward the nurse lady. "You gotta let me see her. I might be able to—"

"Shut your mouth," the guard said, roughly wrenching his arms behind him and spinning him around.

Glancing over his shoulder, Solomon thought he saw a troubled look on the nurse lady's face, a look that said she might just believe him after all. But it wasn't enough to get her to stop the guard from dragging him away.

In the end, he supposed it didn't much matter. The Rhythm would do what it had to do.

And whatever that turned out to be, neither one of them would be able to stop it.

Chapter 38

The man known as DickMan229 lived in a squat, two-story apartment building not far from Blanchard Beach. A big block of cement, it housed about twenty units over-looking a small, oval swimming pool that looked like it had been pissed in at least one time too many.

According to Janovic's Palm Pilot—and a subsequent check of Todd Hastert's arrest record—Hastert lived in one of the upstairs units, apartment 2F. After signing out a fresh new sedan from the motor pool, Blackburn took the ride over, climbed the stairs to the second floor, knocked on Hastert's door—

—and got nothing. No answer.

So he decided to wait.

From his parking spot on the street, he had a good view of the apartment. He'd brought Abby Tolan's murder book along with him, hoping to catch a minute to take another look at it, and figured now was as good a time as any. Clipping a copy of Hastert's mug shot to the visor, he pulled the blue binder onto his lap and cracked it open.

She had been discovered in her studio darkroom by the cleaning crew who regularly serviced the building, which was located in a trendy section of Ocean City proper, just off Main Street. Some hapless janitor had gone in to dump the waste basket and found her on the floor. Or at least parts of her. Piled in the center of the room like firewood.

Her body had been doused with photo chemicals, the bottles scattered around her.

She had been dismembered in a way that was nearly identical to the seven previous victims. Hands and feet severed at the wrists and ankles. Head severed just below the chin. Arms at the shoulder and elbow. Legs at the torso and knee. And the torso itself had been sliced open, the intestines removed and wrapped around it.

This had all been preceded by several vicious knife blows to the chest and abdomen.

And the removal of her left ear.

Crime scene technicians had found traces of her blood in a small shower located near the darkroom. It was assumed that the killer had cleaned up before leaving, but no evidence was found that might lead them to his identity.

Investigators had known immediately that they were dealing with another of Vincent's conquests and a look inside the victim's mouth confirmed it. The now familiar burn marks had been created by what the crime scene techs determined to be a battery-operated PowerBlast cauterizing or line-cutting tool, often used by fly fishermen. This determination, while based on tests done in the laboratory, was considered to be a "best guess."

The tool, which looked much like an oversized fountain pen with a needle-sharp point, was sold via Internet, at thousands of tackle and bait shops, and at approximately twenty different retail department store chains throughout the country, so the chances of narrowing down a purchase were fairly slim.

Time of death was estimated to be between 6:00 and 11:00 P.M. Despite the condition of the body, they had no trouble identifying the victim. Her face and hair matched several of the self-portraits they'd found hanging in the adjacent gallery. Later, fingerprint and dental matches confirmed that she was Abby Tolan.

A search of her purse uncovered a cell phone with a message from "Michael" waiting on it. Because of his recent fame, investigators assumed this to be the victim's husband, Dr. Michael Tolan. When detectives failed to find him at home, they called him at the number on the victim's cell phone and notified him.

Tolan was described by the investigator who made the call—Jerry Rossbach—as "distraught" over the news of his wife's murder. He returned home immediately and was subsequently questioned. Because the investigators had already identified Vincent as the killer—a fact later confirmed by the medical examiner—they did not treat Dr. Tolan as a suspect and questioned him accordingly.

This, to Blackburn's mind, was a mistake. While he understood their reasoning, he felt they should have thrown a few hardballs at Tolan, just to see how well he handled them. It's never fun to beat up on the victim's family, but you never know where it might lead.

According to the victim's profile, Elizabeth Abagail Tolan was thirty-two years old, born in Mississippi, and raised in New Orleans by a single parent, one Margaret Elizabeth Fontaine. Fontaine was a known prostitute.

A search of the crime databases revealed that the younger Fontaine had been arrested twice by the NOPD. The first was a misdemeanor prostitution charge when, at seventeen, she solicited an undercover vice detective. The second was an assault charge at twenty-five, when she attacked a former boyfriend whom, she claimed, had stolen one of her prized cameras.

She was convicted and paid a fine for the first charge, but the second was dropped due to lack of cooperation by the assault victim.

Abby Fontaine's career as a photographer began to

blossom the year she turned twenty-six. Having moved to New York the previous year, she quickly earned a reputation as an Annie Leibovitz in waiting. Her stark black-and-white portraits of up-and-coming rock stars put her on the map, and a feature story in *Rolling Stone* magazine had made her the celebrity photographer of choice. Those who talked about her often used the word "artist."

Fontaine met her husband at age twenty-eight, when she was hired by his publishing company to shoot his portrait for an upcoming book. A year later they were married, and Fontaine, now Abby Tolan, joined her husband in Ocean City, California, where she opened up a studio and gallery.

A list of her clients was found by investigating officers, and several of them were subsequently questioned. None of the interviews proved fruitful to the investigation.

Her calendar for the day of her death had been completely blank. No outgoing calls had been made from her studio or cell phone, and the only incoming call for that night, at 9:00 P.M., had come from her husband, informing her of his impending arrival in Los Angeles.

The lock on the front door to her gallery was jimmied with what crime scene techs believed to be a screwdriver or a pocketknife. The assailant had surprised the victim right there in her darkroom and offered no mercy. The medical examiner determined that she was dead within seconds of the attack.

The dismembering, however, had taken considerably more time. The weapons of choice had been a steak knife and a hacksaw, both consistent with the previous killings. Neither had been recovered after a thorough search of the premises.

Blackburn looked again at the estimated time of death. Between 6:00 and 11:00 P.M. Tolan had checked into the Beverly Wilshire at around 10:00 P.M. Which gave him plenty of time to have done the deed.

Flipping back to the autopsy report, Blackburn read through it and found a detailed description and photographs of the emoticon burned into Abby Tolan's lower lip. If the medical reports for the other victims were equally as detailed, then anyone with access to them— authorized or not—would know the secret the Van Gogh task force had tried to keep.

Todd Hastert had worked for the medical examiner's office for three years. Could he have discovered that secret and passed it along to Janovic? Could Janovic have somehow turned around and told Tolan? Or what about Jane Doe? She was at Janovic's apartment. Could *she* be the connection?

Out of the corner of his eye, Blackburn saw movement on the apartment building's second-floor walkway. Two lowlifes, a man and a woman in scruffy street clothes, were walking along the railing that overlooked the pool, headed straight for apartment 2F.

When they reached Hastert's door, the man knocked. Pounded, actually. Blackburn could hear it echoing across the parking lot.

"Hey, Todd! Open up!"

When Hastert didn't answer, the man pounded the door again while the woman jiggled the knob.

Still no response.

The man and woman said something to each other, then the man looked around to make sure no one was watching. Reaching into his pocket, he brought out a wad of keys, selected one, then gestured to the woman.

She reached into the handbag slung over her shoulder and pulled out what looked like a small ratchet wrench as the man inserted the key into the lock. Taking the wrench from her, he used it like a hammer, tapping it against the back edge of the key.

A bump job. Blackburn was witnessing a B & E.

As the man and woman opened the door and headed inside, Blackburn climbed out of his car and crossed the lot, moving past the pool to the stairway alcove.

He was halfway to the second floor when he heard a scream.

A woman's scream.

Blackburn bolted, taking the steps two at a time. When he reached the second-floor walkway, the door to 2F burst open and the woman tore out of it, heading in Blackburn's direction, her expression a mixture of revulsion and terror.

Blackburn pulled his weapon. "Police! Stop right there."

Surprise filled her eyes as she came to a sudden stop. He moved quickly to her and shoved her against the wall, face first, keeping an eye on the open doorway. "Where's your boyfriend?"

The woman started crying now. ". . . still inside."

"What happened in there? Why'd you scream?"

". . . He . . . there's a . . ."

Before she could finish, the man came through the doorway, a shell-shocked look on his face.

Blackburn immediately leveled his Glock at him. "Down! Down on the ground! Now! Hands behind your head!"

The man halted in his tracks and threw his hands up, lowering to his knees.

"Don't stop," Blackburn told him. "Get all the way dow—"

In a single, fluid motion, the woman brought her arm up, sweeping a hand back toward Blackburn's face. He jerked back, but felt a sudden stinging sensation across his forehead. And just as he realized she was carrying a box cutter, blood began to fill his eyes and he stumbled back, hitting the railing.

He brought his Glock around toward her, but his vision was blurred and she was moving too fast. Rushing forward, she slammed her palms against his chest and—

—Blackburn lost his balance, falling backward over the railing. He tried to grab hold, but his fingers merely brushed the painted metal and he was suddenly hurtling downward, blinded now by the blood in his eyes, legs and arms flailing.

Time seemed suspended as he waited for the impact, certain that the moment his head hit the cement he'd be—as his old man used to say—deader than a squashed frog.

Then something amazing happened.

The impact came, and it hurt, but it wasn't cement he hit. It was water. Glorious, piss-contaminated, unchlorinated, hasn't-been-cleaned-in-a-month pool water. And before he knew it he was instinctively sucking in a breath—

—as the water surrounded him and he plunged deep into the ice-cold swamp.

By the time he managed to get back to the surface, the two lowlifes were long gone. Blood started to fill his eyes again and he realized she had cut him pretty good. An inch and a half lower and he'd probably be a blind man.

He stuck his head back in the water, clearing away the blood, knowing he had to be inviting a serious infection. He then brought his arm up against his forehead, trying to stop the flow with his coat sleeve.

Feeling foolish nonetheless, he waded toward the pool steps and climbed out, spotting his Glock on the cement a couple yards away. Surprisingly, despite the commotion, there didn't seem to be any neighbors gawking at him.

Snatching it up, he returned it to its holster, then, keeping his arm to his forehead, moved across the lot to his car. Popping the trunk, he took off his tie, peeled off his coat and shirt, then wrung out the shirt, dribbling rancid pool water into the gutter.

His forehead was still bleeding like crazy.

He found the standard first-aid kit tucked in a corner of the trunk, opened it, unrolled a wad of gauze, and pressed it to his wound. The gauze immediately turned crimson.

Head wounds were always a pain in the ass.

Dumping the pad, he unrolled more gauze, pressed it to his forehead and did his best to tape it in place. Quickly slipping his damp shirt back on, he closed the trunk and crossed back toward the apartment building's stairway alcove.

He was feeling a little woozy.

Working his way up to the second floor again, he took the walkway toward apartment 2F. As he went, he looked down past the railing to see how far he'd fallen, fairly certain that if he'd hit cement instead of water, he'd be dead.

Cursing himself for allowing the woman to get the upper hand on him, he pushed through the door to 2F and immediately understood why the two had been so anxious to leave.

The apartment itself was nothing special. A few sticks of cheap furniture, a stereo and TV, and a small kitchenette. The place looked lived-in but undisturbed.

The smell, however, was unmistakable.

Following his nose, Blackburn navigated a narrow hallway until he reached the source:

A small bathroom. Just enough room for a sink, a toilet, a tub, and not much more.

Except, of course, for the bloody body parts stacked inside the tub.

Hands, feet, arms, legs, torso.

And the head, which was facing the doorway, lifeless eyes frozen open and staring directly at Blackburn.

The lifeless eyes of Todd Hastert.

Chapter 39

The paramedic tossed the bloody gauze aside and put a butterfly bandage on Blackburn's forehead.

"Cut's pretty deep," he said. "You might want to come to the hospital, get some stitches."

"Maybe later."

Blackburn thought about what that would look like, imagining the cops at the station house calling him *Frank*enstein. Not that he cared what they thought, but it would just be another in a long list of annoyances he'd have to endure.

He thanked the paramedic and headed back upstairs to where Rossbach, Worsley, and a couple other task force members—along with a crime scene unit—were crowded into Todd Hastert's tiny apartment.

Worsley scowled at him when he walked in the door. "Thanks for dripping pool water all over the crime scene, genius."

Blackburn ignored him and approached Rossbach, whose gaze immediately went to Blackburn's forehead.

"Jesus. Half an inch lower and you woulda lost your—"

"I know, I know. You call Carmody? She'll want to be part of this."

"There's already enough cooks in this kitchen."

"So what're we cooking?"

Rossbach sighed. "Assistant M.E. says it's there. The mark. We're definitely looking at another Vincent hit."

Blackburn shook his head. "I'm not buying it. Do we have a time of death?"

"Sometime last night, between ten and midnight."

"So this guy was done first. Before Janovic."

"It's looking that way."

"Makes me think it's even less likely that Vincent did this. Two in one night? Not really his style."

"What the fuck is his style, Frank? I've been thinking about this sonofabitch for over a year now and I still can't figure him out."

"Don't forget the two victims knew each other. You take a look at Hastert's bank records, I'll lay odds you'll find some recent deposits. Somebody paying him off."

"For what?"

"Same as Janovic. To keep his mouth shut. They were partners."

"What the hell are you talking about?"

"It's Tolan," Blackburn said. "Hastert used to work at the medical examiner's office. Which means he could've known Vincent's M.O. Either he or Janovic leaked crime scene details to Tolan, and when they figured out what he used them for, they put the finger on him."

"And you think Tolan got tired of paying, so he did *this*?"

"That's the long and the short of it."

"Where's the connection? How does Tolan even know these guys?"

"Good question."

"Well, until you work it out, hot shot, I'm running on the assumption that Vincent's our man."

"Big mistake, Jerry. Vincent's in the wind and has been for a year."

Rossbach snorted. "I think it's safe to say you're in the

minority with that opinion. But I won't hold it against you."

Fuck you, Blackburn thought, but said nothing. Instead, he just shrugged and pushed past him, moving deeper into the apartment.

Navigating the narrow hallway, he passed the bathroom, where crime scene techs were carefully cataloging and bagging the body parts.

Hastert's bedroom had about as much personality as the rest of the place. A queen-sized bed, dresser and nightstand. The bed unmade. Dirty clothes scattered on the floor.

If Hastert was collecting money, he wasn't spending it here.

Taking out a pair of latex gloves he'd gotten from the crime scene kit in the trunk of his car, Blackburn snapped them on and started working the room, opening and closing drawers in the dresser, finding a sparse assortment of socks and underwear, blue jeans, T-shirts. Nothing even remotely interesting.

In a corner near the bed were three stacks of paperback books. Blackburn crouched next to them and studied the spines. Crime novels, medical thrillers, legal thrillers, horror stories. He recognized a few of the writers. His second wife had been a book nut and some of it had rubbed off on him.

He knew this was a long shot, but taking them one by one, he leafed through the pages, looking for makeshift bookmarks: bank stubs, credit card receipts, anything that might possibly connect the guy to Tolan.

Nothing.

Moving to the nightstand, he pulled the drawer open and found another paperback—something called *The Cleaner*—along with a pair of reading glasses and two prescription bottles.

Picking up one of the bottles, he glanced at the label. Twenty capsules of Vicodin. County General Pharmacy. Prescribed by a Dr. Wilson.

Returning it to the drawer, he picked up the second bottle. The date on the label was a year old. County General Pharmacy again, this one for Paxil—which Blackburn knew to be a depression killer, like Prozac. The name of the doctor was Soren.

Soren, Blackburn thought. That name sounded familiar. Where had he heard it before?

Then it hit him.

Hadn't Tolan once been partnered with a guy named Soren? Back when he was in private practice?

Blackburn was almost sure of it. But if anybody would know, it would be Carmody.

Unclipping his cell phone from his belt, he started to dial before he realized his dunk in the pool had killed it.

Shit.

Crossing back to the hallway, he flagged a crime scene tech. A guy named Abernathy. "You got a phone I can use?"

"Sure, Frank." Abernathy dug his phone out of his pocket, handed it over, and Blackburn quickly punched in Carmody's number.

Her line rang several times, then switched over to voice mail.

What the hell? Why wasn't she answering?

After the message came on and the line beeped, Blackburn said, "Hey, Sue, call dispatch and have them contact me as soon as you get this. My cell phone's kaput and I'm thinking I may have found something here."

He clicked off, knowing his next step was to pick up a new phone, change his clothes, then visit Dr. Soren. He dialed again, and when De Mello picked up, he said, "I need an address."

"Glad you called," De Mello said. "Got a curious little morsel here for you."

"Oh? What's up?"

"I finally heard back from the company who supplied that photo clip of Bikini Girl. They gave me the name of the photographer who sold it to them."

"And? Do we know who the model was?"

"No," De Mello said, "and I doubt we ever will."

"Why?"

"Because the photographer is dead."

"Wonderful. Is there any way we can get hold of his records?"

"You might want to ask Tolan about that. The photographer was his wife."

Chapter 40

Lisa had left four more messages for Michael and still no word from him. In the time since he'd left, the police had gone as well, without explanation. Then Clayton Simm showed up, fresh from a shower.

She spotted him, coming in through one of the private entrances. She knew Michael thought highly of him, but she'd never really understood it. Thought he was a bit too arrogant for his own good.

"What brings you here in the middle of the afternoon?"

"You're lucky I'm here at all," he said, tucking his card key into his breast pocket. "Cops called me. They got a witness they want me to look at. I checked her in this morning."

"SR-three? The Jane Doe?"

"That's the one."

"I thought Michael was covering that."

"So did I. But that asshole cop—whatshisname—told me there was some kind of conflict of interest. Says Michael wants me to take over."

"What conflict?" Lisa asked, immediately thinking of Jane Doe's resemblance to Abby. For some reason, the old man's words flitted through her head. *Un emprenteuse.*

"Beats the hell out of me. I just do what I'm told."

"Well, I hate to be the bearer of bad news, but the police are gone."

Clayton's brow furrowed. "What?"

"I was down in the basement doing a supply check and when I came back they'd all packed up and left."

"Are you fucking kidding me? Do you know how hard it was for me to drag myself out of bed?"

"All they left behind was a uniform posted at the Jane Doe's door, and he won't tell me a thing."

"What about Michael? Is he in there with her?"

She shook her head. "Gone too. Left before lunch. I haven't seen him since, and he won't answer his phone. To tell you the truth, I'm pretty worried about him."

"So what the hell is going on?"

"You tell me. I'm just a nurse, remember? I couldn't even get Michael to spill."

Clayton's frown deepened. He was not a happy man. Probably needed his beauty sleep.

"Fuck it," he said, then started off toward the seclusion ward.

"Where are you going?"

"I'm here, I might as well check in on her. See what all the fuss is about."

They went in together, looking through the glass at Jane Doe, who barely seemed to have moved since the last time Lisa had been in here.

"Hey, hey," Cassie said, the moment she saw Clayton. "What brings you out of your cave?"

Lisa had always suspected Cassie had a crush on Clayton, but whenever they were together—which wasn't often thanks to opposing shifts—she chided him like a younger sister.

As the two exchanged quips, Lisa tuned them out and kept her gaze on Jane Doe. Try as she might, she couldn't get what the old man had told her out of her head. He was certifiable, no doubt about that. But while she had never been the superstitious type, there was something about this woman—the resemblance that somehow seemed *more* than a resemblance—that gave weight to his words.

Un emprenteuse. A borrower.

Could it be true? Could Abby be in there somewhere, struggling for control?

"You're out of your friggin' mind," Clayton said.

Feeling as if her thoughts had suddenly been invaded, Lisa returned her focus to Cassie and Clayton's conversation. Clayton seemed more agitated than ever.

"I'm just telling you what I saw," Cassie said, looking defensive. "Dr. Tolan saw it too. Both of her eyes are brown."

"Impossible. Heterochromia isn't something you just . . ."

He paused then, his gaze once again resting on Jane Doe. He moved closer to the glass. "Is this some kind of practical joke? Who is that woman?"

Lisa joined him at the window, but couldn't figure out what he was staring at. "What's wrong?"

"I think I'm being punked, is what. Any minute now some idiot from *That '70s Show* is gonna poke his head in here and say boo."

"What are you talking about?"

"That isn't the same woman I examined this morning. Look at her shoulder."

"Come on, Clay," Cassie said. "You're being ridiculous. I've been on watch all day and . . ."

Now *she* paused, her jaw going slack. She punched a key on her keyboard and the computer screen switched to camera view, an overhead shot of the patient. Clicking the mouse, she zoomed in on Jane Doe's left shoulder.

"Holy crap," she said. "That's impossible."

Clayton turned away from the glass. "I don't know what kind of game you people are playing, but you can tell Michael or that knucklehead cop or whoever's behind this that I don't appreciate dragging my ass out of bed to be made a fool of."

He headed out the door, Lisa watching him, thoroughly bewildered. "Would somebody like to tell me what the hell is going on?"

Cassie pointed to the computer monitor. "Her tattoo. The Hello Kitty tattoo."

"What tattoo? I don't see one."

"That's the thing," Cassie said. "It's gone."

FIVE

The Man Who Tempted Fate

Chapter 41

In the dream, she was with him.

They were walking together through the darkness, careful to stay close, her hands tightly clutching his arm. She was frightened—they both were—but in a good way. The kind of fright you feel on a roller coaster or watching a scary movie.

They came to a stop in front of the old hospital, its looming malevolence making them press a little closer together. The open front doors were missing, and the black hole that stood in their place was like an invitation to some dark hell.

After a moment, Abby held up her camera—the Canon Digital SLR she carried with her everywhere she went—and said, "I'm going in."

This surprised Tolan, but he nodded. "I'll go with you."

"No, Michael, you have to stay here."

"Why?"

"Too dangerous," she said. "You have to wait your turn."

Tolan stared at that black doorway. The "good" fright he'd felt only a moment ago didn't seem so good anymore.

"I don't want to wait," he said. "I want to be with you."

"You'll be with me soon enough. You have to break away for now. You have to let go."

"I don't want to."

She smiled at him then, leaned up and kissed him. "I don't want to either, darling. But it isn't about us. It isn't our choice."

"I don't understand."

"There's nothing *to* understand. It's the way. The Rhythm. The heartbeat."

"The heartbeat?" Tolan said. "What does that mean?"

She let go of him then, started toward the doorway. He tried to grab her arm, but his hand went right through her, as if she were made of vapor.

"Abby, wait."

"I'll see you again, Michael. I'm closer than you think. Much closer. Just ask the old man. He knows."

"Old man? What old man?"

She stood at the doorway now, a step away from the darkness. "This is where it happens, Michael. Where it all comes together and balance is restored."

"I don't understand."

"Listen . . ." she said. "Don't you hear it? Someone's calling you."

At first he wasn't sure what she was talking about. Then a distant buzzing filled his ears, coming in short, steady spurts. He turned, looking for the source of it. Saw nothing but the night. The trees. The mountains.

"I'll see you soon, Michael."

He turned back to her and her camera was raised to her eye, pointed at him. Then the flash went off, momentarily blinding him.

When it finally cleared she was gone.

"Abby?"

He stared at that darkened doorway, wondering if she'd ever really been there at all.

He awoke to the buzzing sound.

His phone, vibrating.

He was lying on a floor, but he wasn't sure *whose* floor until he sat upright and the world spinning around him began to slow and come into focus.

Then he recognized the place immediately. The oriental rugs. The off-white sofa and chairs. The abstract painting on the wall above the fireplace. The carpeted stairs leading to the bedroom. The steady sound of waves rolling in.

The beach house. Lisa's beach house.

He was sitting on her living-room floor.

But how had he gotten here?

His body ached, as if every one of his muscles had been hammered with a baseball bat. His jaw was on fire. Even his toes ached.

Realizing it was almost dark outside, he checked his watch: 5:30 P.M.

Jesus.

The last thing he remembered was sitting in his car in the hospital parking lot, trying to recover from a sudden panic attack.

Mama got trouble
Mama got sin
Mama got bills to pay again.

But that had been close to noon, which meant he'd somehow lost over five hours.

Five full hours.

Every one of them a blank.

His phone was still buzzing. He turned, looking around until he saw it on the floor near the sofa. He was about to reach for it when it stopped, kicking over to voice mail.

He looked around the room again. "Lisa?"

He waited a moment, but got no answer.

Climbing to his feet, he swayed slightly, then checked the table near her front door. There was a small basket there, where she usually left her keys, but it was empty.

"Lisa?"

No response. Was she even here?

Maybe she'd taken her keys upstairs with her. She did that sometimes, then spent half an hour trying to remember where she'd left them.

But the place seemed empty. Except for the sound of the waves, it was as silent as a new morning. Deciding to check anyway, he moved to the stairway, about to take the first step, when his phone buzzed again, stirring up images of a dream he'd had.

The old hospital. A dark doorway.

Abby?

He turned, watching it vibrate, knowing instinctively who the caller was, wondering if he should let it ring. But a moment later, he was standing over it, then snatching it up, flipping it open.

"Hello?"

"You're finally awake," the voice said. "I hope you enjoyed your sleep, Doctor. You've needed it for so long."

Heat blossomed in the pit of Tolan's stomach, an image flashing through his mind. Darkness. A narrow beam of light shining in his eyes.

And pain. Indescribable pain.

His muscles tightened involuntarily. "What did you do to me?"

"Nothing special. Just had a little fun." A pause. "Now I'm about to give you the credit you've been so anxious to receive. Han van Meegeren will look like a rank amateur by the time this night is over."

Tolan said nothing. Didn't know what to say. More images were hurtling through his mind now. Moving so quickly that he couldn't decipher them.

"You still there, Doctor?"

"Yes."

"I take it you haven't been upstairs yet."

Tolan's heart skipped. He turned abruptly, looking toward the stairway. He glanced toward the top of the steps, where darkness waited.

"Dr. Tolan?"

"What?"

"If we're going to have a conversation, you'll have to respond to my questions. *Have you been upstairs?*"

"No," Tolan said, his dread deepening. "What have you done?"

"There's a little anniversary present waiting for you there. A friend of yours. We had a lot of fun with her this afternoon."

Another image flashed through Tolan's mind: a blade piercing flesh. Then, as if he was only now becoming fully aware of his surroundings—of *himself*—he glanced down at the front of his shirt.

It was covered with blood. Drying blood.

Oh, Jesus, no.

Lisa?

"You sonofabitch."

"Me? This is all about you now, remember?"

"No," Tolan said. "You did this. You. Not me. And I swear to God if you hurt her, I'll hunt you down and kill you, you fucking animal."

"That's the spirit. Keep it up, Doctor. You're making this easier and easier. Why don't you get upstairs now? Assess the damage you've done."

Tolan looked again at his bloody shirt, then toward the top of the stairs, wondering what waited for him up there.

"You're on your own now, Doctor. I have to admit, I'm quite anxious to see how you'll wiggle out of this one."

"Fuck you," Tolan said, then hurled the phone at the nearest wall with every bit of strength he had. It broke into three pieces and dropped to the floor, leaving an indentation in the wall.

Moving to the stairway, Tolan stared up at the darkness, hesitating only a moment before he started upward, his dread deepening with each step he took.

As he reached the second-floor landing, he heard water running. Lisa's shower.

He looked down the short hallway at her closed bedroom door. But he didn't hesitate this time. Crossing to it, he put his hand on the knob, then, mustering up his courage, turned it and pushed inside.

The sound of the shower was much louder in here and he could see that her bathroom door was hanging open.

Moving past the bed, he stepped through the doorway and looked toward the shower, at its pebbled glass enclosure.

The image was distorted, but he could see someone—a woman—sitting on the tile inside, water cascading down on her head.

No. Please, no.

"Lisa?"

No answer. Tolan slowly moved to the shower door and pulled it open, nausea bubbling up in his chest as he stared down at a face frozen in death, eyes wide open, mouth agape, as if she'd been caught by surprise.

But it wasn't Lisa.

The woman who sat there, her blouse ripped open, her abdomen a gaping crimson hole, her intestines snaking toward the drain, floating in a swirl of bloodied water—

—was Sue Carmody.

Detective Sue Carmody.

Tolan's legs went numb. He stared at her, trying to keep the nausea at bay.

And as awful as this tableau was, it was rendered even more horrifying by the simple fact that Carmody was missing her left ear.

Tolan backed away from her.

Why? he thought. Why is this happening?

"Michael?"

He jerked around to find Lisa standing in her bedroom doorway, a look of concern on her face.

She moved toward him. "I just got your text message. Thank God you're here, I . . ."

The words caught in her throat as her attention was abruptly drawn to the blood on his shirt, then past him to the running water, the shower stall, the carnage that waited there.

She said nothing for a long moment, her expression a mix of revulsion and disbelief as her brain caught up to what her eyes were seeing.

Then, in a voice that was barely a croak, she said, "Oh, my God, Michael. Oh, my God."

Chapter 42

Dr. Ned Soren wasn't an easy guy to pin down.

A typical day, Blackburn discovered, was spent bouncing between his office on Terrington Avenue, the psych ward at County General, and the Bayside Country Club, where he played golf three afternoons a week.

According to his secretary, a cute little Angelina Jolie wannabe (who was definitely more "be" than "wanna"), today was a golf day. But by the time Blackburn reached the country club it was already dark outside, and he had a sneaking suspicion that any golf-related activities were over and done with.

The closest Blackburn had ever come to playing the game was the hour he'd spent hacking at balls on the municipal driving range while surveilling a suspected pedophile. But he had enough sense to know that once the scorecards were tallied and the clubs were back in the bag, the players usually drove their little electric go-carts straight to the nearest bar.

Blackburn was able to zero in on his target the moment he pulled into the country club parking lot. There were a dozen or so of the aforementioned go-carts parked atop a small embankment, surrounding a structure that sported the name The 19th Hole.

Originality was obviously not the goal here.

On the drive over, Blackburn had considered the information he now had. There were two possible connections between Hastert, Janovic, and Tolan—the first being Soren, and the second being Jane Doe herself. She'd worked for Abby Tolan as a model and, in turn, may have known her husband. Was it possible they were having an affair? Was that why Tolan had reacted the way he did when he saw her?

Unless Blackburn could get either Soren or Jane to admit to the connection, his chances of proving anything against Tolan were slim. And considering Jane's condition, it was doubtful he'd get anything from her anytime soon.

So Soren was his man.

Blackburn didn't bother with the formality of checking in at the country club guest desk. Instead, he trudged up the embankment and went straight into the bar.

The tables were packed, mostly with men sporting deep tans and dressed in the standard-issue golfer uniform: polo shirts and slacks of various nauseating colors. A good 80 percent of them were already half in the bag, while the other 20 were borderline comatose. Blackburn didn't even want to *think* about what the parking lot would look like in a couple hours.

Although he had managed to change into a new suit shortly after leaving the Hastert crime scene, his lack of appropriately casual attire and the lovely bandage adorning his forehead got him quite a few drunken stares as he approached the bartender.

The noise level was just a few decibels below deafening. Leaning in close, Blackburn showed the guy his badge and said, "Dr. Ned Soren."

The bartender's gaze zeroed in on Blackburn's forehead,

then quickly shifted, scanning the room. He pointed. "Table six. The one with the black stripe."

Blackburn turned in the direction of the finger. Across the room, four boisterous men sat hammering back what looked like Scotch ale, the one on the farthest side of the table wearing a badly sunburned nose and a tasteful gray knit polo with a fat black stripe across the chest.

Blackburn nodded thanks and headed over, showing his badge again when he reached the table. "Dr. Soren?"

Soren looked up in surprise, his gaze shifting from the badge to Blackburn's forehead, Blackburn beginning to understand how it might feel to be a top-heavy female.

"Yes?" Soren said.

"I need to talk to you about a patient of yours."

"A patient? Is something wrong?"

"You mind if we step outside?"

Soren frowned now. He was fairly well lit, but still had enough presence of mind to be protective of his clientele. "If you're here to ask me questions about a patient, Officer, I'm not sure I can be of much help. Patient-doctor privilege and all that."

The other guys around the table started nodding. Apparently they were doctors as well.

"Does that extend to the dead ones?"

There was a momentary trace of alarm on Soren's face, but it quickly passed. "Yes, I'm afraid it does."

"I'll tell you what," Blackburn said. "Why don't we step outside and if my questions get too invasive you can slap me down. But at least give me the courtesy of letting me ask them first."

Soren looked around the table at his buddies. One of them, an old geezer with a bright pink bald spot, said, "Careful, Ned, he sounds like a tricky bastard."

This must have been funny in the world of the marginally sober, because they all laughed. Blackburn was still trying to figure out where the joke was when Soren scraped back his chair and got to his feet. "I'm all yours, Officer. I need a smoke anyway."

Blackburn gestured toward the door. "After you."

Chapter 43

Once she had assessed the situation, Lisa immediately went into mop-up mode.

Tolan had seen it a million times in the years they'd known each other, whenever she was faced with any kind of crisis. At home. At the hospital. There'd be that initial moment of shock, then she'd put on her game face and go to work, her focus so narrow that it seemed as if everything else around her had ceased to exist.

He'd once asked her about it and she'd said that she'd always had the ability to remove herself from the emotion of a situation. To concentrate solely on the task that needed to be done and save the nervous breakdowns for later.

But what lay before her this time wasn't a simple task.

There was a dead woman in her shower. A dead woman with her guts ripped open. A dead woman missing her left ear.

The full weight of that fact had not completely hit Tolan. He knew he was in shock himself and it would take awhile for the numbness now creeping through his entire body to wear off. He figured it was the same for Lisa. And his only concern at that moment was convincing her he wasn't a killer.

"I didn't do this," he said. "This wasn't me."

Lisa ignored the comment and stepped past him into

the bathroom. Reaching into the shower, she shut off the spigot, then turned to Tolan, her expression fixed and emotionless.

"Get the comforter off the bed," she said.

Tolan hesitated. "We need to call the police. Call Blackburn."

She glanced at his shirt. "If we call the police, you'll spend the rest of your life in jail."

"I didn't do this."

"I hate to break it to you, Michael, but that's not how it looks. Now get the comforter."

Tolan didn't argue. As he moved to the bed and stripped off its lavender cover, he heard Lisa banging around in the medicine cabinet. When he got back to the bathroom, she was wearing a pair of latex gloves. She took the comforter from him and handed him a pair.

"Put these on."

As he did, she lay the comforter on the bathroom tile and spread it out. Then, reaching into the shower again, she carefully retrieved Sue Carmody's lower intestine from the drain and did her best to pack it back into the abdominal cavity.

Tolan felt a wave of nausea wash over him again. He had a medical degree, yes, and had seen some pretty horrific things in his time, but something about the matter-of-fact way in which Lisa handled those intestines made him want to puke.

He looked into Sue Carmody's lifeless eyes, and couldn't help thinking about how excited she'd been only hours before, after he'd told them about Vincent's phone calls. An intense sadness overcame him and he struggled to contain it.

Lisa, however, was all business.

"Grab her legs," she said.

"Lisa, we can't do this."

"We don't have a choice."

"Why would you want to risk your life, your career—"

"For godsakes, Michael, we've known each other for fifteen years and you still haven't figured me out? This is what I *do*. I take care of things. I take care of you. I always have and I always will. Now shut up and grab her legs."

"This is the road to hell," he said.

"Better than the road to prison."

Despite his protests, Tolan knew she was right. Nobody would believe this wasn't his doing. He had a feeling even Lisa didn't believe it.

He bent down and grabbed hold of Sue Carmody's ankles, which were wet with shower water.

Trying not to stare at the gaping wound in her abdomen, he waited while Lisa grabbed her wrists, then helped her hoist the body onto the blanket.

"I need you to know this, Lisa. I need you to understand I didn't kill her."

"That isn't how it'll look to the police."

"Maybe not, but this wasn't me. It was Vincent. The body, the blood on my shirt. He's setting me up."

She dropped Sue Carmody's arms and looked at him. "Vincent? What are you talking about?"

"Those crank phone calls I got this morning? The ones I was so evasive about? They weren't just a prank. They were real."

Lisa's brow furrowed. "From Vincent? *The* Vincent?"

Tolan nodded. "He says he didn't kill Abby. And he thinks *I* did. Thinks I'm some kind of psychotic plagiarist."

"And you told this to the police."

Tolan nodded.

"Which explains why they were all over the hospital this morning."

"Right," Tolan said. "But now Vincent is looking for revenge. First he kills some guy on The Avenue, now this."

Lisa's frown momentarily deepened, then her face went blank. "Help me roll her up."

Tolan looked down at Sue Carmody's body again, his instinct for survival overruling any hesitation he felt.

"God forgive us."

"God gave up on us a long time ago," Lisa said.

Then the doorbell rang.

Chapter 44

The moment Soren lit up, Blackburn wished he had a cigarette of his own. But he'd never made it through an entire day without succumbing to temptation and was determined to make this one an exception.

So rather than bum a smoke, he said, "I think you know a friend of mine."

"Oh?"

"Michael Tolan. We've worked together on a couple cases. He used to be your partner, right?"

"Yes," Soren said, exhaling a plume of smoke. Then the alarm returned to his face. "This isn't about Michael, is it? The dead patient?"

The question surprised Blackburn. "Is Tolan a patient too?"

Soren shook his head, looking a bit befuddled. "No—I mean, that's privileged. He's okay, isn't he?"

"As far as I know, he's fine."

"Then who are we talking about?"

"A guy by the name of Hastert," Blackburn said. "Todd Hastert."

Soren took a moment to search the memory banks, but seemed to draw a blank.

"You prescribed Paxil to him a little over a year ago.

He filled it at the County General Pharmacy, so I'm assuming he might've been a pro bono patient."

Still no sign of recognition. And it seemed unforced. Genuine. "And he's dead?"

"I'm afraid so. Somebody carved him up pretty good last night." Blackburn reached into his coat pocket and brought out Hastert's mug shot. "Maybe this will refresh your memory."

Soren took a long drag off his cigarette and squinted at the photo. Nodding now, he exhaled and said, "Right. I saw him a few times at the hospital clinic. But that's about all I'm willing to say."

"The man was murdered, Doc."

"That doesn't change the law. Or my duty to my patients."

"Did he ever express any concerns to you? That someone might be threatening him?"

"I haven't seen him in over a year. So I highly doubt anything he may have said would have much bearing on the here and now."

"What about Dr. Tolan? Did he ever treat the patient?"

Soren was about to put the cigarette between his lips again, when he paused. "Why don't you ask *him*?"

"I would, if I could find him."

"What does that mean?"

"He's MIA," Blackburn said. "And I have reason to believe he may be in danger."

This wasn't strictly a lie, of course. Tolan was certainly in danger of being arrested. But Soren didn't need to know that.

"Danger? What kind of danger? Does this have something to do with Hastert?"

"I'm afraid it does," Blackburn said. "I think there may be a connection between the two, but I'm not sure what it is, at this point. Which is why I asked if Tolan ever treated him."

Soren thought about this a moment, the new information seeming to compound both his alarm and his befuddlement. "As far as I can remember, Michael never even met the man. He didn't do much pro bono work. Didn't have time."

This wasn't what Blackburn wanted to hear. "So you don't know of any threats Hastert may have made against him?"

"No," Soren said. "None whatsoever."

"What about the other way around?"

"What?"

"You were his partner, I assume you knew his wife?"

"Yes, of course. But what—"

"How would you characterize their relationship?"

"They were in love," Soren said. "Probably more than any two people I've ever known. They had their share of problems, but—"

"What kind of problems?"

"They fought sometimes, just like anyone else."

"So is Tolan capable of violence?"

Soren said nothing for a moment, his inebriated brain trying to process the turn in the conversation about four questions too late. "What's going on here, Officer? Is Michael in danger—or is he in *trouble*?"

Blackburn shrugged. "Six of one, half a dozen the other."

Soren's face hardened. "You fucking asshole."

"Just doing my job, Doc."

"You think Michael killed Hastert? Is that what this is all about?"

"Among other things."

Soren shook his head. "That's completely preposterous. I've known him for years and I've never seen him lift a finger against anyone. He doesn't have it in him."

"What about his wife? You said they fought."

"Yes, but . . ." Soren paused, starting to put it together now. "Jesus Christ," he said. "This isn't about Hastert at all. It's about Abby. You think Michael killed Abby."

"I'm more interested in what *you* think. Is it possible Tolan was having an affair? Screwing around on her?"

Soren flicked the cigarette at him. "Fuck you."

"You don't want to be assaulting a police officer, Doc."

"So arrest me."

"If it comes to that, trust me, I will. But I'd rather hear what you have to say about Tolan. What are you treating him for?"

Soren turned. "This conversation is over."

Blackburn grabbed his arm. "Did he ever confess to you, Doc?"

"Don't be ridiculous. Let go of me."

But Blackburn didn't let go. "What about Todd Hastert? Did he ever brag about his job? Maybe mention something about the Vincent murders? Pass along a little inside information that you turned around and gave to Tolan?"

"I said let *go* of me." Soren wrenched his arm free. "I have no idea what you're talking about. If Hastert was guarding some kind of state secret, then I suggest you go to County General and start slinging your accusations there. That's where he spent most of his time." He paused. "As for Michael, there's nothing you could ever say to convince me he hurt Abby. Not one thing. So do me a favor and fuck off."

Soren turned again and headed back inside.

This time Blackburn let him go.

Chapter 45

Kat Pendergast waited what seemed an eternity before the door opened.

She wasn't quite sure why they were here. After an extended shift this morning, and all the drama on the fourth floor, she had gone home and crawled into bed without even bothering to shower. She'd gone straight to sleep and stayed that way until her alarm clock kicked her awake again.

She was halfway through dinner when her phone rang, the watch commander telling her he was short-handed and needed her and Hogan to start their shift early.

Which meant another long night.

The minute they reported in, they were told about the alert out on Dr. Michael Tolan and were instructed to check out the girlfriend's place, a two-story beach house in Baycliff.

Kat didn't know much about Tolan, but she knew the alert had been initiated by Frank Blackburn and that was good enough for her.

Unlike most of her fellow officers—hell, most of the squad, for that matter—Kat liked Frank. She knew that every time she walked away from him he was ogling her ass, but that didn't bother her. She'd put a lot of time into making it a view worth ogling, so if people weren't going to appreciate it, what was the point?

Besides, Frank's backside wasn't so bad either. And while she might not admit it out loud, she'd thought more than once about what it would be like to grab a couple handfuls while he did whatever he wanted with those nice big hands of his.

They'd been circling each other for over a month now, the circle getting smaller with each pass. Sooner or later, there'd be a head-on collision and Kat was looking forward to it.

But back to reality. While Hogan shone his flashlight into the girlfriend's car, a sparkling new silver BMW parked in the drive, Kat leaned on the doorbell again.

They knew the girlfriend was inside. Had seen her turn in from down the block, where they'd been waiting for the last half hour. So Kat couldn't quite understand what was taking so long.

She was about to ring the bell again when the door finally opened a crack and an attractive woman in her early thirties peeked out. Her hair was wet. Looked like she was wearing a bathrobe. She'd obviously been in the shower.

Which reminded Kat that she'd never taken one herself. She suddenly felt sticky and gross.

"Lisa Paymer?"

"Yes?"

"Sorry to bother you, ma'am, but we're here about a Dr. Michael Tolan."

Paymer's face fell and she opened the door wider. "My God, is he hurt?"

Kat realized she should have phrased that differently. "No, ma'am, it isn't that. We're looking for him, is all. We were hoping he might be here."

"Here?" Paymer said. "I haven't seen him since this morning."

"At the hospital?"

"Yes, I've tried calling him, but he doesn't answer, and I've been worried sick. Why are you looking for him? Is he in some kind of trouble?"

"I'm afraid I don't know the answer to that. Would you mind if we came in and took a look around?"

"I told you, he's not here."

"It's just a formality," Kat said. "Part of the job. And it's entirely up to you."

Paymer hesitated a moment, then gestured them inside. "Be my guest."

Kat nodded to Hogan and he moved around the BMW and joined her, the two of them stepping into a nicely appointed living room with oriental rugs and off-white furniture. It looked like a photo out of *House Beautiful*. The kind Kat usually found herself drooling over while she waited her turn at the dental clinic.

She and Hogan took a perfunctory look around, Hogan sticking his head through a doorway that led into the kitchen, then moving down a short hallway to what looked to be an extra bedroom.

Kat glanced toward a set of carpeted steps that led to the second floor, but decided not to bother going upstairs. Paymer had seemed genuinely surprised that they were looking for Tolan, and her willingness to let them search the place was a fair indication that she wasn't hiding anything.

A moment later, Hogan returned, and Kat knew from his expression that he thought this was as much of a waste of time as she did.

They exchanged a look, then moved back to the front doorway. "Sorry to bother you, ma'am."

"You don't want to go upstairs?"

"I think we're okay," Kat said. "Sorry for the intrusion."

As they were about to step outside, Paymer said, "Wait."

Kat turned to see her digging through her purse on the coffee table. She brought out a business card and handed it to Kat.

"If you do find him, please call me right away. Both my home and cell are on there."

Kat glanced at the card, nodded, then unsnapped her shirt pocket and slipped it in.

"You have a good evening," she said, then went outside.

When the door closed behind them, Hogan whistled. "Wish they grew 'em like that at my hospital."

"Keep your voice down, dumbass. She might hear you."

Hogan waved her off as they headed down the drive to their cruiser. "I'm sure she's used to it. But I'll lay odds she didn't buy that house with the money she earned cleaning up after crazies."

Kat nodded. "I'm guessing she's daddy's little rich girl. She's got that pampered look."

"You gotta give her credit for taking a job at Baycliff."

Kat was about to agree with him when her cell phone bleeped. She dug it out and clicked it on. "Pendergast."

"Hey, hot stuff, you on duty yet?"

Frank Blackburn.

Kat stifled a smile. "Unfortunately, yes. They called us in early. What's up?"

"I've got a favor to ask you and your partner. Strictly off the books."

Kat glanced at Hogan. "What do you need?"

"A lookout."

"For what?"

"What else?" Blackburn said. "A little B and E."

Chapter 46

When the front door closed, Tolan let out a breath.

He was pretty sure he'd been holding it ever since the doorbell rang. He hadn't been able to hear much of what was going on downstairs, but it was enough to let him know that the police were looking for him.

The question was, why?

Did they know about Carmody?

A moment later, Lisa was back upstairs, pulling open the closet door. It was a big walk-in adjacent to her bedroom that provided plenty of room for both Tolan—

—and the body.

Lisa had taken her bathrobe off and was standing there in her bra and panties. As the light spilled inside, illuminating the rolled-up comforter that lay at Tolan's feet, the absurdity of the situation suddenly hit him.

What the hell were they doing?

Instead of hiding from the police he should have called out to them. Instead of helping to get rid of a body, a cop's body, no less—a cop he *knew*—he should have reported the death immediately.

But he hadn't. Because Lisa was right. They would assume that he, not Vincent, had killed Sue Carmody. And before he had a chance to explain, his arms would be yanked behind him, his wrists cuffed, and he'd be spending the rest of his life in a jail cell.

And how, exactly, *would* he explain this?

Because, despite his protests, something Vincent had said kept running through his mind:

We had a lot of fun with her this afternoon.

It was the *we* that got to him. The *we*, accompanied by his bloodied shirt and his jacked-up memory. He'd had another blackout. Another gap in time. This one bigger than ever.

The image of a blade piercing flesh once again flitted through his mind.

Who, he wondered, was holding that blade?

Lisa stepped into a pair of blue jeans. "We need to get her downstairs."

"Why are the police looking for me?"

"They wouldn't elaborate." She fastened the jeans and grabbed a T-shirt from a hook on the door. "But I guess I could have invited them to dinner. Maybe they would've told me all about it."

It was a pointed jab, and he knew he deserved it.

"Look, I'm sorry. I thought I was protecting you."

"That's *my* job, remember?"

She pulled the T-shirt over her head, the words BEST IN SHOW plastered across her chest.

"What happened at the hospital?" Tolan asked. "After I left?"

She gestured to Carmody's body. "Apparently this did. Now help me get her downstairs."

Tolan said nothing, reluctantly doing what he was told, grabbing one end of the blanket as Lisa grabbed the other.

But he could barely concentrate on the task. There was another part of Vincent's *we* that concerned him. Another possibility that had been floating on the distant horizon ever since the night Abby was murdered. Ever since that first blackout.

He thought about his mother and those tumultuous days up in their Arrowhead Springs cabin. She was a nasty woman, prone to vicious mood swings, who took her unhappiness out on Tolan and his father. He could remember hiding in the closet as they fought, his mother using his dad as a verbal punching bag, telling him what a loser he was, bragging about the lovers she'd had, men who were so much better at satisfying her than he ever was.

Tolan had later learned that she'd been in the throes of a classic dissociative episode, as clear a case of multiple personalities that anyone had ever seen. Many years later she had described the feeling to him—the loss of time, the conversations she'd had with the "others."

"Like phone calls from the dead," she'd told him.

"Phone calls from the dead?"

"That's right. Talking to me over an invisible telephone line. A line running all through my brain, cutting it into sections, you know? And in each one of those sections, I've got a nice little friend just waiting to—"

"Michael? Are you still with me?"

They were halfway down the stairs now, awkwardly carrying the blanket-wrapped body between them, trying not to leak blood on the carpet or bump it against the wall. And though he'd heard Lisa's question, he said nothing to her, still thinking about Vincent's phone calls and wondering. Wondering if it was possible—if he should even *entertain* the notion that the calls he'd gotten . . .

He could barely bring himself to think it.

That the calls he'd gotten were not real.

What if they were nothing more than a troubled mind's way of filtering out the truth?

Phone calls in his head.

Phone calls from the dead.

How much of this day, this anniversary of death, was a product of his imagination? Jane Doe saying his name, looking so uncannily like Abby, those haunted hazel eyes, the shifting, undulating facial bones—some of which he knew to be, at least in part, a delusion. So why not the rest of it?

Maybe beneath it all, down in the part of his mind where darkness dwelled, where the animal crouched, watching, waiting . . . maybe down there he knew the truth, the real explanation.

That he *had* killed Sue Carmody.

That he *had* killed Abby.

And, who knows, all those years ago in college, after he'd been spurned by Anna Marie Colson, rejected in favor of a law student—a *law* student, for godsakes—maybe he'd killed her, too. Shot her and her new boyfriend dead in the street.

Tolan frowned.

He couldn't remember the last time he'd thought about Anna Marie, so why was she suddenly making an appearance now?

Another image flitted through his mind. Not a knife this time, but the penlight, shining in his eyes. Something being shoved into his mouth.

A bite bar?

Then he remembered how much his jaw had ached when he awoke. What the hell was going on here?

"Careful," Lisa said. "You almost hit her head."

Her voice brought him back to the here and now, as they cleared the last step. Tolan almost said, "What difference does it make?" but cursed himself the moment he thought it. No matter how Carmody had wound up in this state, she still deserved his respect.

"We'll take her out the side door," Lisa said.

They carried her through the living room into the kitchen and laid her on the linoleum.

"Where's her car?" Lisa asked.

"I don't know."

"Did *you* bring her here? I saw yours parked in the garage."

"I don't *know*," Tolan said. "I don't remember anything since I left the hospital."

"We'd better leave yours inside. The police will be looking for it." She turned then, heading back toward the living room. "Go change your clothes and meet me back here in five minutes."

Tolan looked down at the blood on his shirt, then shifted his gaze to Carmody's body, wishing he could teleport to some distant planet.

Beam me up, Scotty.

The side door led from the kitchen to a small, sheltered courtyard. Beyond that was an alleyway that separated Lisa's house from her neighbor's. A seasonal resident, the neighbor was rarely here this time of year, leaving the alleyway secluded and quiet, even this early in the night. The only illumination was a distant string of streetlights that didn't come on until cars passed.

The chances of anyone seeing them were slim. If they were careful, if they timed it right, nobody would ever know that Sue Carmody had been here.

Nobody but Tolan. And Lisa.

And Vincent?

No, Tolan thought. Not even Vincent.

Chapter 47

Blackburn was waiting in his sedan when the squad car pulled up behind him. A moment later, Kat Pendergast and her partner, Dave Hogan, got out, Kat frowning as she approached his window.

"What happened to your head?"

Blackburn caught himself touching the butterfly bandage. He'd almost forgotten about it.

"A lesson on how not to subdue an armed suspect," he said. "I'll have to tell you about it sometime."

She nodded, then gestured to the row of houses lining the street. It was a cul-de-sac in the middle of Bryant Park, an unassuming, upper-middle-class neighborhood. "So which one is Tolan's?"

Blackburn pointed to a small three bedroom/two bath in the center of the curve. According to De Mello, Tolan had lived here for six years, four of them with his wife.

There was no car in the drive.

No lights on inside.

"You sure he isn't hiding in there somewhere?" Kat asked.

"You sure he wasn't at the girlfriend's place?"

She shrugged. "Like I said when you called, I don't think so. But I could be wrong."

"So could I," Blackburn said as he popped open his

door and climbed out, "but I've got a feeling he's still in the wind."

"And you just want us to wait here, right? Give you the heads-up in case he decides to show?"

"That's the general idea."

"What about the neighbors? Won't they be curious? Wonder why we're hanging around?"

Blackburn looked at the surrounding houses, saw lights in the kitchen and living-room windows, families going about their business, living their lives.

"Let 'em wonder," he said.

"You do realize we'll be breaking about a hundred different laws."

"Just one, actually. Maybe two. But we're on a fact-finding mission, remember?"

"What about a search warrant?"

After his conversation with Soren, Blackburn had pretty much convinced himself that Soren wasn't Tolan's connection to Hastert and Janovic. Soren didn't strike Blackburn as the kind of guy who would let himself get caught in the middle of a blackmail scheme. Especially one that involved multiple murders.

But with Psycho Bitch currently incapacitated, Blackburn needed to find some other connection, some concrete piece of evidence that linked Tolan to the two victims. If for no other reason than to confirm that he was on the right track with this thing.

But he knew a judge would never allow him to go on a hunting expedition. Not without probable cause.

So he'd go in anyway, see what he could find, and worry about the search warrant later.

"Look," he told Kat, "if you don't feel comfortable about this, feel free to—"

"I want to go in with you," she said.

Blackburn saw the excitement on her face, but shook his head. "No way."

"Come on, Frank. Hogan can handle lookout. And you could use another pair of eyes."

"Not gonna happen."

"Why?"

"This isn't a date, Kat. We aren't talking about a movie and a milkshake."

"Yeah?" She leaned in close to him then, whispering in his ear. "If you ever *want* that milkshake, you'd better reconsider."

Blackburn stared at her, not doubting for a moment what she meant by that. A bold move, to be sure. An ultimatum. Appealing to his baser instincts.

And he liked that. Hell, he *loved* it—especially the reward being offered.

But the moment he thought about the visual she had so generously supplied him, an image of Carmody intruded. Carmody, lying across her bed, pulling him toward her. Carmody, who still hadn't bothered to return his last phone call.

He had no reason to feel loyal to the woman. Had every reason *not* to be. But sitting in that hospital cafeteria today, he'd felt a renewed vibe between them. That old spark. An intangible link that a loner like Blackburn didn't often find.

And for all his sexual bravado, he hadn't slept with another woman since that night of drunken bliss.

But he also knew that Carmody was a dead end. Treated him with about the same amount of dignity she'd afford a piece of used toilet paper. More interested in advancing her career than getting involved with an overbearing jerk like him.

So why the sudden conflict?

Why was he wasting his time fretting over a cold fish when he had a potential sure thing standing right here in front of him? All he had to say was *yes*.

Maybe having a second set of eyes in there wasn't a bad idea after all.

"Well?" Kat said.

Blackburn stared at her. God, she was cute. He didn't need much more convincing.

"What are you doing for dinner Saturday night?"

Chapter 48

"Turn left," Lisa said.

She had lined her trunk with black Hefty bags before they put the body inside. The trunk was small, but they managed to get Carmody to fit with a minimum of fuss.

A minimum of fuss, Tolan thought. How callous is that?

They were driving now, Tolan behind the wheel of Lisa's BMW. He was still in shock, letting her take the lead, continually amazed by her calm under fire, and continually grateful that she was willing to take this risk for him.

But how could she?

How could she remain so loyal to a monster?

Because if he'd done this, if he had butchered Carmody, that's exactly what he was.

Something stirred at the periphery of his brain, like an image from a dream. Abby standing near a dark doorway.

"Where are we taking her?" he asked.

"The old hospital."

"The old hospital? We can't just dump her there."

"We don't have much choice."

"But—"

"Nobody goes up there anymore, Michael. And there are plenty of places to hide a body."

He glanced at her and saw the set look on her face, her expression unreadable. This was beyond the usual focused concentration now. Something deeper. Colder.

"Why are you doing this, Lisa? How can you even be in the same car with me?"

"I already told you why."

"No, this is above and beyond. You think I killed her. You probably think I killed Abby, too."

They pulled onto Baycliff Drive now, winding up the mountain.

She looked at him. "It doesn't matter, Michael. Don't you know that by now? I love you. I've always loved you. You're my lost soul."

"Your what?"

She shook her head. "If you don't get it by now, there's no point in trying to explain it to you."

"No," Tolan insisted. "Tell me. What do you mean?"

"It's something the old man said. That I looked like a woman in search of a lost soul. I think it's fitting. Don't you?"

Another image from the dream assaulted Tolan. Abby pointing her camera. A flash of light.

Ask the old man, Michael. He knows.

"Who are you talking about? What old man?"

"The police brought him in today. He had some interesting things to say about your new girlfriend."

"My what?"

Lisa sighed. "Jane Doe, Michael, Jane Doe. But according to him, that's not who she really is. Not now, at least. And I think you already know that."

Tolan tried to find a suitable response to this, but couldn't. His mind was reeling.

Lisa pointed. "Take the access road."

"Lisa—"

"Turn."

He did as he was told, pulling onto a narrow road that snaked through the mountains toward the old hospital. He waited as Lisa gathered herself to tell him whatever it was she was trying to tell him.

After a moment, she spoke. "You remember when Abby used to say, 'Careful, now, the rhythm is gonna get you'?"

Tolan nodded. "What about it?"

"I always figured she got it from that song. I mean, she did, but she didn't really use it in the same way. For her it was a warning."

"It's just something she said. I never really gave it much thought."

"Neither did I, until today, when the old man started talking about it."

"About what? The song?"

"No, Michael, pay attention. The Rhythm. The way of The Rhythm." A pause. "Abby was from Louisiana, just like him."

It's the way, Michael. The Rhythm. The heartbeat.

"Maybe you should back up and tell me who the hell this old man is."

"First, I need you to tell me something."

He said nothing. Waited.

"Why did you leave the hospital today? Why did you take off without saying anything?"

Tolan hesitated, thinking about what he'd seen and heard in that seclusion room. Early this morning, he had chastised Blackburn for his insensitive use of labels, but there was no better way to describe what he'd been through.

"You'll think I'm nuts."

"I doubt it," she said. "Just answer the question. Tell me why you left."

He hesitated again, wondering how much he should say.

But what exactly did he have to lose? Things couldn't be much worse than they were right now.

So he told her. Told his story from the beginning. About the blackout the night Abby died, and again today, just before finding Carmody in her shower. About the details of Vincent's phone calls and his fear that they might not be real. About Jane's changing eyes, the disappearing needle tracks. About the song that only he and Abby knew, the shifting facial bones, the words she spoke. Saying his name.

It was an unburdening. A confession.

The confession of a madman.

Because he now knew that's what he was.

Lisa said nothing as he spoke, staring out her window into the night.

"The missing ear was the kicker," he said. "I had a panic attack, ran to my car, then . . . nothing. Until I woke up on your living-room floor."

They were silent as he rounded a curve, threading his way through the tangle of pepper trees, then into a clearing where the old hospital stood, illuminated only by the moon.

The place was a throwback to a more primitive time. A time when the mentally ill needed to be hidden from the world. Shunned.

As he pulled into the front drive, Tolan couldn't help feeling the heat of a thousand eyes on him. The ghosts of the many patients who had come and gone over the years.

Watching him.

Judging him.

When he finally brought the car to a stop, Lisa turned to him. "I knew this was coming, you know. I guess it's pretty ironic it happens today of all days."

Tolan was puzzled. "You knew *what* was coming?"

"This moment. The moment you finally realize what you're capable of. What you did to Abby." She paused. "Sooner or later it had to catch up to you."

What he did to Abby.

"You *knew*? You've known about her all along?"

"Yes," she said.

Tolan was at a loss. ". . . How?"

"The same way I know about Detective Carmody. And Anna Marie Colson."

He just looked at her. *"What?"*

"Come on, Michael. Do you really think this is the first time I've helped you?"

Chapter 49

Like the lowlifes who had broken into Hastert's apartment, Blackburn always kept a ring of bump keys handy. Such keys were once a well-kept secret in the locksmith's arsenal, an essential tool for quick and easy entry. But it didn't take long for the home-invasion crowd to catch on.

The keys were of various makes, each with its grooves filed down to the lowest cut, allowing it to be used in just about any lock that accepted that particular make of key. Once the key was inserted, the locksmith or thief—or, in this case, cop—would lightly "bump" the back of it with a screwdriver, or some other blunt instrument, until the key turned and the lock opened.

The process was so simple, a kid could do it. And Blackburn had no doubt that more than a few had.

After he and Kat took a quick look around the perimeter of the house, they decided to go in through the rear door. There were two locks, the knob and a deadbolt, but Blackburn had no trouble bumping them both.

"I knew those hands were good for something," Kat said.

The moment they were inside they flicked on their Mag-Lites, illuminating a basic, upscale tract home: kitchen attached to a sunken living room. Hallway leading to a bathroom and three bedrooms.

"Where do you want to start?" Kat asked.

Blackburn handed her a pair of crime scene gloves, then shone his light toward the bedroom doors. "Most people keep their secrets in their closets. You take the first one, I'll take the last, and we'll meet in the middle."

"A head-on collision."

"Huh?"

"Nothing. Just thinking out loud. What exactly are we looking for?"

"Bank statements, check stubs. The most recent ones you can find. Patient files would be nice."

"Janovic?"

"Or the new victim—Hastert."

"Good luck."

"I can dream, can't I?" He gestured for her to get started. "Make sure you put everything back where you got it. We don't want to leave any footprints."

"Roger."

As Kat pulled her gloves on and headed for the first bedroom, Blackburn navigated the narrow hallway until he reached the last door. Resting a hand on the butt of his holstered Glock, he pushed inside, shone the light around.

The master bedroom.

King-size bed, double-wide dresser, closet to the left, bathroom to the right. Nothing special. The wall above the bed featured a stark black-and-white photograph of Tolan, awash in sunlight, standing in a large, open room with high windows.

Taken by the wife, no doubt.

On closer inspection, Blackburn realized it was shot at the old Baycliff Hospital. A gathering spot. A Day Room. He remembered seeing this and several more like it in *The New Times* magazine, shortly after Abby's murder.

He took a quick look through the dresser drawers,

making sure that every sock, every pair of boxers remained in place, but found nothing of interest.

Moving to the closet, he slid open the door, shone his light inside, and found the usual assortment of clothes and shoes. A set of pristine golf clubs were buried in a corner, looking as if they'd been sitting there since the day they were purchased.

Undoubtedly the product of peer pressure.

The shelf above held a few boxes, their handwritten labels chronicling several years' worth of tax returns. Blackburn pulled the most recent year down and quickly rifled through it, found a couple of check registers. A scan of their contents, however, yielded nothing of use.

Replacing the box, he closed the closet and turned, sweeping the flashlight beam around the room again.

He decided to move on.

The center bedroom was a home office. Functional and unpretentious. Bookcases holding a mix of hardcover and paperback books, both fiction and nonfiction.

Another reader, like Hastert.

The closet was a bust. A couple of coats hanging inside, more books piled on the shelf above them.

Shutting the closet door, he moved to a desk that was pushed up against the far wall, its blotter littered with various pieces of paperwork and mail. Blackburn quickly looked through them, but again found nothing of interest.

Sliding open the bottom drawer, he was hoping to see a row of hanging file folders, but instead found even more books, most of them snooze-inducing tomes covering a variety of mental health issues.

One of them had Tolan's byline and the title *What Color Is Your Anger?* Blackburn pulled it out and leafed through it, vaguely remembering that it had been a bestseller a couple years back. The book that put Tolan on the map.

As far as Blackburn could tell, there was nothing special about it. Just a retread of every other self-help book out there, this one assigning colors to our various moods, followed by an armchair analysis of what triggers them.

It was all gobbledygook to Blackburn and seemed out of character for Tolan. As if he'd been slumming in the world of pop psychology. Why the public and the press latched on to this kind of nonsense was anybody's guess. One of the many mysteries of our culture.

He was returning this masterpiece to its designated spot when he realized he'd missed something in the back of the drawer, wedged behind the rest of the books. Quickly moving them out of the way, he reached in and pulled out a box. A rectangular metal box with a padlock attached.

Blackburn felt a tiny surge of adrenaline that was immediately offset by puzzlement.

It was a tackle box.

The kind fishermen use.

But if this connected in the way he thought it might, that didn't make sense. It didn't make sense at all.

Still, he had to wonder, if you're using a box like this to store your fishing tackle, why not keep it in the garage with the rest of your gear? Assuming Tolan had any. Why stick it in the back of a desk drawer, hidden by a bunch of books?

Setting it on the desktop, Blackburn rattled the padlock, but it was securely fastened. Bump keys wouldn't be any help with this, but a properly bent paper clip would.

He had just found one in the top desk drawer when Kat's voice rang out from the adjoining bedroom.

"Hey, Frank, I think I've got something here."

Snatching up the tackle box and carrying it with him, he moved down the hallway to the next room, which had been set up as a den.

Sofa. Armchairs. TV.

Kat stood near the closet, a box of her own at her feet. This one made of battered cardboard.

"The shelf in there is full of these," she said. "All labeled. Old mementos and stuff." She held out a newspaper clipping. "Take a look at this."

Blackburn set the tackle box on the floor, then took the clipping from her and shone his light on it. It was a fifteen-year-old article taken from the *LA Times*, yellowed with age, its headline reading:

COED AND BOYFRIEND GUNNED DOWN

The story that followed told of a young UCLA student named Anna Marie Colson, who had been gunned down one night while she and her boyfriend were returning from a walk to Westwood Village. Several of Colson's roommates had been questioned, including one Michael Edward Tolan, a pre-med student whom police said was Colson's former boyfriend.

While Tolan was initially a "person of interest," no charges were ever brought, and the official conclusion was that the murders were the result of a random mugging.

A photo accompanied the article. The coed and several of her roommates. Six in all.

One of them was clearly Tolan. Much younger. Happier than Blackburn had ever seen him. And sitting on his lap was a cute brunette with a cheerleader's smile.

Anna Marie Colson.

"The wife wasn't his first," Blackburn said. "The sonofabitch did it before."

"Exactly what I was thinking."

Blackburn continued to stare at the photo, looking at all those fresh young faces, none of them knowing that they had a killer among them.

But how could they? How can you look in someone's eyes and really know what's behind them?

Tolan had certainly fooled Blackburn. And Blackburn was a professional.

"What's that?"

He looked up to see Kat gesturing toward his feet.

The tackle box. He'd forgotten about it.

"I'm not sure," he said, "but we're about to find out." Folding the article, he stuck it in his shirt pocket.

"Shouldn't I return that? I thought you said no footprints."

"What he doesn't know won't hurt him."

Picking up the tackle box, Blackburn carried it to an armchair and sat, pulling it into his lap. Then he took the paper clip from his coat pocket, bent it straight, and went to work on the padlock.

Unfortunately, it was tougher than he'd expected.

"Let me try," Kat said, crouching next to him.

Taking the paper clip, she attacked the lock, working it like a seasoned pro. Less than half a minute later, it was open.

She saw Blackburn's look and grinned. "Gym class, senior year. I pulled a lot of locker room pranks."

"What I would've given to be a fly on that wall."

Her grin widened as he pulled the lock free and set it aside. Flipping up the latch, he carefully swung the lid of the tackle box open and shone his light on it.

There was a tray full of fishing lures on top. Weights. A spool of line. A couple of cork floats. Everything quite innocent and unremarkable.

Blackburn hooked the tray's handle with a finger and pulled it out, setting it on the floor.

Then he froze.

Holy shit.

"What? What've you got?"

"What *don't* I have is the question."

Reaching into the bottom of the box, he pulled out a fat, pen-shaped object, the words *PowerBlast 2000* printed on the side.

The cauterizing tool.

Beneath it lay a small hacksaw and a razor-sharp kitchen knife. And next to that was a stack of photographs.

Blackburn pulled them out and stared at them. The same photos he'd seen on the printed web page Tolan had given him. Dismembered bodies arranged in several different configurations. The last of the photos were shots of Abby Tolan. Her eyes cut out.

Kat eyed the contents of the box. "Is this what I think it is?"

Blackburn nodded. "The whole goddamn enchilada."

"The murder kit, right? *Vincent's* murder kit."

Blackburn nodded again, knowing this didn't quite fit—that something was off—but was unable to refute the evidence in front of him. There was no other conclusion he could reach.

Dr. Michael Tolan wasn't a simple wife killer.

Dr. Michael Tolan was Vincent Van Gogh.

But before Blackburn could fully process the magnitude of this sudden revelation, he noticed something else in the box. Reaching a hand under the hacksaw, he pulled out a large plastic Ziplock bag and held it up, shining his flashlight beam at it.

"You've gotta be kidding me," Kat said, her face going pale.

Inside the bag, strung on a piece of nylon fishing line, was a necklace of severed ears, all but one of them as cracked and withered as old orange peels.

That one, however, stood out like a teenager in an octogenarian chorus line.

It was a new addition to the collection. A fresh souvenir.

Pink and raw and bloody.

And it was the sight of that ear—or more precisely, the earlobe—that sent the skittering of tiny feet along Blackburn's spine.

"No," he said quietly. "Not this."

"What?" Kat asked. "What's wrong?"

Blackburn suddenly felt sick to his stomach, the slop he'd eaten for lunch defying gravity and doing a barrel roll up his esophagus.

His whole body began to shake.

This can't be true. Please tell me it isn't true.

But it was. He knew it was. Knew it with unwavering certainty.

Because fastened to that fresh pink earlobe—

—was a tiny red ruby.

A tiny red ruby he'd seen just a few short hours ago.

A gift from a loving father. A birthstone.

Sue Carmody's birthstone.

Chapter 50

Tolan was in a daze.

"I was there, Michael. I saw it all."

It was one thing to believe you might be a monster and another thing altogether to have it confirmed so matter-of-factly. Yet here Lisa sat, telling him what he'd dreaded hearing for a year now.

"You remember those photos Abby took of me on my birthday?"

"Yes," he said.

"She called me a couple weeks later, told me to come by the gallery and pick them up. I showed up after work, but when I went inside, I heard you two in back, arguing. I should've left right there and then, but I didn't. I couldn't help myself. I peeked around the corner and saw you waving that box at her."

"The condoms . . ."

She nodded.

"What was I saying?"

Lisa paused a moment. Swallowed. This was obviously difficult for her. "You called her a whore . . . Then she slapped you."

Tolan thought about that slap, but was unable to penetrate the darkness that stretched beyond it.

"Keep going," he said.

"You just stood there, as if you couldn't believe she'd done that, your face a blank. Then you seemed to disappear into yourself, while someone else took over."

"Someone else," Tolan repeated.

Just like his mother.

She'd called it the changing of the guard. And it was usually followed by an attack on his father. A flurry of fists against his chest.

She'd be screaming at him and Tolan would run to the closet and hide, finding comfort in the darkness. But no matter how hard he pressed his hands against his ears, he couldn't shut out the sound of his mother's voice. Just as he couldn't now shut out the truth.

"What happened next?" he asked, not sure he wanted to hear this.

Lisa's gaze shifted to a spot outside her window, unable to look at him as she summoned up the memory.

"There was a knife on Abby's work table. She'd been eating apples or something. One minute you were standing there and . . . and the next you suddenly grabbed it and started stabbing her. She didn't even see it coming."

The coldness that had enveloped Lisa earlier was long gone. A tear rolled down her cheek.

"When you were done, you just dropped into a chair and stared at the wall. At one of her photographs. The one you have hanging over your bed now."

"And you saw the whole thing?"

She nodded. "I was in shock. It happened so fast, and I just stood there, frozen. There you were, covered in blood, Abby dead at your feet." More tears filled her eyes. "It was Anna Marie all over again."

Anna Marie?

So it was true. He was responsible for her death too.

Jesus, he thought. Will it ever end?

"You don't remember that night, do you? The night Anna Marie died."

He didn't know what he remembered at this point.

"Clive and Kruger and the others were all out partying, but I stayed back because I wasn't feeling well, and you said you needed to go to the library."

No, Tolan thought. He hadn't gone to the library. He'd stayed home to study. He was almost sure of it.

"Then about eleven o'clock, you came home in a panic, babbling on about calling the police. You had a gun wrapped up in your sweater."

Jesus. Had he had another blackout? How often had he lost time and never even known it?

"The thing is," Lisa continued, "you didn't even have to do it. Anna told me the night before that she was planning to dump the law student and come back to you."

"I don't believe this. I don't believe any of it."

"Believe it, Michael. I helped you clean up. Helped you get rid of the gun. And when the police questioned all of us, I lied and said you'd been with me all night."

"Why would you do that?"

"I told you. Because I love you. I've always loved you."

"And the night Abby died?"

"The same thing. There was a lot of blood, but I put you in the shower, helped you clean up, got you into your car and on the road. I don't think you said three words to me the whole time."

"And what about my alibi?"

"You didn't need one, thanks to Vincent."

It took Tolan a moment to realize what she was saying, the weight of that realization nearly flooring him. He stared at Lisa with new eyes.

"*You?* You did that to her?"

"I had to, Michael. Don't you see? I had to protect you. Vincent was in the papers every day for weeks. It only seemed natural to blame it all on him. To keep the police from suspecting you."

Tolan squeezed his eyes shut now and buried his head in his hands. He was no longer interested in the truth. He just wanted to curl up like Jane Doe and die.

He'd spent his entire professional life and a good portion of his childhood dealing with people who suffered from the mildest phobias to the most severe psychosis. But until this moment, he had never fully understood or appreciated their pain.

To realize that he was one of them was like being told he had only a week to live. And Lisa, out of some misplaced sense of loyalty or twisted love, had done the unthinkable. Had done it for him.

She may have kept him from going to jail, but this moment, this pain, this realization was worse than the most hellish day in prison. Bile stung the back of his throat and he swallowed hard, trying to keep from throwing up.

"There's something else you need to know," she said.

Tolan opened his eyes and looked up at her, unable to even imagine what that something might be.

"What?"

"You won't believe me, but I swear to God it's true."

"Tell me."

"All those things you saw in seclusion room three? Abby's eyes? Her face? You didn't imagine them. They weren't a delusion. They were real."

She was talking crazy now. "Real?"

She nodded, then said words Tolan never thought he'd hear. Impossible words. Damaging words.

Words that inexplicably filled him with hope.

"She's back, Michael. Abby's back. And she's alive."

Chapter 51

Blackburn's hands shook as he took out the new phone he'd picked up at the station house and quickly punched in Carmody's number. After several rings the line switched over to voice mail.

The nausea that had been crowding his stomach intensified. He felt like he was about to do a Linda Blair all over Kat's crisp black uniform.

Clicking off, he immediately dialed again. A different number this time.

De Mello answered on the third ring.

"Fred, are you still at the squad?"

"Yeah, I was just packing up. I've got a few things on the fire, but I figured I could follow them up at—"

"Drop all that and sit your ass down," Blackburn said.

"Why? What's up?"

"I need you to do a GPS trace on Carmody's cell phone."

"Carmody? But—"

"Just do it, Fred. Now." He gave him his new number. "Call me back as soon as you locate her."

"Is Carmody okay?"

"That's what I want to find out." He clicked off and turned to Kat. "Here's what I need you to do."

"Shoot."

"Clean this place up, get everything back where it belongs, but leave the tackle box open on Tolan's desktop and break one of the windows. Then I want you and Hogan to drive to the nearest pay phone and call 911."

"Why?"

"You're gonna report a break-in, anonymously. Give them Tolan's address. And the minute the call comes out over the radio, you respond."

Kat nodded, immediately understanding. This would give them probable cause to enter the premises and "discover" the evidence laying out in plain sight.

It was an old tried-and-true ruse, and Blackburn had never lost any sleep over using it.

"Where will you be?" Kat asked.

"Wherever De Mello sends me."

Five minutes later, he was on the road and traveling, heading in the only direction he knew to go. Toward where he'd last left Carmody.

Toward Baycliff Hospital.

As he waited for De Mello's call, he ran the evidence through his head, still thinking that something didn't quite fit right. What he'd found in that desk drawer was like pure gold to an investigator, but it seemed too convenient somehow. Too staged.

If Tolan was Vincent, then Blackburn's extortion theory went right out the window. Why would Tolan need to buy Hastert's and Janovic's silence? Why would he need them at all?

Because if Tolan was Vincent he'd already *know* about the burn marks. He'd be the *originator* of the burn marks.

It was the same damn stumbling block as before, only from the opposite direction this time.

Someone had surely butchered Hastert and Janovic. Someone using Vincent's mark. And every instinct Blackburn had said that the two victims were involved in a blackmail scheme. The reason for their murders.

But if Tolan wasn't the target of that scheme, who was?

Blackburn let the events of the day tumble through his head and kept coming back to the phone calls Tolan had attributed to Vincent.

Was it possible that they weren't phony after all? That they *hadn't* been the product of a guilty conscience? Had Tolan been telling the truth about them all along?

Blackburn dialed his phone again, hoping to catch the squad's resident computer tech, Billy Warren, still in his office.

No such luck.

Dialing dispatch, he asked for Billy's home phone number, then got him on the line in three rings.

"Billy, this is Frank Blackburn."

A pause. "Hey, Frank, what's up?"

"Got a question for you."

"I'm in the middle of *Jeopardy* here, man. Can it wait?"

Blackburn ignored him. "I need to know if it's possible for somebody from the outside, some hacker, to go in and change official cell phone records."

Billy seemed distracted. "Like how?"

"Like wiping away any trace of a specific call. Making it look like that call never happened."

"What's a cattle prod?"

"What?"

"Sorry, man. *Jeopardy* question."

"Do me a fucking favor and focus," Blackburn said.

"Yeah, yeah. You want to know if it's possible to sanitize a cell phone record, right?"

Blackburn sighed. "Yes."

"As long as the company's network is accessible, then yeah, it's possible. They try to wire in all kinds of security protections, firewalls and such, but an enterprising hacker can worm his way through all that bullshit and do just about anything he wants. How do you think we ended up with our last president?"

"And he could erase just one or two entries?"

"Sure," Billy said. "He could add some too. Hell, he could throw in the latest Bruins-Trojans score if he wanted to." Another pause, then, "So does that answer your question, man? I've got a game to get back to."

Blackburn told him it did and hung up, thinking again about the events of the day. Tolan had said that Vincent threatened him, believing he'd been used as a scapegoat for the wife's murder.

So was it possible that Vincent had erased those threats from the record? The use of an untraceable server for the website photos indicated at least some skill with computers.

Could Vincent be pulling a reverse whammy on Tolan?

If you looked at it that way, it all started to hang together.

Something like this:

Tolan somehow comes across the secret of the emoticon. If not through Soren or Jane Doe, then directly from Hastert, whom he may have treated at County General. Soren had said Tolan didn't do much pro bono work, but that didn't negate the possibility.

A few months after Abby Tolan is murdered—reportedly Vincent's eighth victim—Hastert and his buddy Janovic put it all together and finger Tolan, threatening to expose him. Tolan gets tired of draining his bank account and does what has to be done. He kills them both, again making it look like a serial perp at work.

Vincent, in the meantime—the real Vincent—uses the

anniversary of the wife's death to get even with Tolan for stealing his thunder. Instead of simply giving credit where credit is due, why not let Tolan take the fall for *all* of the murders? Why not frame a guilty man?

The question was, how did Carmody fit in?

Was she part of the frame?

One last victim to help seal the deal?

Blackburn felt sick. He didn't want to believe it, didn't want to believe that the ear in that bag was Carmody's, yet there was no denying that ruby birthstone.

But maybe he was wrong.

Please, God, let him be wrong.

Popping open the glove compartment, he sent up a small prayer that whoever drove this car last had been a smoker and had left behind his stash.

Miracle of miracles, he found a crumpled pack of Winstons inside, one lonely, battered cigarette still in the pack. Shaking it out, he stuck it in his mouth, pressed the in-dash lighter, waited for it to pop out, then fired up the Winston.

The smoke in his lungs felt wonderful.

Chapter 52

"Alive? Why would you say something like that?"

"Because it's true," Lisa said. "Abby's alive. What you saw in that room today was real. Every bit of it. Just like the old man said."

"What is your obsession with this old man?"

Then it hit him. Something Blackburn had mentioned early this morning about an old homeless coot claiming he knew Jane Doe. Could this be the old man she was talking about?

"You have to believe me, Michael. I saw it with my own eyes. I knew it was all true the minute Cassie showed me the tattoo."

"What tattoo?"

"The Hello Kitty tattoo."

"On Jane's shoulder?"

"The one that *used* to be there. Cassie showed me the observation tapes. It was like a special effect from a movie. We saw it fade right before our eyes. I think Cassie was ready for a nice tall drink after that."

Tolan felt the flesh on his head prickle.

"Let me get this straight," he said. "You're telling me the Hello Kitty tattoo is gone? Completely gone?"

Lisa nodded. "Just like the needle marks, the eyes, and everything else you saw."

No, Tolan thought. It couldn't be right. This kind of nonsense went against everything he believed in.

But hadn't Clay reported a case of heterochromia? Hadn't Cassie confirmed the change in Jane's eyes? Hadn't Blackburn claimed he'd seen the needle marks? Hadn't Jane sung that goddamn song?

> *Mama got trouble*
> *Mama got sin*
> *Mama got bills to pay again.*

Tolan had thought he was losing his mind, but if Cassie and Blackburn and Lisa and Clay had also seen these things, was it possible that Lisa was right? That his delusion was not a delusion at all?

"It's her, Michael. It's Abby. She's a borrower. *Un emprenteuse.*"

"A what?"

"It's what the old man called her. She's come back from the dead, and borrowed a friend's body to do it."

Tolan tried to grasp this idea, but couldn't get past the absurdity of it. He'd spent his life looking for rational answers to people's problems, looking for ways to explain away their delusions and their superstitions. Yet despite this resistance, part of him wanted to believe. Could it really be Abby lying on that hospital bed?

"Why?" he said. "Why would she want to come back?"

"Why do you think? She's not here for a glorious reunion. You killed her, Michael. You butchered her."

"No," he said. "I don't believe it, I—"

"Stop it. You know it's true."

"Then why can't I remember? Why can't I remember any of them? Abby. Anna. Carmody."

"Because you've blocked it. Just like your . . ." She

paused, looking up sharply. "What was that? Did you hear that?"

He had no idea what she was talking about.

"It sounded like a cell phone ringing. I thought I heard it before."

She popped open her door and climbed out, moving around the front of the car. Tolan opened his own door and joined her.

She pointed toward the forest of pepper trees. "It came from in there."

Tolan stared into the darkness, but his mind was somewhere else. All he could think about was Abby. *His* Abby. Lying on that hospital bed.

"I don't hear it now. Maybe I'm just being paranoid." Lisa turned, looking toward the trunk of the car. "We'd better get that body inside. There's an old incinerator in the basement. We can hide her in there."

But Tolan wasn't listening. He started for the pepper trees. "I have to go to Abby. I have to make it right."

As if in response to this, the wind kicked up, rustling the leaves, whistling in the black windows and doorways of the old hospital.

Lisa grabbed his arm. "What are you doing?"

"I have to go to her. She came here for me."

"What you have to do is help me with this body or neither of us is going anywhere."

"No," he said, wrenching free. "She needs me."

"She doesn't *need* you, Michael. She wants to kill you."

"I don't care," he said, starting for the trees again. "I have to see her. I have to make it right."

"Stop, Michael! It's too late."

He stopped dead then and turned, dread once again filling his gut. "What do you mean it's too late? What did you do?"

"It's already in motion. She'll be dead by the time you get there."

He advanced on her, overtaken by a sudden rage. *"What did you do?"*

Lisa brought her hands up and backed against the car. "I did what I had to. I went back to the old man, set it up with him. I would've done it myself, but I got your text message and—"

"To do what?"

"To keep her from hurting you. From hurting us! She's evil, Michael. Don't you understand that?"

"You sent him after her?"

"Yes," she said, then quickly shook her head. "No. He's only helping. Because he knows how dangerous she is. He knows what kind of damage she can do."

Tolan felt his rage build, accompanied by the growing roar of the wind through the trees. It was as if that wind was swirling inside of him.

Was this how it had been with Abby?

With Anna Marie?

"Who else?" he shouted, forcing Lisa to raise her hands even higher, to ward him off. "Who else did you send after her?"

Lisa said nothing for a moment, her eyes again filling with tears. "I did it for you, Michael. For us."

"Who?" he shouted.

She lowered her hands, her lips trembling as she finally answered his question.

"Bobby Fremont."

Then, in the distance beyond the trees, a fire alarm began to ring.

SIX

The Children Who Brought Balance to the World

Chapter 53

Ten minutes before the alarm went off, before The Rhythm gave its final push, bringing all of the elements together in the old, dead hospital, Solomon St. Fort thought about what he was supposed to do and hoped it would all go the way they'd planned.

When the nurse lady came to him earlier that day and told him what she'd seen and who she was trying to protect, he had readily agreed to help her. If the woman who wasn't quite Myra had not yet completed her transformation, there was still a chance he could reverse the process and make her go back to wherever she'd come from.

He didn't know if the incantations his grandfather had once taught him would work. He'd never had to use them himself and wasn't even sure if Papi ever had. But it was worth a try if it meant getting Myra back.

And he knew now that for him, personally, this day had been about much more than Myra.

It was about redemption. The redemption of a soul scarred by a lie. A lie he had been telling himself for far too long.

If The Rhythm didn't want him here, it would've kept him away. His "yes" to the nurse lady, his agreement to do this deed—at (he might add) incredible risk to his own life and limb—was all part of The Rhythm's plan.

So at the appointed time, a time chosen to take maximum advantage of the security crew's shift change, Solomon climbed off the bunk he'd been assigned, then went into the hallway, around the corner and, careful to stay one step behind the motorized video cam as it panned the adjoining hallway, approached a locked door marked AUTHORIZED STAFF ONLY.

Using the key card the nurse lady had given him, he went through that door and found himself on a stairway leading down to the basement. A moment later, he was standing in the basement itself.

It was exactly as described: a row of storage lockers adjacent to a maze of pipes. Mounted on the far wall was his first target, the electrical panel, a column of switches that controlled power to the entire detention unit.

Sitting on the floor below it was a flashlight and an umbrella.

Grabbing them both, Solomon stared at the switches, each of them labeled for a different part of the detention unit. He turned off the backup power first, then, sending up a prayer to God and Henry and Papi and his sweet departed mother, reached up and switched off the main power line.

The shouting began almost immediately.

A few minutes later, Solomon was upstairs in one of the main corridors, using the flashlight to help him navigate in the dark. Patients all over the detention ward were calling out for lights, spilling out of the Day Room into the corridors. Those in seclusion banged on their cell doors, screaming obscenities, as a frazzled staff and security crew struggled to maintain order.

Without hesitation, Solomon moved to his second target: a locked fire alarm mounted on the wall. Inserting a key, he turned it, flipped open the door, and pulled the alarm. He had wondered if it would work with the juice off, but the nurse lady had assured him it ran on a separate power system.

And, boy, was she right about that. The racket it made was loud enough to curdle cheese. The moment it went off, Solomon opened the umbrella as water valves came alive overhead.

Target three, coming up.

As the hospital erupted in chaos, Solomon rounded another corner and made his way to the seclusion rooms. The moment he stepped foot in the corridor, a light shone in his face and someone said, "Who the hell are you?"

It was a police officer, posted outside seclusion room three. He was holding a hand above his head in a fruitless attempt to stay dry. Solomon gave him a concerned look and said, "The guards sent me to fetch you. Up in front. They need help with the evacuation."

"What about the people in here?"

"They'll get their turn, but right now they need you up front." Solomon held out the umbrella and was immediately hit by a shower of cold water. "Here, take this."

The guard took it, said, "Thanks," and headed around the corner.

Solomon then turned to his new target: seclusion room six.

At the wire-mesh window stood a kid of about twenty, looking so calm and quiet you'd think he was a monk saying his evening prayer.

But the moment Solomon shone his light on the glass, the kid's eyes brightened, lips curling into a grin.

Solomon had seen him before, in the shower room, when two guards had escorted the kid inside. They took him to a spigot and stood back, their hands resting lightly on their weapons as they watched him undress and shower.

He'd looked dangerous then. But now, up close and

personal, he looked downright lethal. Which, Solomon had to admit, gave him pause.

But the nurse lady had assured him that the kid could help them get Myra out of here, and if anything went wrong, he looked like just the type of guy you'd want on your side. So Solomon pressed the intercom button and said, "You're Bobby, right?"

"Just open the door, old man."

Solomon figured he'd take that as a yes, then punched a code into the keypad. The moment it buzzed, the door flew wide and Bobby Fremont stepped into the corridor.

"Why'd you give away the umbrella, you useless turd?"

Solomon ignored the insult and pointed to seclusion room three. "She's in there."

"I know where she is. You think I'm a fuckin' moron?"

Fremont crossed the corridor and stood before the door to SR-3. "Open it up."

Solomon moved up to the glass and tried to peer inside, but it was too dark to see anything.

"Come on, goddamn it. Open it."

Turning to the keypad, Solomon punched in the code.

"Be quick," he said. "We've gotta get her out of here before that cop comes back."

"Fuck you," Fremont told him. "I'm gonna enjoy this ride for as long as I want."

"What's that supposed to mean?"

Fremont snatched the flashlight from him. "You did your job, old man, now go tell Lisa that this bitch is as good as dead."

Then he put a hand on Solomon's chest and pushed.

Solomon stumbled back, nearly losing his footing on the wet floor.

Had he just heard what he thought he'd heard?

Was Fremont planning to *kill* Myra?

No, no—that couldn't be right. They were supposed to

take her out to the parking lot and meet up with the nurse lady.

Regaining his balance, Solomon moved toward the kid, watching as Fremont shone the flashlight beam into the darkness and aimed it at the bed.

But the bed was empty.

"What the fuck?"

Fremont stepped past the threshold and swept the light around the room.

The woman was nowhere in sight.

"What is this?" he growled. "Lisa promised me some prime pussy, so where the hell is it?"

Then, as if in answer to the question, they both heard a sound. A faint whimper. Coming from overhead.

It sounded more animal than human.

Fremont aimed the flashlight beam toward the ceiling. And despite Solomon's concerns about this young punk's intentions, what he saw there made his entire body go numb.

"Holy shit," Fremont said.

A moment later, he wasn't saying anything.

He was too busy screaming.

Chapter 54

It started to rain.

Blackburn crushed out the last of the Winston and flipped his wipers on, wondering when the hell De Mello was gonna call back and give him that location. He had been headed in the direction of Baycliff just out of instinct, but for all he knew, it was the wrong direction altogether.

He was about to pull to the side of the road, debating whether to try calling Carmody again, in the dim hope that he'd been wrong about that severed ear.

Then his cell phone bleeped.

"I don't know what the holdup was," De Mello said, "but they've got it pinpointed."

"Where is she?"

"Baycliff—sort of."

"Sort of? What the hell does that mean?"

"The tracker shows her up the hill a bit. Somewhere between the new hospital and the ruins. From the satellite photos, it looks like she's in the trees."

The pepper trees. They grew like weeds up there.

Not liking the sound of this, Blackburn reminded himself that they were only tracking Carmody's phone, not Carmody herself. But then the thought of that little detail made him feel even worse.

"You okay, Frank? You sound a little tense."

"Hunky-dory," Blackburn said.

"Don't worry about Carmody, I'm sure she's fine. The cell signal up there isn't worth shit."

He hadn't told De Mello about the ear.

And what De Mello hadn't mentioned was that a phone caught in a dead zone doesn't ring. It goes straight to voice mail.

Carmody's had been ringing like crazy.

And if her phone was caught in a dead zone, the GPS trace wouldn't have worked.

"By the way," De Mello continued, "we just got an anonymous squeal on a possible break-in at Tolan's house. Hogan and Pendergast are picking it up."

"Nothing on Tolan himself?"

"Not yet. But he's bound to show up sooner or later."

Probably later, Blackburn thought. A lot later.

He thanked De Mello, told him to get his ass home, then hung up.

Sticking his flasher on the dashboard, he flicked it on, hit the siren, and bore down on the gas pedal.

Five minutes later, Blackburn was tearing up the hill toward Pepper Mountain Mesa. As he closed in on Baycliff, he cut the siren and heard a sound—the piercing ring of a fire alarm.

Pulling into the parking lot, he saw no sign of the car he'd left for Carmody, and was surprised to see staff and patients piling out of the detention unit, as well as the hospital proper. While the main building was still lit, the EDU itself was dark, as if someone had cut the electricity.

And this was no orderly evacuation.

The patients were unruly and wild, staff and security having a tough time containing them. Half of them were soaked to the bone, but Blackburn couldn't tell if this was because of the rain—which was quickly turning into a thunderstorm—or if the overhead sprinklers had gone off inside.

For some reason, it all reminded him of a scene from *Night of the Living Dead*.

Spotting an OCPD uniform carrying an umbrella—talk about prepared—Blackburn skidded to a stop in the middle of the aisle, jumped out, and ran toward him, showing him his badge.

"What's happening here?"

"What's it look like? A fuckin' mess, that's what."

Blackburn gestured toward the detention unit. "Is Detective Carmody inside?"

The uniform shook his head. "I just got on duty, but the guy I replaced said she took off hours ago."

Shit, Blackburn thought. He'd known it was too much to hope for.

As the cop moved past him to grab one of the wayward patients, Blackburn turned, looking off toward the trees. It was raining fairly hard now and a handful of patients were running for shelter as EDU staff members tried desperately to corral them.

Blackburn followed, crossing the wide lawn toward a narrow pathway with a NO TRESSPASSING sign. He was halfway to it when a hand grabbed his arm.

He turned sharply, expecting it to be one of the nutcases, but was surprised to see it was the old man from The Avenue. The one who said he knew Psycho Bitch.

And he didn't look good.

His eyes were wide with shock, the front of his hospital garb ripped open and covered with blood. His neck was crosshatched with severe lacerations, his left shin sliced open and bleeding, and he barely had the power to stand. He looked as if he'd been attacked by a wild animal.

"You've gotta stop her," he said.

"Who? Who did this?"

"You know who. The woman. The one who used to be Myra. She's one of the children now. The children of the drum. Just like Henry."

Blackburn had no earthly idea what the old man was talking about, could easily have dismissed it as the ravings of a lunatic, but there was something in those eyes of his that told Blackburn he needed to listen.

"Where is she?"

The old man did his best to point toward the trees. It looked as if it was a Herculean effort just to lift the finger. ". . . In there. You gotta stop her . . . before she hurts someone else. You gotta . . ."

He faltered then, falling to one knee, and Blackburn grabbed hold of him. The rain was coming down in sheets now, soaking them both, a pool of bloody water forming on the grass beneath them.

"How did she do this to you? Does she have a knife?"

The old man managed a negative shake of the head, then turned his face toward the sky, letting the rain wash over him.

"Reminds me of Katrina," he said. "He shoulda taken me then for what I did. Instead, he helped me."

"Who?"

The old man coughed, bringing up a bubble of blood. "Henry. My brother, Henry." He didn't speak for a moment, disappearing into a memory. Then he looked at Blackburn and said, "Can you keep a secret?"

Blackburn knew the old man was dying. Nobody could survive this kind of punishment. "Yes."

"I've been lying to myself all these years. We do that a lot, don't we? Lie to ourselves."

Blackburn nodded, his feelings for Carmody immediately coming to mind.

"We keep lying and lying and when you mix that in

with all the booze, after a while the truth don't matter much anymore. The lie is what we remember. The stories we make up to keep us from going crazy for what we've done."

He faltered again, coughing up more blood. Then he said, "I loved my little brother. I don't know why I pushed him in front of that police car . . . but . . . but my instincts just told me to. It was The Rhythm. The Rhythm makin' me do it. Keepin' the world synchronized."

He paused, trying to catch his breath. "I don't know why Henry went after that drunk-ass cop instead of me. I deserved it more. But there musta been a reason for it. Somethin' he had to do to restore the balance. And he musta known this day was comin'."

The old man looked up at the sky again. "You knew, didn't you, Henry? You knew it all along."

As if in answer—and Blackburn wouldn't have believed this if he hadn't witnessed it himself—thunder rumbled and rolled, shaking the earth beneath them.

The old man closed his eyes, listening to some inner voice, then said, "Forgive me, little brother. Please forgive me . . ."

Then his body weight shifted in Blackburn's hands and he slumped forward.

Dead.

Blackburn stared at him a long moment, listening to the thunder recede, to the sound of the chaos around him, feeling the rain soak through to his skin, still not sure what the old man had been talking about.

But his confession—if that's what it was—his expression of regret for deeds long past, cut Blackburn right to the bone.

Carefully laying the old man on the grass, he turned toward the trees and ran.

Chapter 55

Tolan knew there was a pathway in here, but he couldn't find it.

He didn't have a flashlight, so his vision was limited. Yet despite the rain, there was enough moonlight filtering through the trees to keep him from being completely blind.

The moment he'd heard the fire alarm, he had headed straight for the forest, Lisa calling out for him to stop. But he'd ignored her, still reeling from the revelations of what he'd done, what they'd both done, and of her willingness to go so far to protect him.

A day that had started with a simple but terrifying threat—imagined or otherwise—had now spiraled so far out of control that Tolan didn't think he would ever regain his balance. The things he'd learned about himself—the horrible atrocities he had committed—made him believe that if he were to look into a mirror he'd see a demon staring back at him.

But if what Lisa had said was true, if The Rhythm or the heartbeat or whatever it was had worked its magic and there was even a chance that Abby had returned, then he'd do everything he could to keep her from harm.

He just hoped he wasn't too late.

He thought about that night in Abby's studio, what Lisa

had witnessed, the fury that had overcome him, made him do the unthinkable, and he didn't care about her warnings. He didn't care whether Abby was dangerous or why she'd come here.

Or what she might do to him.

Because, in truth, he deserved whatever punishment he got. And this one small act of redemption could well be the key to his personal salvation.

Running through the trees, he thought he saw the trail ahead, a narrow unpaved path that snaked through the forest. But as he drew closer he realized he had somehow gotten turned around and the trail was no longer in sight.

Had he doubled back without realizing it?

He couldn't be sure.

What he *did* realize was that he was suddenly lost, unable to determine which direction he needed to go.

A vision of Bobby Fremont looming over Abby filled his head, and he came to an abrupt stop, squeezing his eyes shut, willing it to go away.

As he stood there, the rain filtering down on him through the trees, he was struck by a new notion:

If what Lisa said was true, that the things he'd seen in seclusion room three were real, that Abby was back, was it also possible that he hadn't imagined Vincent after all? Could those phone calls have been as real as he'd thought they were?

And if so, was Vincent out here somewhere, watching him squirm like a bug under a pin?

A cell phone bleeped, startling Tolan.

Faint, but unmistakable. Somewhere nearby.

Opening his eyes, he looked around, did a full three-sixty, and saw nothing but the forest and the darkness.

It bleeped again and he turned toward the sound, pinpointing its location. Focusing his gaze, he saw a dim light shining in the distance. Dark shapes.

Moving through a tight cluster of trees, he stepped over a pocket of fallen branches and came to a small clearing that was littered with the bones of abandoned cars. He knew now that he *had* doubled back, was close to the access road that he and Lisa had taken to the old hospital.

Among those old bones was a shiny new carcass.

A Crown Victoria.

Frank Blackburn's unmarked squad car.

The rear passenger door hung wide, the overhead light burning, the sound of the bleeping telephone coming from inside.

His stomach clutching up, Tolan approached. He could see that the backseat was soaked with blood, and there was no doubt in his mind that a killing had taken place in there. A butchering.

Sue Carmody?

No matter how hard he tried to remember it, he could not put that knife in his own hand.

Had it been Vincent after all? Was this one killing Tolan wouldn't have to take credit for?

He knew he shouldn't be thinking about this. None of it mattered anymore. He was wasting time. He had to find his bearings and get to the hospital, get to Abby. But that one small kernel of hope buoyed him, and he wasn't sure why.

Turning in his tracks, he studied the slope of the earth, trying to determine which way to go now, listening as the cell phone bleeped one last time, then went silent.

And just as he'd made his decision, had chosen what path to take, a bright white beam of light assaulted him, and a familiar voice said, "Don't move or I'll blow your fucking head off."

"Lock your fingers behind your neck," the voice said.

Its owner was standing near the tight cluster of trees, a

flashlight in one hand, a gun in the other, his hair plastered down by the rain, his clothing soaked, a butterfly bandage adorning his forehead.

Blackburn.

Tolan had to squint to see him. Raising his hands, he locked them behind his head.

"Where's Carmody?"

Tolan hesitated, not knowing what to tell him. If he told him the truth—however vague that might be—Blackburn would surely pull the trigger, and Tolan needed to stay alive long enough to find Abby.

"Please," he said. "I have to get to the hospital."

The flashlight beam didn't waver. "You don't look hurt to me. Down on your knees."

Tolan did as he was told, twigs crackling beneath him. Overhead, the wind continued to howl through the tree-tops.

"Where is she?" Blackburn said. "What did you do with her?"

"Please, I don't have time for this. I have to find Abby."

"Abby?"

Realizing his slip, Tolan quickly corrected himself. "Jane. Jane Doe. I have to get to her."

"I'm afraid you're too late for that."

Tolan's heartbeat quickened. "What?"

"It's a mess down there. She escaped. Along with a bunch of other nut jobs."

"How do you know that?"

"One of the patients told me. An old man."

The old man again.

"He had a run-in with her and he wasn't in too good of shape. Said she came this way."

Tolan's gaze shifted to the dark silhouettes of the trees. Did this mean that Bobby Fremont had failed? That Abby was safe?

Was she in here somewhere? Hiding?

"I don't know what kind of weapon she's carrying, but she ripped the shit out of him. And frankly, I don't give a damn right now. I just wanna know what you did with . . ."

He stopped talking then, aiming the flashlight beam at the Crown Victoria behind Tolan.

"Motherfucker," he muttered, moving a step closer. "What did you do to her?"

There was a sudden rustling sound nearby, a flash of movement through the trees—

—and it wasn't the wind.

Blackburn stopped and swept the flashlight around, illuminating the darkness. "What was that?"

Tolan turned. Abby?

Another rustling sound, this time coming from the opposite side of the clearing. Higher in the trees, like the flutter of bat wings.

Blackburn pointed the flashlight toward it, but caught nothing in its beam. It was an unguarded moment and Tolan wondered if he should jump to his feet and run—

—but Blackburn quickly brought the light down again and shone it in his face.

"You can try," he said. "But you won't get very—"

Another sound abruptly cut him off.

A thudding sound.

Blackburn exhaled sharply and went down, the flashlight tumbling to the ground in front of him.

Tolan watched him fall, then looked up to see Lisa standing over him, a thick tree branch in hand. She tossed it aside and crouched over Blackburn, prying the gun out of his fingers. He was either out cold or dead.

"Get up," Lisa told Tolan. "You heard what he said. Your precious Abby is loose, and I'll be damned if I'll let her hurt you. We need to finish what we came here to do."

Blackburn stirred and Lisa pointed the gun at his head, about to pull the trigger.

Tolan sprang to his feet. "Lisa, no!"

"I have to," she said. "He saw you. He knows."

"No, it's one thing to want to help me, to clean up after me, but you're not a murderer. Don't do it."

"What difference does it make?"

"More than you can know," Tolan said. "Trust me on this. I'd give anything to take back the things I've done."

There was a flutter of movement again.

In the trees behind Lisa. A flash of white.

Abby?

Crossing to Blackburn, Tolan picked up the flashlight and pointed it, seeing nothing.

Then, another flutter, off to his right. A faint whisper:

"A lie stands on one leg, the truth on two . . ."

He and Lisa exchanged quick looks as he swept the beam toward it.

Again nothing.

"A lie stands on one leg, the truth on two . . ."

"Oh, my God," Lisa said, panic filling her eyes.

Another flutter, off to the left now.

"A lie stands on one leg, the truth on two . . ."

Tolan swept the light in that direction—

—and there she was, crouched at the base of a pepper tree, looking out at them with dark, feral eyes. Not the product of a deluded mind, but real. Very real.

"Abby," he said, feeling a sudden, overwhelming ache, accompanied by an unbridled sense of relief.

She was alive. She was alive and she was back and she didn't look dangerous at all. She was the same woman he'd met five years ago, the same woman who had taken him into her bed, into her heart.

His lost soul.

"Oh, my God," Lisa said again in a trembling voice, and brought the gun up to fire.

"No!" Tolan shouted, hitting her arm with the flashlight. The gun cracked, the shot went astray, and when Tolan returned his gaze to Abby—

—she was gone.

Chapter 56

"Jesus," a voice said. "What the hell happened to you?"

Blackburn had a mouthful of twigs.

He opened his eyes and spit, then realized he was lying on the ground. His head felt as if it had ballooned to twice its size.

Turning on his side, he looked upward toward the source of the voice. All he could see were two overlapping circles of a light.

Double vision.

Shit.

"Somebody sure did a number on you," the voice said.

Then hands grabbed him, pulling him upright.

Clayton Simm crouched next to him, aiming a flashlight toward his head, fingers immediately going to the butterfly bandage, then moving to a spot just above Blackburn's temple.

There was something wet there and Blackburn winced, pain shooting through him.

"This is bad," Simm said. "You don't want to be moving around too much."

"What are you doing out here?"

"Fire alarm. Some of our patients got loose. I thought I heard a gunshot. Did one of them attack you?"

"No," Blackburn said, fighting confusion. "Maybe. I

don't know." He squinted at Simm. "You picked the perfect time to finally show up."

"Yeah, thanks for dragging me out of bed, then disappearing on me. I figured if I'm awake, I might as well be doing something useful."

"Good, then help me to my feet."

"I don't think you should be—"

"Just do it."

Simm stood up, then reached a hand out and pulled Blackburn to his feet. The world started spinning and Blackburn grabbed ahold of Simm's arm to steady himself.

"I told you. You might want to sit back down. I'll go get you some help."

Blackburn said nothing, thinking he might toss his cookies. He tried searching the ground, but the double vision persisted. "Where's my Glock?"

Simm swept his flashlight beam around the area, but came up empty. "Don't see it." Then he spotted something and stooped to pick it up.

Blackburn swayed again and Simm quickly caught him. "You drop this?"

It was a scrap of newspaper. The article on Anna Marie Colson that Kat had found in Tolan's house. It must've slipped out of his coat pocket when he fell.

It was wet, but not soaked through. Simm shone his light on it, staring at the photograph of the college roommates. Blackburn looked too, trying to get his vision to clear, the image swimming before him, then finally coming into focus.

He stared at the fresh young faces, surprised by what he saw. Something he hadn't noticed before. One of the roommates looking *away* from the camera, not at it, wearing an odd expression.

"Is that Michael?" Simm asked.

Blackburn shifted his gaze to Tolan's smiling face, then snatched the article away from Simm and stuck it back in his pocket.

"I need to get up to the old hospital."

"What the hell for?"

"Just help me get back to the trail. I'll be fine after that."

"Not likely," Simm said. "I let go, you'll fall flat on your face."

Blackburn brushed a wet leaf off his cheek. "Wouldn't be the first time."

Tolan weaved in and out of the trees, finally clearing the last of them, then stepped onto the grounds of the old hospital, where the rain came down hard, turning the battered driveway to mud.

After the shot, he thought he'd seen Abby again, several yards in the distance, and had taken off after her without looking back, leaving Lisa in his wake.

"No, Michael! You can't trust her! She's not what you think she is!"

But Tolan didn't listen. Nothing she could say could stop him. Not after he'd seen that face. That beautiful face with its striking brown eyes.

All he wanted was to make things right. To put his arms around Abby, to hold her, to tell her how sorry he was for what he'd done.

But now, as he stood at the edge of the forest, rain battering his face, he saw no sign of her, and the glimmer of excitement he'd felt only moments ago began to morph into the first seeds of despair.

From across the drive, the wide black mouth of the hospital's main doorway seemed to call to him, beckoning him to enter.

He shone Blackburn's flashlight toward it.

Was she inside?

A sudden feeling of déjà vu washed over him. A memory of Abby standing in the darkness of that doorway. Like something from a dream.

This is where it happens, Michael. Where it all comes together and balance is restored.

Steeling himself, Tolan crossed the drive and went inside.

"Michael!"

As Lisa watched him disappear through the doorway, she felt heartsick.

After all she'd done for him, all the sacrifices she'd made, all these years she had put her own interests aside to love him and protect him and what does he do?

He ignores her. Leaves her behind. Humiliated.

And all because of that *thing*.

Because of Abby.

Always Abby.

Lisa had spent the last year—the last *fifteen* years—coddling him, nurturing his wounded heart, promising to always be there, even during the darkest moments of grief.

And what had it gotten her?

She was always second string in his eyes.

The consolation prize.

When they made love, she knew he was thinking of Abby. He'd even said her name once, not realizing it. But Lisa had never mentioned it to him, had never complained.

Was there nothing she could do to make him see her?

She was a beautiful woman. A lot of men had told her so. She'd felt their stares, their unchecked desire, but she'd never responded, never led them on.

Because her heart was Michael's. Always had been. Always would be. No matter how he treated her.

No matter who he chased after.

And she'd thought it was finally working this time, this year together, only to see it destroyed by that woman. That aberration.

But Lisa was an optimist. She knew this night would soon pass, this terrible day would be over, and when she was done cleaning up—a chore she had been born to perform—everything would be on track again, and she'd have another chance to make Michael's heart hers.

But she needed to catch him first.

And Abby.

Before something terrible happened. Like the old man had warned.

Hurrying through the rain, Blackburn's gun clutched in her hand, she glanced at her BMW parked out front and stopped in her tracks.

A chill ran through her.

The trunk was open.

She hadn't opened it, had she?

No, she knew she hadn't.

Moving around for a better view, she looked inside and felt her stomach drop. The blanket was there, soaked with rainwater and blood—

—but the body was gone.

Sue Carmody's body was gone.

Michael? Could he have taken it?

No, he didn't have time. She'd just seen him a moment ago.

Could it have been Abby?

That seemed even less likely.

But if it was neither of them, then who?

"Hey!" a voice shouted.

Lisa wheeled around and saw Detective Blackburn emerge from the trees, a bloody gash in the side of his head. Clayton Simm, of all people, was propping him up, looking just as surprised as she was.

"Don't fucking move," Blackburn shouted. "Stay where you are!"

She should have shot the sonofabitch when she'd had the chance. Shouldn't have listened to Michael, let him talk her out of it.

Oh, well. Better late than never.

As the two men approached, she brought the gun up and squeezed the trigger.

Chapter 57

When the gun came up, Blackburn dove.

"Holy Christ," Simm shouted, diving in the opposite direction.

Then the shots rang out, one after another, bullets ricocheting around them, Simm scrambling for cover in the trees as Blackburn rolled on the muddy pavement, narrowly avoiding a hit.

Pain shot through his head, and when he looked up, his vision had doubled again—two overlapping images of Tolan's girlfriend turning away and running into the old hospital.

A moment later, she was gone.

Climbing to his feet, Blackburn staggered, then regained his balance, his head throbbing, the wound leaking a lot more than he would have liked.

He turned to check on Simm, to make sure he wasn't hit, but didn't see him anywhere around. The poor guy was probably halfway back to Baycliff by now, shitting his pants as he ran.

Feeling as if he'd just stepped off an overcranked merry-go-round, Blackburn staggered toward the open doorway.

Halfway there, he had to stop, resting against the BMW. That was when he noticed the open trunk and the bloody blanket. And he had no doubt that there had once been a body inside.

The body of Sue Carmody.

He'd known she was dead the moment he saw that ruby earring. And whatever thin hope he'd carried for her survival had already washed away in the rain.

Tolan barely heard the shots.

They were little more than faint popping sounds, part of some other world, just like the wind and the rain.

This building, this hospital—with its charred and crumbling walls and shattered glass and broken tiles and peeling paint, with its long, shadowy corridors and darkened rooms—was a world unto itself.

He remembered it in more detail than he thought he would. But it looked different at night, the decay seeming more sinister in the darkness.

Yet, oddly enough, he felt comforted. His last good moments had been spent within these walls, with a woman he would always love.

Sensing she was here somewhere, Tolan worked his way down the corridor and turned a corner to find a broad staircase leading up to the second floor.

Abby had loved that staircase. Snapped a dozen or so photographs that day, taking her time, trying to get just the right angle, as she always had.

He could feel her now. A ghost, perhaps—or was it the real thing?—hiding in the shadows above.

He heard a sound from up there and swept the flashlight beam toward the top of the stairs. It flickered and grew dim. Probably damaged by the rain.

"Abby?"

His voice bounced off the walls, but it was the only voice he heard.

No one answered.

He banged his hand against the flashlight and for a moment it grew brighter, then flickered again and went out.

Shit.

Another sound came from the top of the stairs.

A whimper?

Tossing the flashlight aside, Tolan took the steps two at a time and plunged into the darkness of the second floor, moving down a long hallway, the only illumination coming from the far end, where pale moonlight shone in through a broken window.

There was movement down there. A shadow in the light.

"Abby?"

Picking up speed, Tolan barreled toward the end of the corridor and ran smack into something hard and metallic, banging his shin. Wincing in pain, he stumbled forward and landed on his hands and knees.

Sonofabitch.

Turning, he saw that he'd tripped over a portable generator, its thick electrical cord snaking toward a small, windowless room.

What was *that* for?

Was someone living up here?

Tolan rubbed his shin, waiting for the pain to subside, then got to his feet and approached the room, a sudden memory stirring in his brain. That feeling of déjà vu.

There was a table in the center, slanted slightly toward the floor, and next to it sat a rolling cart with an ECT machine atop it.

Hanging above it all was a blackened ceiling, holding the charred remains of a light fixture with missing bulbs.

He'd seen that fixture before.

But when?

Before he could give it too much thought, he heard the sound again and turned, listening carefully.

Not a whimper this time, but the faint echo of someone crying.

Tolan quickly followed it until he found himself in another long hallway. At the far end, open double doors led to a room he remembered from his time here with Abby.

The Day Room.

She'd taken his photo in there, the one that now hung over his bed.

Moving down the hall, he passed through the doorway into a cavernous room lined with high, wire-mesh windows, moonlight slanting toward its center, illuminating a grouping of dilapidated tables and chairs, each of them bolted to the floor.

A small figure was huddled near the foot of one of the tables, half hidden in the shadows.

Abby.

Tolan stopped, the sight of her riveting him to the spot.

Sensing his presence, she turned, looking up at him with wet, lucid eyes. "Michael?"

At the sound of her voice, Tolan felt something loosen inside his chest, a flood of emotion washing through him.

Rising, Abby held out her arms to him, opening them wide.

"It's me, Michael. I've come back to you."

And then he was across the room and in her arms, pulling her close, holding her so tight he thought she might break, but she didn't seem to mind, the tears coming again, and he was crying too, unable to contain himself.

"It took me so long to get here," she whispered. "I tried so hard to get here. I thought I was too late."

"It's all right, Abby. You're here now. You're with me."

They held each other for a long moment, Tolan overcome by joy and guilt, not wanting to think about what he'd done to her. The savagery.

"I won't lie to you," she said finally, as if she knew

exactly what was going through his mind. "You hurt me, Michael. So many times in those last few days. And then that night . . ."

"I'm so sorry," he said, squeezing her tighter, fighting his tears.

"But that's not why I'm here," she continued. "None of that matters. Not now. Not anymore."

He pulled away from her, surprised. "How can you say that? What I did to you is unforgivable."

"No, Michael—"

"—I don't even remember it. I don't *want* to remember." He closed his eyes, hearing Lisa's voice in his head. "But she told me what she saw. She saw it all."

"What are you talking about? Who?"

"Lisa. She was there that night. And she told me more than I wanted to know."

Abby frowned. "What did she tell you?"

"Everything. Everything that happened. The fight. The knife in my hand. The blood . . ." More tears filled his eyes. "I never wanted to hurt you, Abby. Never. Please believe that."

Abby just stared at him for a moment, as if she wasn't quite sure what he was trying to say. Then sudden realization set in and she pulled him toward her. "Oh, my God, Michael, no . . . Don't blame yourself for this. It isn't your fault."

Tolan pulled away from her again. ". . . *What?*"

"I can't believe she's got you thinking this way. It wasn't you. It wasn't you at all."

Tolan was confused. "What are saying?"

"Lisa's *lying* to you. Everything about her is a lie. That's why I came back. To *warn* you about her."

"Warn me?"

"You can't trust anything she tells you," Abby said. "*You* weren't the one holding the knife. *She* was."

And as Tolan tried to process these words, Lisa stepped into the doorway and pointed Blackburn's gun directly at Abby's chest.

"I think it's time for you to go now."

Chapter 58

Blackburn was halfway up the stairs when he heard the echo of voices.

For a moment he thought they might be the voices inside his own head, the way everything was so jangled up in there. He felt dizzy and nauseous and wished he could just lie down and sleep for a long, long time.

But when you're on a mission, there's no time for sleep. When you're on a mission, you keep climbing, keep walking, keep going until you reach your stated objective, no matter how difficult that may be.

And while Blackburn's objective at this particular moment was not noble, not smart, and most decidedly not danger-free—especially when you considered the fact that his Glock had been stolen from him—it was all he had to keep him upright.

The thing that drove him.

Ever since he'd seen that ruby earring, then the bloody blanket in the trunk of the BMW, the sense of loss he'd felt, the sense of finality, the realization that he would never again see Sue Carmody alive, told him exactly what that objective needed to be.

He was no longer looking to catch a killer.

He was looking to kill one.

Funny thing was, the man he'd initially suspected was

no longer the one he was after. When he stood with Clayton Simm in the forest, looking down at the newspaper photo of those fresh-faced college kids, he was shocked to realize that the only one who wasn't smiling, the only one who wasn't looking directly at the camera—

—was Nurse Lisa Paymer.

A much younger Lisa, to be sure, but it was unmistakably her, as unmistakable as the barely disguised scowl on her face.

And instead of smiling for the camera, she was looking directly at the victim.

At Anna Marie Colson.

And in that moment, Blackburn realized his mistake. Unlike Tolan, he was no expert on the inner workings of the human mind, but that one look into Paymer's soul put it all in perspective for him. What he was dealing with here was a classic obsessive psychotic, and the old, stale proverb rang especially true:

Hell hath no fury like a woman scorned.

When Anna Marie Colson messed with Paymer's man, Paymer had gunned her down. Then, when history repeated itself fourteen years later, Paymer had taken a knife, a PowerBlast cauterizing tool, and had gone to work again.

Her only mistake had been Todd Hastert and Carl Janovic.

Blackburn couldn't give you the wheres and the whys of her introduction to Hastert, but Paymer herself had told him she'd worked at County General, and he was sure that the crucial information about Vincent Van Gogh had been passed along to her there.

A look at Paymer's bank records would undoubtedly yield some interesting activity.

The wild card, of course, was the evidence he'd found in Tolan's house, but he hadn't abandoned his theory that Tolan may have been set up.

Yet none of that really interested Blackburn right now.

For him it was all Paymer, all the time.

And she wouldn't make it through the night.

As Blackburn reached the end of a long hallway, the voices grew louder and more distinct.

"Don't you listen to her, Michael. She's a freak of nature. A goddamn demon."

"Put it down, Lisa. Nobody needs to get hurt."

Blackburn picked up speed—or at least the best approximation of speed he could muster in his condition—and rounded a corner, finding himself in another long hallway, a wide doorway at the far end.

Standing in the room beyond, in a pool of pale moonlight, were three familiar figures: Tolan, Psycho Bitch, and Paymer.

Paymer was holding the gun. *His* gun.

Stopping short, Blackburn quickly ducked into a darkened dooway. His Mag-Lite had disappeared along with his Glock, and he needed a weapon of some kind, something heavy to wield.

It was dark, but he could see that there were several loose chunks of cement on the floor—reminding him of the one Psycho Bitch had tried to use on him this morning. But they'd be too awkward to deal with.

He needed a pipe. A piece of two-by-four.

He wished he'd had enough sense to get the crowbar from that trunk.

Scanning the darkness, he saw nothing he could use and was about to step outside again when he instinctively stopped, sensing a presence behind him.

What the hell?

Hearing the faint shuffling of shoes on cement, Blackburn spun, bringing his arms up defensively, but his reflexes were shot and he moved too slow.

A hard blow to his solar plexus doubled him over, then a fist slammed down on his back. He crumpled to the floor, the world once again spinning.

This was getting tiresome.

Then a dark figure crouched next to him, putting a hand over his mouth.

"Quiet now. Let's let the children have their fun."

Lisa was waving the gun around and Tolan stepped in front of Abby, shielding her. "Lisa, listen to me. . . ."

"Don't you try to protect her, you sonofabitch."

"I'm begging you, leave her alone. You don't have to do this."

"Oh, please, Michael. Are you gonna tell me how much you love me now? Huh? Promise me it'll all be better in the morning?" Her eyes were wild. The eyes of a psychotic.

"Waving that gun around won't get you what you want."

"Won't it? It did before."

Tolan's receptors were on overload, the information coming at him too quickly to be processed. All the things he'd thought about himself, all the damage he thought he'd done, had been a fabrication. A jealous woman's lie. And what frightened him most was that he'd actually allowed himself to believe her.

"She's a whore. You said it yourself. And you just stood there like a pathetic fool and let her slap you."

As she spoke, the information train continued to roll through Tolan's head, transmitting images in rapid-fire succession, a fast-forward replay of Abby's last night on earth.

He was remembering it now.

It was all coming back.

The blackout he'd suffered had not been the product of a dissociative personality at all, but a reaction to severe trauma. The trauma of seeing his wife stabbed to death by his best friend.

"She was cheating on you, Michael. I tried to prove that to you when I put those condoms in her purse. I knew you'd confront her and she'd have to confess."

Tolan heard a rustling behind him as Abby took a step backward, receding into the shadows.

"You're not making any sense," he said. "Abby always considered you a friend. She never did a thing to you."

"She took you away from me, didn't she? And when the two of you started to fight so much, I thought there might be a chance for us. But then you took that little field trip up here and let her snap her precious pictures. I followed you, watched the two of you, and I knew, I knew she'd never let you go. She had her hooks in you and she'd keep them in, for as long as she could."

"She didn't trap me, Lisa. I was in love with her. I'm still in love with her."

Another rustling sound behind him. A small whimper of pain. Tolan turned, peering into the darkness.

"Abby?"

". . . A lie stands on one leg, the truth on two . . ."

He returned his gaze to Lisa. "You hear that? That's you she's talking about."

". . . A lie stands on one leg, the truth on two . . ."

"I did what I had to," Lisa said.

"What about that murder last night? The one on The Avenue? Was that you too?"

"He was threatening us."

"Us?"

"You and me."

There was another murmur behind him. Unintelligible this time.

Tolan eyed the gun, then inched backward toward Abby, trying to see her in the darkness.

"If you wanted her dead, why didn't you just kill her last night, when she walked in on you?"

Lisa's eyes flared. "You think I wouldn't have? I didn't even know she was there. I heard a sound and ran like a scared rabbit."

More rustling behind him.

Something about Abby seemed to be changing and he was reminded of what he'd seen in the seclusion room, the shifting of bones, the missing ear.

"Abby, are you okay?"

Lisa moved toward them, trying to peer into the darkness. "Don't you get it, Michael? It's happening. Just like the old man said. She's one of the children now. The children of the drum."

"Stay away from her."

Lisa leveled the gun. "I can't do that."

"Put it down," he said. "You're not going to hurt her."

"Move! I don't want to hit you too."

But Tolan didn't move.

Face hardening, Lisa shifted her hand, pointing the gun toward the shadows behind him.

"Come out of there, you bitch. Show yourself. Show him what a freak you are."

Her finger brushed the trigger, about to squeeze it, but before she could, a high, piercing shriek filled the room as a figure sprang from the darkness.

And what emerged no longer looked like Abby at all.

Was not even human.

Instead, a sleek, animal-like creature lunged for Lisa as—

—she stumbled back, wide-eyed, ready to fire and—

Tolan shouted, "No!" leaping in front of her as the gun went off, heat blossoming in the center of his chest.

He tumbled to the floor and the gun went off again and then again, followed by an agonizing screech of pain as something or someone fell nearby.

Then silence.

Chapter 59

Someone was crying.

Tolan rolled, reaching up to touch his chest, his hand coming back red and wet.

Turning to see who or what had fallen next to him, he was surprised to find that it wasn't the animal he'd seen only a moment ago, but Abby, her own chest and stomach covered with blood.

Her breathing was shallow, just like his, and he knew that she wasn't long for this world.

Not again, he thought. I can't lose her again.

Reaching across to her, he touched her hand, and she grabbed a hold of his fingers, her words coming out in slow, wet gasps:

". . . It's time, Michael. . . . You can come with me now. . . ."

"Abby, no . . ."

"It's all right . . . we'll be together. . . . We'll always be together. . . ."

"Promise me," he said.

She smiled at him.

"I promise."

Then she squeezed his hand and quietly closed her eyes. And a moment later, as she drifted into death, she began to change again, her face shifting, cheekbones widening, nose growing narrow. And in a few short seconds there was a stranger lying next to him.

Jane Doe Number 314.

But it didn't matter. Tolan knew that he'd be with Abby soon. Because he, too, was starting to drift, listening to the faraway sounds of someone sobbing.

After a moment, Lisa crouched over him, grabbing his hand, tears rolling down her face, and he wondered if hell reserved a special place for people like her.

"Don't you die on me," she cried. "Don't you dare die."

But he *was* dying. It wouldn't be long now.

"I'm so sorry, Michael. Hang on. You've got to hang . . ."

The words suddenly caught in her throat as her eyes went wide, a look of confusion spreading across her face.

Then realization.

Then pain.

". . . that hurts," she said softly, and slumped forward, landing in a heap next to Tolan.

Tolan stared at her, at her lifeless eyes, but was too weak to muster up much surprise. What *did* surprise him was the man standing over her.

A familiar face.

A friend.

None other than Clayton Simm.

And he was holding a bloody scalpel.

He smiled at Tolan, his voice little more than a whisper. "I guess I owe you an apology, Doctor. Frankly, I'm a little embarrassed by this turn of events."

". . . Clay?" Tolan was trying to understand exactly what was happening here. "It was you . . . ? You're . . . ?"

He couldn't get the rest out.

"I think *Vincent* is what you're going for. At least that's what they call me now. Who knows what it'll be tomorrow."

Leaning down, he wiped the scalpel on the sleeve of Lisa's T-shirt. BEST OF SHOW.

"I'm sorry it had to turn out this way. But I guess everyone makes mistakes."

He smiled again, then backed away, disappearing into the shadows.

"Say hello to Han van Meegeren for me."

The moment he was gone, there was a loud crashing sound and Detective Blackburn barreled into the room, looking as if he'd been hit by a very large truck.

He took one look at the mess, said, "Oh, fuck," then collapsed to the floor, out cold.

That was when Tolan closed his eyes for the very last time, Abby's sweet voice in his head:

Sleep, Michael.

Time to sleep now.

SEVEN

The Man Who Said Good-Bye

Chapter 60

They never did find Sue Carmody's body.

What they found instead was a room in the bowels of the old hospital, the room Vincent had been staying in, complete with sleeping bag, a portable stove, and another generator.

There were also mementos of the various Vincent killings:

Jewelry. Photographs. Clothing.

Killing tools.

Two envelopes had also been left behind: one addressed to the Van Gogh task force, and the other to Blackburn himself.

The task force letter laid it all out for them, confirming Blackburn's suspicions. Vincent explained in detail his misguided attempt to infiltrate Tolan's world and set him up as a killer.

He reasoned that since Tolan had tried to blame *him* for Abby's murder—or so he'd thought—the only solution was to give Tolan credit for *all* of the Vincent murders. To expose him as a madman. The mementos he'd left in Tolan's house, the altered cell phone data, and the murder of Sue Carmody had been designed to do just that.

He was, however, happy to admit that he'd been terribly

wrong. And he hoped the untimely demise of Nurse Lisa Paymer made up for his mistake.

It certainly made *him* feel better.

He also told the task force that they'd find the body of the *real* Clayton Simm buried in a vacant lot up in San Mateo, and he thanked the staff of Baycliff Psychiatric for welcoming him into their family.

He was profoundly sorry, he said, for any grief he may have caused.

When Blackburn got the letter addressed to him, he didn't open it right away. He wasn't sure he ever would, although he knew the department had already read it at least fifty times, dusted it for prints, and spent hours debating its contents, hoping to catch the man who had killed one of their bright and shining stars.

Blackburn spent the day of Sue Carmody's funeral stuck in a hospital bed. The gash above his temple took sixty-six stitches, while the one on his forehead took thirty-nine. He had a serious concussion and a ruptured spleen where Vincent had hit him. He was pretty sure that the *Frank*enstein label was already circulating around the station house.

The investigation into the murders of Carl Janovic and Todd Hastert had proven that Blackburn's theory about Lisa Paymer was also correct. She'd been the duty nurse five out of the seven times Hastert had visited County General, and her bank account—which was considerable, thanks to a very rich father—showed regular monthly withdrawals that matched the money given to the dead men.

Two months after the funeral, Blackburn and Kat Pendergast went out to a movie. Three dates later, they finally had that milkshake, and it was just good enough to help Blackburn forget about Carmody for a while.

Later that same night, however, as Kat lay sleeping, he took Vincent's envelope out of his desk drawer, slid a finger under the flap, and opened it.

The letter inside was short and to the point.

Sorry about your partner, it said.

I can send pictures, if you'd like.

Acknowledgments

Once again, I want to thank Kathy Mackel for being my cheerleader throughout the writing of this novel.

Thanks also go to:

Ellie Evans, retired psychiatric nurse, for fact-checking the manuscript. Any mistakes, however, are my own;

Peggy White, for being a terrific sounding board;

My tablemates at Authors at Sea: Ann DiVito, Bill and Sally Hacker, Gloria Hall, Marti Keely, Gail Ryan, Gloria Wood and Karen Yates;

Scott Miller, world's greatest agent, of Trident Media Group;

The folks at St. Martin's Press for their wonderful support; my amazing editors, Marc Resnick of St. Martin's, and on the other side of the ocean, Stef Bierwerth of Macmillan;

My Killer Year crew mates;

My mother, Louise, my sister, Scoti;

My kids, Lani and Matthew, who make a father proud;

And, finally, my wife, Leila, who is my best friend, my biggest supporter, and my greatest love.

KILL HER AGAIN

Chapter 1

The little girl was about to die.

She knew this instinctively, even though the man in the red baseball cap had never uttered so much as a word to her. It was as if she had crawled up inside his brain and could read his innermost thoughts.

Thoughts of darkness. And dead things.

Lots of dead things.

The little girl wasn't a stranger to death herself. She'd seen it firsthand, at six years old, when Mr. Stinky got hit by a bus. A lot of the details were hazy now, but she remembered she was playing hopscotch with Suzie at the time, Mr. Stinky running circles around them on the driveway, barking like crazy.

Then, for some reason, he had decided to dart out into the street. Saw a cat or something. And the city bus that usually came down their block at nine o'clock every morning came late that day, showing up out of nowhere as if it had been waiting for Mr. Stinky to make his move.

The little girl had been waiting too, waiting for Suzie to finish her turn, watching her friend skip from square to square, when she heard the roar of the bus and looked up to see its front bumper smack Mr. Stinky right in the head. It knocked him into the air like one of her old stuffed animals, his legs flopping as he did a kind of slow-motion somersault, then landed on the blacktop.

He didn't move after that.

And the bus driver didn't stop.

The little girl screamed and ran into the street, even though she knew her mother would yell at her. And there was Mr. Stinky, lying on the ground like a bag of broken toys, his glazed eyes staring up at her, as lifeless as the two black buttons on her favorite Sunday School dress.

There wasn't any blood, but she knew he was gone, knew he was dead, and he would never come back to her no matter how much she begged him to as she cradled him in her arms and cried and cried.

That had been four years ago.

But she still missed Mr. Stinky and sometimes wished she could be with him again, to feel him press his head against her arm, or put his paw on her knee, whenever he wanted her to pet him.

Maybe she'd get that wish.

Maybe he was up there in heaven somewhere, waiting for her.

Lying in the backseat of the car, her wrists and ankles bound, her mouth taped shut, the little girl stared up at that greasy red baseball cap and wondered where the man was taking her.

The road bumped beneath them, tree shadows flickering across the ceiling, and from what little she could see of the darkening sky, she thought they were headed into a forest of some kind. Not like the forest she'd camped in with her mom and dad, with the sun and a lake and fishing poles, but a dark and scary Hansel and Gretel kind of place, where kids like her were cooked and eaten.

The little girl's stomach burned something awful, like that night not long ago when she'd eaten too much lemon meringue pie. She wanted to throw up, wanted to release it all over the backseat, because she knew, without a doubt, that her time was almost up. The end was near.

That, just like Mr. Stinky, it was *her* turn to—

"Hey, McBride, you awake?"

Anna McBride blinked, then turned from the passenger window to look at her new partner. Ted Royer. He seemed to be speaking to her from the far end of a long, dark corridor.

She blinked again and shook her head slightly, trying to clear her mind, a deep sense of dread bubbling in the pit of her stomach as the corridor finally widened, then disappeared altogether.

The darkness, however, didn't. It was a little past one A.M.

"Is that yes or no?" Royer asked.

"Yes," Anna said, clearing her throat. "I was thinking, is all. Daydreaming."

But that wasn't exactly the truth. The truth was much deeper than a simple daydream. And certainly more frightening.

Special Agent Anna McBride was losing her mind.

"Let's get something straight right up front," Royer said. He was seated behind the wheel of their bureau transport, a black Ford Explorer. He drove with the casual self-assurance of a career brick agent, a man who had spent many years in the field. "If we're gonna be working together—and from all appearances it looks like we are— then I'm gonna need you to stay alert and keep focused. You think you can manage that?"

There was an edge of impatience to his voice. Anna

knew that this new partnership had not been his choice, that it was merely the luck of the draw that had thrown them together. And she was pretty sure Royer considered it *bad* luck.

But she didn't care about that right now. She had more pressing things to think about than an unstable work relationship.

Like an unstable mind.

As much as she wanted to believe that she'd fallen asleep for a moment, had let the hum of the engine lull her into the Land of Nod, she knew she'd been wide awake, and that what she'd just experienced had not been a dream at all. Not this time.

The question was, what exactly was it?

"Yo, McBride. Am I getting through to you?"

Anna nodded. "Message loud and clear."

Royer gave her a sideways glance. "You're not gonna be one of those, are you?"

"One of what?"

"Smart asses." He returned his gaze to the road, which seemed to stretch out forever into the desert darkness, all prairie brush and cactus. The view was as foreign to Anna as a lunar landscape. "I'll tell you right now, I've had my fill of smart-ass partners, always trying to be clever, but usually at the expense of good investigative work. Too busy listening to their own bullshit to notice anything else."

Anna was tempted to tell him she thought this might be a case of the kettle and the pot, but stopped just short of letting the words fly. Instead she said, "You don't have to worry about me. No bullshit. And I'll stay focused."

This was an outright lie, of course. Staying focused was not her strong suit these days.

"I'm not gonna kid you," Royer said. "The truth is, none of us really want you here."

"I'm beginning to see that."

Another sideways glance. "There you go with the smart-ass shit again. I'm surprised they didn't ship you straight to South Dakota. Who'd you have to blow to get this assignment, anyway?"

Anna bit her tongue. Anything she said right now would only egg Royer on and all she wanted to do was shut him the hell up. The Glock 9 on her hip was calling out to her, but she resisted the urge to put a bullet in his brain. A feeling she'd been fighting since the moment she'd met him.

She had arrived in Victorville two days ago, less than a week after the doctors had proclaimed her fit for duty, and a little over a month after the blow-up in south San Francisco.

She didn't like thinking about that night, had known the moment it exploded in their faces that she would be the designated scapegoat, as she should be. It was all her fault.

But thinking about it had not turned out to be the problem. Ever since she'd jolted awake to a dark hospital room, a nasty set of stitches on the side of her face to remind her of the mistake she'd made, the majority of her mind's real estate had been occupied by only one thing:

The vision. The dream. Nightmares so vivid they had her waking up in a cold sweat every night. Fleeting thoughts and images that all but disappeared the moment she opened her eyes.

A little girl in trouble.

A little girl who was about to die.

"Here's the drill," Royer said. "We get to Ludlow, you stand there and keep your mouth shut. These jurisdictional disputes can get a little tricky, so I'll do all the talking."

"I thought they invited us in?"

"They did, but the request came from the County Undersheriff himself, so it's unlikely the rank and file are gonna be too thrilled about a coupla feds sticking their noses in the pond."

"I've seen my share of pissed-off locals. I think I can handle myself."

"Yeah," Royer said, wagging his finger at her scar, which, despite several sessions with CoverGirl, had proven impossible to hide. "I can see that."

This silenced her. It was her turn to shoot *him* a glance, but his concentration was centered on the road ahead, and he didn't seem to notice.

Or did he?

Was he baiting her? Hoping she'd give him an excuse to send her packing?

The Victorville Resident Agency—one of the bureau's L.A. satellite stations—wasn't any paradise, but Royer was right, she *should* be in South Dakota. She'd only managed to stay in California because Daddy dear had connections in the Justice Department.

But it was doubtful even South Dakota wanted her.

Nobody did.

"I'll keep my mouth shut," she said, surrendering to Royer's contempt, knowing she'd have to swallow a lot of pride to make this partnership work. She'd spent a lifetime ramping toward a career that had unraveled in just a few short minutes, so she wasn't about to squander what was likely her one and only second chance, no matter how much it pained her.

Besides, pride was the least of her concerns at the moment. The visions had obviously begun to escalate. They were coming during her waking hours now. And despite what the doctors had told the Victorville AIC, she knew she wasn't even remotely fit for duty yet.

And until she was, she'd simply have to fake it.

"Looks like we're here," Royer said, and sure enough,

the lights of Ludlow, California, twinkled in the distance ahead, a dusty oasis in the middle of the Mojave Desert.

Anna wondered how people lived out here, wondered what compelled them to seek out the isolation and the dry, oven-like temperatures. Places like this were scattered throughout Southern California, with no apparent connection to the rest of the world.

Maybe that in itself was the attraction.

"You might want to brace yourself," Royer said. "I'm told the scene is pretty grisly."

Anna didn't mind.

Maybe grisly was just the distraction she needed.

Chapter 2

It was small as houses go. A worn, two-bedroom box made of brick and stucco, surrounded by a low, sagging wooden fence and fronted by a tiny patch of earth that had never held much more than a few desert weeds.

Anna had always harbored the notion that everything looked better at night. More stylized. Romantic. But there was no romance here. The house was a desolate and dreary reflection of the neighborhood—and town—it occupied.

A half dozen county sheriff's vehicles were parked haphazardly in the street out front, a coroner's van backed into the driveway, its rear doors hanging open.

Several neighbors stood watching from across the street, a mix of old and young, fat and thin, clothed and half naked, every one of them with leathery, sun-baked complexions that added a good ten years to their appearance.

The first thing Anna noticed as she climbed out of the cool interior of the Explorer was the oppressive summer heat. Middle of the night and it had to be over a hundred degrees. She felt as if someone had thrown a thick, wool blanket around her and she wanted desperately to take off her coat. That, however, wasn't about to happen unless Royer took his off first, and Anna wasn't holding her breath.

Good thing, too, because Royer actually *buttoned* his coat before flashing his creds at a nearby deputy. Ducking under the yellow crime-scene tape, he headed for the open front door.

Anna followed, but before they reached the porch, a sinewy guy in a Western shirt, jeans, and cowboy boots stepped into the doorway.

"Agent Royer?"

His voice was a deep, somber baritone, but there was no hint of hostility on his face as he moved forward and held out a hand to shake.

Royer shook it, looking mildly surprised by the man's courtesy.

"That's right," he said. "Deputy Worthington?"

Worthington nodded. "Sheriff's Homicide. But call me Jake." His gaze shifted to Anna, lingering briefly on the scar before finding her eyes. "And you are?"

Royer cut her off before she had a chance to respond. "This is Agent McBride."

"Welcome to Ludlow," Worthington said, as Anna grabbed his outstretched hand.

She'd always hated shaking hands with a man, feeling awkward whenever she did it, wondering how to negotiate the task. Squeeze too hard and she might come off as some desperate female trying to prove herself, while not hard enough painted her as weak and ineffective. Finding a balance was tough, and the moment was usually stiff and uncomfortable.

Anna managed to get through this one with a minimum of fuss, however, and was relieved when Worthington didn't hang on longer than necessary.

"I've gotta warn you both that what you're about to see

isn't pretty. We've got more than one deputy that almost lost his dinner over it, including me."

"The minute it stops bothering you," Anna said, "you'd better start thinking about a change of careers."

Royer shot her a frown, but Worthington nodded solemnly, then handed them each a pair of latex gloves and gestured for them to follow him inside. "Let's get to it."

Royer didn't wait for Anna or offer her the chance to go in first. She was, she realized, merely an accessory here. A show of force that didn't really translate into action. This was Royer's party, and she was the annoying little sister whom Mom had foisted on the big kids.

Her only sense of satisfaction came from the fact that Royer had been wrong about the reception. Worthington seemed genuinely glad to see them.

Pausing at the doorway, she turned as she snapped on the gloves, taking another look at the neighborhood, at the ramshackle houses that lined the street. She had a feeling that even out here in the desert, a street like this was no stranger to violence. There'd have to be something extra-special going on inside to gather such a crowd at one-thirty in the morning.

Grisly, Royer had warned her. Not pretty.

Turning back toward the house, Anna stepped past the threshold and took it all in.

The first thing she noticed was the blood. It was hard not to, considering it was everywhere, arterial spray all over the furniture and walls. She didn't need gloves, she needed a haz-mat suit.

A split second after the blood registered in her brain, the smell hit her, the same smell that accompanied too many of the homicide scenes she'd been to.

Urine and feces.

It's the thing they never told you about in movies and

television: that when some people die violently, they evacuate their bladder and bowels. From rock stars to anonymous paupers, it isn't unusual to find them swimming in their own waste.

Mix that with the scent of the blood and rotting entrails and you've got the smell of death.

A smell you never got used to.

Royer and Worthington were standing over a body on the right side of an unkempt, standard-issue living room. A couple of coroner's men stood nearby, waiting to bag it.

The victim was female, possibly thirty years old, although it was hard to tell, thanks to the way the body had been carved up. The killer had been quite liberal with the use of his weapon, which had been sharp enough to cut very deep.

More blood soaked the sofa cushions just above the spot where the body lay, and Anna figured this was where the victim had been killed. She felt the Lean Cuisine meatloaf she'd scarfed for dinner start to back up on her, but forced it down. She wasn't about to give Royer any more ammunition against her.

Not that he needed any.

When she joined them, he said, "What took you?"

She ignored the question and stared down at the corpse, feeling a sudden sense of sadness wash through her. She didn't know this poor woman, didn't know anything about her, but nobody deserved to be displayed like this to a room full of strangers.

Anna looked at Worthington. "Who is she?"

"Rita Fairweather. Twenty-seven-year-old single mother of two."

Christ, Anna thought. Only a year younger than me.

"She worked at a bar in town, place called The Well. Was there until about eleven P.M." He gestured to the blood on the walls. "Near as we can figure it, it was pretty much a blitzkrieg attack. They never saw it coming."

"They?" Royer said, raising his eyebrows.

Worthington hitched a finger, and they followed him across the room through a doorway that led to a small, dingy kitchen. Lying on the faded linoleum in a sticky pool of blood was a man of indeterminate age, multiple stab wounds to his chest. An unopened can of Colt 45 lay at his feet.

"One of her boyfriends from the bar," Worthington said. "John Meacham. Poor sonofabitch picked the wrong night to get horny."

Anna noticed something on his neck and crouched down for a closer look. The flesh was slightly pink, with two fresh, reddish marks about half an inch apart.

"Looks like he used a stun gun on this one," she said.

Worthington nodded. "That's what we're thinking. We'll know for sure once the M.E. gets him on the table."

Anna stood up. "You say Fairweather has kids. Where are they?"

"Ahh," Worthington said. "The reason you two are here."

He turned again, crossing through the living room to a narrow hallway. As Anna and Royer followed, she began to get a vague feeling of deja vu.

There was a bathroom at the far end of the hall, and two bedroom doors on either side, facing each other. Worthington led them to the one on the left, to yet another body—a teenage girl, her mouth taped shut, her wrists and ankles bound, more stab wounds.

An image flashed through Anna's mind—

—the little girl, bound and gagged in the backseat of a car—

Anna blinked it away, forcing herself to concentrate on the room, which was largely occupied by two twin beds and a parade of stuffed animals and action figures. One of the beds sported Los Angeles Dodgers bedsheets, while the other carried a pastel pink comforter covered with a throwback to Anna's own childhood: My Little Ponies.

A bookshelf to her right held dozens of children's books, including some of Anna's own favorites. *Little House on the Prairie. Through the Looking Glass. The Wonderful Wizard of Oz.*

She remembered many a night, her mother perched on the edge of her bed, reading aloud to her, and she wondered if Rita Fairweather had ever had the chance to do the same.

Worthington gestured to the body on the floor.

"Tammy Garrett. The family babysitter. She looked after the kids three nights a week."

She couldn't have been more than fifteen, sixteen years old. Plump. Baby-faced.

"And the kids?" Anna asked, already knowing the answer.

"Like I said, the reason you two are here."

Worthington moved to the nightstand between the two beds and, with his gloved right hand, picked up a small digital camera, pressed a button, and handed it to Anna.

"Evan and Kimberly."

Anna looked down at the photograph on the tiny LCD screen. A woman whom she assumed was Rita Fairweather stood with her two young children, a boy and girl, on the grounds of what looked like a carnival. There was a Ferris wheel in the distance and directly behind them, the black hole of a doorway led to what a gaudily painted sign said was DR. DEMON'S HOUSE OF A THOUSAND MIRRORS.

Something stirred at the periphery of Anna's brain—another image flash, too fast to decipher, accompanied by a sudden unexplained rush of vertigo.

Acutely aware that the deterioration of her mind was still in progress, and that the distraction of blood and feces and dead bodies had been temporary at best, she waited for the dizziness to pass.

"You all right?" Worthington asked.

She knew her face must be showing her distress. "Fine," she said. "Just a little touch of nausea."

He nodded, offering her a grim smile. "Like you said, the minute it stops bothering you, you'd better start thinking about a change of careers."

Anna managed a smile in return, but Royer was having none of it. Giving her an impatient scowl, he snatched the camera out of her hands and stared down at the image of Rita Fairweather and her kids.

"Where was this shot?"

"High school football field. Carnival comes through town every year. Still here, as a matter of fact, so the photo is recent."

"I take it they're missing?"

Nothing like stating the obvious.

"No sign of 'em," Worthington said. "And being so close to Nevada and all, we figure there's a fairly good chance they were taken across the state line."

There was no guarantee that this had happened, of course, but Worthington had been smart enough to hedge his bets and call in the FBI. Crossing state lines automatically made it a federal case, and the Ludlow County Sheriff's Department was undoubtedly ill-prepared for a crime of this magnitude—which explained the complete lack of hostility toward a couple of federal outsiders. They were anxious to hand it off.

"What about the father?" Royer asked. "He still in the picture?"

"Dead two years, according to the neighbors."

"Is there a ransom note?" Anna asked.

It seemed like a ridiculous question. Who was left to pay ransom? And even if she were still alive, Rita Fairweather obviously wouldn't be able to afford one.

But you never knew whether there was a rich relative somewhere in the picture, and for all of her faults, Anna believed in being thorough.

"No notes, nothing," Worthington said. "I figure we're dealing with a predator—and not just any predator at that."

"What do you mean?"

"This'll sound a little crazy, but you work a crime scene long enough, the victims start to talk to you."

"And what are they telling you?"

"That whoever did this, it wasn't his first time. He's had practice, and a lot of it."

Anna thought about the serial perps she'd studied back at Quantico. Sociopathic savages who brutalized and tortured their victims, treating them with less sympathy, less mercy, than they would a bug on a wall. It was true that many of them had been victimized themselves, but this was a reason for their behavior, not an excuse, and she knew that should she ever encounter one in the wild, she wouldn't hesitate to blow him away.

Just as this thought entered Anna's mind, her gaze fell to the camera in Royer's hand, to the photograph still on screen. But it wasn't the children she saw, it was the Ferris wheel, the house of mirrors.

Then, all at once, a rush of images came at her as if they were being poured from a box full of puzzle pieces, flickering past her mind's eye so rapidly that she was once again overcome by vertigo, a dizziness so strong she had to grab on to Worthington's arm for support.

"What is it?" he asked. "What's wrong?"

But the onslaught was so overpowering that her brain couldn't form the words to answer him, the images continuing to assault her—

—a spray of blood—

—the bound little girl—

—the man in the red baseball cap—

—tree shadows flickering across a tattered car ceiling—

—an ornate locket swinging from a rearview mirror—

Anna stumbled back, nearly losing her footing as she turned and hurried through the doorway. Stepping quickly down the hall, she crossed the living room and went outside, pulling her coat off as she moved, trying to get some air, trying desperately to purge her brain of these terrible images—

—a dark corridor of trees—

—a remote clearing—

—a suitcase full of bloody knives—

Then finally, thankfully, the last of them flitted by as she leaned a hand against the wall and closed her eyes, wondering what the hell was happening to her, wondering if she was indeed going mad.